LAST WALK IN THE PARK

Claremary P. Sweeney

Publisher's Information

Author contact: claremarypsweeney@yahoo.com
Author website: https://claremarypsweeney.carrd.co
Author blog: AroundZuZusBarn.com

Cover and map design by Zachary Perry

ISBN 978-1-953080-24-0

1. Mystery 2. Claremary P. Sweeney 3. Westerly, Rhode Island 4. Women Sleuths 5. Harriet and Stephen Wilcox 6. Westerly Library 7. Wilcox Park

Copyright 2022 by Claremary P. Sweeney

ALL RIGHTS RESERVED

No part of this work covered by the copyright herein may be reproduced, transmitted, stored, or used in any form or by any means graphic, electronic, or mechanical, including but not limited to photocopying, scanning, digitizing, taping, Web distribution, information networks, or information storage and retrieval systems, except as permitted by Section 107 or 108 of the 1976 United States Copyright Act, without the prior permission of the author.

This book is a work of fiction. Names, characters, and incidents are the product of the author's imagination and are fictionalized. Any resemblance to actual persons, living or dead is coincidental.

DEDICATION

Charle,
if only we could return to our days of holding hands ...

Westerly, Rhode Island

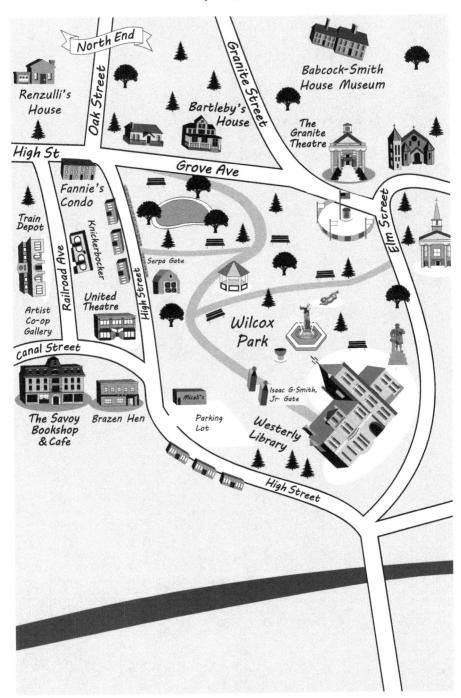

Westerly, Rhode Island

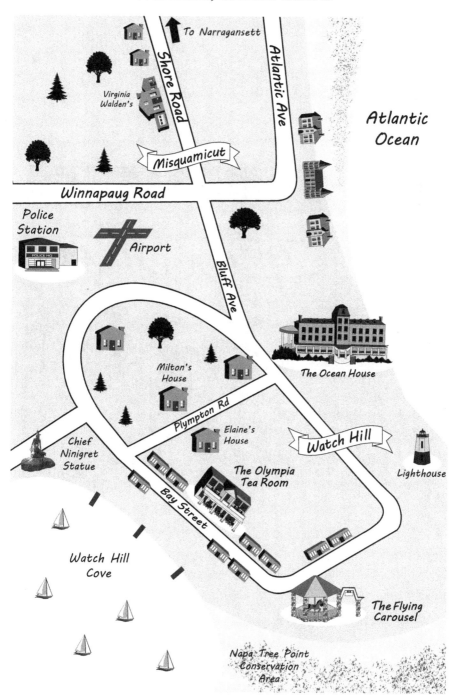

*There is nothing to writing.
All you do is sit down at a typewriter and bleed.*
Ernest Hemingway

Friday, December 6

BARTLEBY SCHNELLING SLIPPED UNDER the cover of the bookshop's entryway. Glancing back toward the train depot, he suddenly felt anxious, unsure if he'd been followed. His old instincts had begun to fail him. Turning to gaze through the plate glass into a room filled with rows of bookcases, he tugged at the fingers of the thick suede glove with his teeth. It dangled from his mouth before plopping onto the black and white octagon tilework, covering part of the **V** in SAVOY. He looked over his shoulder to the sidewalk before making the call. A brief message was followed by a beep, then crackling sounds. A series of repetitive tones signaled he'd been disconnected before finishing his warning to her. *Low battery? The weather? Maybe the brick building?* As he stooped to retrieve his glove, he spied a movement in front of the book stacks. *A ghost? No. Not inside. Outside. A reflection.* He stood up, alert to the sound of footsteps. A couple passed by the doorway arm-in-arm.

Inside, he could see the well-worn brown leather couch and club chairs and the battered old steamer trunk. A sign, hand-written in neon green magic marker, was taped to the glass.

SORRY – CLOSING AT 6 PM DUE TO IMPENDING STORM.

Underneath the words was a yellow happy face with a blue teardrop under one eye.

Had it been an hour earlier, he'd have stepped out of the bleak weather. His young friend Terry would have been working behind the counter in the bookshop's café and she'd have served him his usual cup of warm herbal tea. He could use it right now. It had been a stressful series of days since he'd seen her on Tuesday morning.

A stooped figure came out of the darkness slowly limping across the street, then halting underneath the United Theatre marquee before moving on. The sleet commenced hitting the sidewalk in earnest. Unzipping his jacket, Bartleby removed the portfolio. Inside was a manila envelope. Looking around quickly, he folded it in half, pushing it through the brass mail slot and feeling relief when he heard it plop on the floor. He tucked his cellphone into the portfolio and hugged it against his chest. Stepping out from the protection of the recess, he headed up Canal Street toward Wilcox Park.

Bartleby veered left on High Street, making it to the park's Serpa Gate before a fierce onslaught of rain began pelting him, cutting against his skin. He ducked his head down inside the fur-lined hood, turning sideways to bear the brunt of the driving wind. In that moment, he thought he detected someone in the shadows of the storage barn to his right, just inside the entrance. He froze in place for a brief second before moving forward. A few minutes more and he would be across the meadow and safely inside the old Victorian house on Grove Avenue where he'd grown up. Colorful fairy lights enwrapping the winter-bare tree limbs, glimmered overhead.

He took a deep breath and hastened his pace. He'd underestimated the intensity of the gathering storm that stalked him from the train station to the park. The lamp in his front window had been set on a timer. He scrinched his eyes and stared straight ahead, past the ice skating pond, intent on finding that familiar beacon in the storm.

Suddenly, a powerful shove propelled him downward. Bartleby dropped the portfolio. His hood fell back as his head was slammed against cold, wet stone. He turned on his side looking up at his assailant now bending over him. Recognition and shock. Recoiling in fear, desperate to escape, he crawled away on his stomach only to meet with the frigid sting of the icy water in the dark pool. A pull on his boots forced him down under the murkiness. He struggled weakly, unable to breathe for a brief moment in time, and then there was nothing. Overhead, the twinkling lights clung to swaying branches. Stand-ins for stars hidden behind ominous, swirling black clouds.

Throughout the night, the storm would rage and in the early morning hours, rain and sleet would turn into a heavy, wet snowfall. A thick, white blanket gradually would cover the glassy pane of thin ice on Wilcox Pond where Bartleby's frail body now lay at rest while in the distance a church bell tolled the passing hours.

∼

Rick called out from the kitchen, "Honey, your cell's ringing."

"I'll be right there. Answer it for me." Ruth came into the room as her husband was pressing a button on her phone. She dumped an armload of dishtowels and tablecloths on the counter top.

Rick shrugged as he placed the phone into her outstretched hand. "I saved the message but it's garbled. Maybe you can understand it?"

She listened, "Ruth, it's Bar … crucial I … or death … meet … careful … when you …. Please don't …"

She replayed it, then checked the caller ID. "I didn't understand most of what he said but I recognize the caller. Bartleby Schnelling. One of the writers enrolled in the Local Authors' Program at the Westerly Library." She shrugged and put the phone in her sweater pocket.

"That's the guy you told me about. The one who's writing the thriller based on his time as a spy." Rick helped her fold the linens and place them into the pantry drawers.

"I'm not sure if he was actually an official government operative or part of some covert group. He hasn't been transparent about those details. I think he believes it adds to the 'allure of the mysterious' he informs me he's trying to develop. He was supposed to be in New York this week consulting with someone before finishing the book. And he also mentioned going to see his publisher."

"Do you think the call was important?"

"It's most likely something to do with his novel. We made plans to get together without the rest of group on Sunday. He has his own set ideas and isn't really open to suggestion from others."

"Is the book any good?"

"I've read the chapters he's submitted. His writing style is quite polished although a bit terse. It's not at all the way he speaks. He tries the patience of some in the group whenever he goes off on one of his tangents."

"So, he talks like a woman but writes like Hemingway?"

His wife didn't fall for the bait, realizing he was attempting to goad her into reacting with his stereotypical comment about women.

He tried again. "Papa! Now there was a man's man."

Sophia suddenly appeared in the doorway of the kitchen. "I heard that, Rick," she informed him. "And for your information, women use twice as many words in a day as men because it's necessary to repeat everything we say to them."

"I stand corrected," Rick chuckled. It was one thing to tease his wife, but he knew enough not to get in a war of words with his feisty sister-in-law.

"And as far as Ernest Hemingway is concerned, I don't care how many concussions he had. There's no excuse for his atrocious, narcissistic behavior." She turned and left the room only to return a second later. "And one more thing about that cad whose work you admire." She wagged her right index finger high in the air. "Wives should not be treated like automobiles to be traded in every few years for a newer model."

She made her exit casting a warning look at Gino who called after her, "I wouldn't trade you in, Honey. Not evah. 'Til death us do pot."

They waited to see if Sophia returned with something else to add. After a minute, Ruth deemed it was safe. She whispered to her husband, "Wise man. He knows he'd never live to tell about it."

Rick whispered back, "I'd still sign up for one of your classes if you put *For Whom the Bell Tolls* on the syllabus."

Sophia chimed in from the dining room, "It might end up tolling for thee!"

Ruth quickly changed the subject, continuing their discussion about Bartleby.

"He really doesn't need me to guide him along like the others in the writing group. His manuscript is already in good shape and the agency has assigned him an editor. He complains about the woman at every session. He told me he joined the class because Fannie MacAlister, the librarian, suggested he get some help with completing the final chapters. Oh, well, I'll call him back later."

Rick picked up his hammer and climbed a step stool. "Great, because right now I need your eagle eye to help me make sure this shelf is level."

"And what if it turns out to be slightly off kilter?" she asked.

Gino added his two cents from the pantry. "Have you ever known my brotha ta do anything off kilta? When you're done wid dat, one of yous kin unpack dose mugs." He was busy arranging dishware in the glass-paned cupboards.

"It's fine, Rick." Ruth stepped back to look around the room and carefully removed the lid from the blue Dutch Girl cookie jar. "This was always on my grandmother's kitchen table when I was little. Filled with homemade treats for me when I came to visit." She took out a sugar cookie for her brother-in-law. "Gino, everything looks wonderful. If it weren't for you and Sophia, this place would never be ready for Christmas."

Sophia poked her head in again. "It's the least we can do now that we'll be moving in with you."

Earlier in the fall, Rick had received a large inheritance. Lenore Duckworth, an old friend, had left him a sizable sum of money and properties. He and Ruth had decided to move from their five-room ranch in Kingston into the Duckworth mansion in Narragansett overlooking the Atlantic Ocean. They soon realized the "house" would be much too large for them to manage alone.

Rick was using his time and resources to help establish an arts and cultural center in Westerly. It was a massive project. The old Montgomery Ward Building was recently connected with the United Theatre next door and modern spaces were being constructed for live performances, artist galleries, cinemas, and classrooms. He'd once owned a gallery in Greenwich Village before moving to Rhode Island and worked now as a professional photographer and a teacher in the Art Department at the University of Rhode Island.

Ruth was busy teaching English classes at the university and had agreed to mentor a small group of local authors to guide them in polishing their works for potential publication. They'd discussed options and decided to ask Rick's brother Gino and his wife Sophia to move in and help them.

"Kara and Stewart just pulled up the driveway," Sophia announced. "Perfect timing. The roast is done and the table's set." She rushed to open the door. Ignoring the two adults, she spoke directly to the baby in Stewart's arms. "Hello, and how's my sweet little girl today? Let's get you out of this nasty weather."

Stewart handed Celia to her. "I need to bring in the last of the boxes we picked up from your old house before the rain gets any worse."

"I'll send Gino out to help you." To Kara she said, "Just hang your coat in the closet and come into the library to get warm."

"Wow, this place looks amazing." Kara walked around taking in the pine scented greenery that festooned the doors and windows in the stately parlor rooms located on either side of the hall. "And I'll bet you made every wreath by hand."

"It didn't take that long." Sophia was on the couch in front of the fireplace removing Celia's snowsuit. "Look at this adorable angel in her pretty little dress. I'm glad I had her colors done. That shade of gold is definitely perfect for you, my dear." The infant smiled and cooed.

"Thanks to you, she has enough holiday outfits for all the twelve days of Christmas and then some. Where do you find the time to sew, Sophia? I'd sooner use safety pins than replace any missing buttons on my clothes." Kara hung up her coat and continued to look around at the floor-to-ceiling windows, their wide ledges covered with white-twig trees and fragrant beeswax candles nestled among juniper branches, pinecones, and berries. The enormous mahogany mantle held shining brass candlesticks and golden bells tucked into holly boughs.

Ruth joined them, bending to give her friend a kiss on the cheek. "Well, the gang's all here, and most of the work is already done. We're set to move in tonight for good."

Stewart hung his overcoat in the closet and stood looking at them from the doorway. "You're coping well with all of the recent changes in your life. I'm glad to hear you're not leaving your position at the college to live a life of leisure. Will you still find time to join me for lunch at the University Club?"

"Of course. But we'll continue splitting the check."

The two were professors at the University of Rhode Island. They enjoyed each other's company and had been friends from Ruth's first day on campus many years ago when she'd asked Stewart for directions to the English Department offices. He was setting up equipment on the quadrangle with his teaching assistant in preparation for one of his classes and offered to personally escort her to Independence Hall. She later returned the favor by introducing him to her best friend Kara, at the time, a detective on the South Kingstown Police Force. Ruth proudly proclaimed she possessed a secret power to recognize kindred spirits when she gave the toast as maid of honor at their wedding.

Rick came in to announce dinner was ready. "I've never used this oven before and I didn't want to overcook the roast. I'm sorry we don't have time for cocktails but Gino has chosen a really nice local wine for dinner."

"Yeah, I'll be your some-o-lee-air this evening. I picked up a few bottles at WinterHawk Vineyards and da Malbec is gonna flow tanight cuz we all got a lot ta celebrate."

While Sophia settled Celia into a specially cushioned highchair next to her, the others went into the kitchen and came out with platters and serving bowls which they placed on a table gleaming with gold-rimmed china and polished silver. As the storm raged outside and the waves could be heard crashing against the rocks below, the friends enjoyed this festive meal as they had enjoyed many meals together in the past.

"I have to admit, Stewart and I are curious about your decision to move in here." Kara directed her question at Sophia, but Gino jumped in."

"I been workin at the Courthouse Center for the Arts since I came here and lately I been lookin for something where I kin use more a my talents."

Kara had observed the dynamics of their little band of friends over the past few years and had come to realize it was always Gino they went to when they needed to get the practical things done. He was good at everything. He was an expert carpenter, a licensed electrician, and great with anything having to do with plumbing. He had more connections than a Providence politician, and he had an amazing eye for design. He was the genius behind some of the most memorable holiday display windows when he worked in New York. Gino might still be working in the city if not for a scaffolding accident that had severely injured him. When he was released from the hospital, Sophia had brought him to Rhode Island where his brother Rick had found him a job at the Center and helped with his rehab while she worked as a nurse at South County Hospital. In the end, they realized they'd fallen in love with South Kingstown and decided to stay.

"I'm ready ta turn responsibility over to my young assistant. Da place needs new blood and da kid's got some preddy good ideas," Gino said resignedly.

"And since the house we were living in went along with the job, when Rick asked Gino to manage the properties he'd inherited, we didn't have to think twice," Sophia added.

"The mansion has more than enough room. We were overjoyed when Gino and Sophia agreed. It's a plan that will work out well for all of us," Ruth declared.

"I know he wouldn't tell anyone, but Rick generously offered to pay my tuition if I wanted to go to med school full time. I love my job at the hospital but that was a dream I never thought would happen. I didn't take him up on the offer, but the money we'll save living here will help if I get accepted."

"When you get accepted," Ruth corrected her. "This house is enormous. Sophia and Gino will have the entire east wing to themselves. It's a perfect plan that benefits all of us. Sophia has even prepared guest rooms for you on the second floor if you ever decide to stay over. And, of course, there's the nursery for when Celia visits. We probably should have turned this place into a bed and breakfast, but Rick has always wanted to live along the ocean. So, here we are!"

Rick raised his wine glass, "Here's to old friends and new beginnings."

"Speaking of old friends, where are the three amigos tonight?" Stewart asked.

"Clay is holding a rehearsal for the Kingston Village Christmas Carolers and Arthur and Samuel are at the Elks Club trying to pick up dates to take to Vida's Christmas Party," Ruth informed them.

"I almost forgot. They stopped by earlier to drop this off. " Rick took a note from his shirt pocket and read it out loud. "Please be advised that you're hereby invited to Vida Koranski's Annual Christmas Party to celebrate National Ugly Christmas Sweater Day on Friday, December 20. Ugly sweaters are required. All other clothing is optional. A prize will be awarded for the grossest sweater in the room. Be there or be square."

"I guess we all know what we're doing on the third Friday in December. If any of you don't have a sweater, I have a couple of extra I knitted."

"Sophia, I can't imagine you creating anything ugly," Kara said and everyone nodded in agreement.

"I'm sure they're ugly in a tasteful sort of way," Stewart said. "I may need one. I took out my favorite sweater yesterday, to get ready for the holiday season, and the white snowmen had turned a splotchy olive shade. I think I may have splattered sauce on me when I was cooking." The others stole knowing glances across the table.

Stewart was highly respected for the brilliant scientist he was, but his closest friends were not enamored with his culinary skills, better-known as "kitchen experiments". They were often called in to act as his test rats. Part of the novelty in the recipes he concocted was not just the incongruous ingredients he chose to mix together, but the monochromatic color scheme he often used. Last year, everything on the Langley table during the holiday season came in different shades of green. During one meal, Gino commented out loud, "I never knew dare was so many cullas of green in da world!" And then whispered to Sophia, " Maybe I shoulda ordered us a pizza?"

Stewart had taken Gino's observation as a compliment and rewarded him with extra containers of leftovers to bring home. Sophia later apologized to Kara for not returning the containers re-filled with home-baked goods, as she would normally do. "No matter how hard I tried, I couldn't get those stains out of the Tupperware. They were inside and out! I finally gave up and threw them away. And you know I recycle everything. What is that man using for food coloring?"

"I find it safer not to ask. He loves to cook and I don't, so I tend to encourage him, effusively praising whatever he makes," Kara explained.

"Perhaps if you took samples of some of that stuff into work at the forensics lab and dissected it, you wouldn't be so supportive," Sophia suggested.

"I'd rather not. Ignorance is bliss and I haven't been poisoned, yet."

"Yet being the operative word," Ruth suggested.

"Gino won't open the refrigerator at your house since the day he reached in to get a beer and found body parts festering in the cold cuts bin," Sophia reminded her.

"Those were goose livers and they weren't festering. They were marinating in Stewart's special sauce," Kara corrected her.

"Special being the operative word." Sophia placed her index finger on her tongue and pretended to gag.

Sophia had become somewhat less critical and more open-minded about his "inspired creations" over time. "I have a sweater I think you'll love, Stewart. I call it my 'Figgie Pudding Jumper'. It's mostly brown and will hide future stains well," she assured him.

"It doesn't matter how ugly our sweaters are, they'll never be as gross as that purple one with the bangles Vida chose to wear to our wedding," Rick reminded them and the conversation turned to their celebrations the previous Christmas.

"Will you be going any place special for your anniversary?" Kara asked.

"No, we're too busy getting the house in order and I have workshops scheduled at the Westerly Library throughout December and possibly January, if more time is needed."

"How are the murder mysteries coming along?"

"My first few meetings with the group have been more or less introductory. I've been familiarizing myself with their writing styles. When we begin to discuss their plots in earnest, I'm hoping you'll come to a meeting to share your expertise. Unlike you, murder is not my forte."

"Of course. Are there any story lines you're finding particularly intriguing?" Kara was curious.

"It's a motley crew. I have a married couple from the North End neighborhood who are writing a mystery together. At our first meeting, the husband proudly informed everyone he'd published two non-fiction books when he taught at U Conn - before he opened his insurance agency. They were both math texts for college freshmen." Ruth grimaced, raising a dubious eyebrow, which caused them to laugh. "His wife Carolynn is a high school English teacher I met at a conference. She showed me her writing and I thought it had promise. Then there's an older man, Milton. He's in his eighties, but looks much younger and is extremely agile. He jogs around his neighborhood in Watch Hill every day. His memoir is about life on the horse racing circuit and the murder of a jockey, which he helped to solve. My favorite mystery, I must admit, is the stage play. You've met Terry Ricitelli. I introduced you at the Savoy Bookshop."

"I remember. She's the quiet, young woman who was enrolled in one of your classes last year before she dropped out. You tried to get her to stay."

"Right. She's painfully self-conscious and I noticed she had difficulty communicating with the other students. But her writing made up for her lack of articulation in class. I've encouraged her to continue writing. She's talented and the drama she's working on is promising. It's a psychological thriller. That reminds me, could you listen to this message from Bartleby? He's the one I told you about. The spy." Ruth called up the message and waited until Kara returned the phone to her. "Can you figure out what he was trying to tell me? Do you think it sounded urgent?"

"I distinctly heard the words *crucial* and *death*. Now you have me wondering."

"I redialed but didn't get an answer. I'll try again tomorrow and let you know if I find out anything else."

After the last of the wine was poured and coffee was served, they all helped to clear the table. Gino took charge of loading the dishwasher, as he maintained there was a right way and a wrong way to do this for optimum sanitary results with no streaks or fogging on the glassware.

Ruth glanced out the kitchen window, "I checked the weather and it appears we're going to get some heavy snowfall later. The roads could be pretty icy. Do you want to stay here tonight?"

"I would take you up on that, but now that we have the dogs, we'll need to get home to let them out. And if we lose power, Stewart will want to start up the generator. But thanks for the offer." Kara gently took her daughter from the nest of pillows on the couch and Ruth helped to put on the white fur snowsuit and hat that contrasted well with Celia's dark brown skin and curly hair.

"There's my little snow bunny." Sophia tucked the black ringlets into her godchild's hood and gave her a goodbye hug.

After they'd left and Gino and Sophia had retired for the night, Ruth and Rick made themselves comfortable in front of the fire. She listened again to the phone message. "I have a feeling Bartleby had something important to tell me. I probably shouldn't worry. It could be about the book or maybe he wanted me to know he'd be at the workshop tomorrow afternoon?"

"There's a good chance it will be canceled because of the snow." Rick got up to look outside.

The grandfather clock struck midnight. "It's much too late to call him now."

Placing another log on the fire, Rick added, "It's not as though it's a matter of life and death. I'm sure it can wait until morning."

The church bell tolled twelve times, announcing for anyone still wandering about in the storm that the old day had ended and a new day had begun. Lying on the bottom of Wilcox Pond under a blanket of white, Bartleby Schnelling couldn't hear a sound.

*I don't need an alarm clock.
My ideas wake me.*
Ray Bradbury

Saturday, December 7

THE SOUND OF AN engine revving in the driveway woke Rick and he opened the curtains to look outside. Below, the headlights of a truck moved steadily back and forth in the darkness. He dressed and went downstairs where his wife and sister-in-law were having coffee at the kitchen table.

"How long has Gino been up?" Rick asked.

"Since before five and it's all your fault," Sophia informed him. "You bought him that plow attachment for the front of his truck. He was like a child on Christmas morning when he woke up to snow covering everything."

"He loved playing in the snow when we were kids. Our yard was filled with ice sculptures, igloos, and forts." Rick smiled at the memory.

"He's cleared all of the stairs and walkways and when he's done with the drive, he says he's going over to the Langley's to plow them out. He called at six to inform them." Ruth yawned and took another sip of coffee.

"I'm sure they appreciated the wake-up call. Well, as long as we're all up, I'll make us breakfast," Rick offered.

"I'm going to turn on the TV to see what's been canceled." Sophia left the room.

Ruth shut her eyes for a minute. "We've had a grand total of four hours sleep, it's still dark out, and we're drinking coffee in the kitchen. So much for a life of leisure!"

Rick patted her on the back. "Looks like we may be snowbound. It'll give us a chance to finish unpacking the last few boxes and then we can take a nap."

"Sounds like a good plan. Here's a better one – we could skip the unpacking and go straight to the nap," she suggested.

Sophia returned as Rick was placing a platter of French toast on the table. "Parking bans are in effect. Looks like you won't be having your workshop at the library. Everything's canceled," she said to Ruth. "I'll probably volunteer to do a shift at the hospital. I'm sure some of the nurses won't be able to get there until the side roads are cleared. Gino can give me a ride on his snowmobile."

Rick went out to call his brother inside to join them for breakfast.

Gino stood in the middle of the kitchen shaking off snow. "It's just da beginning of December and we got our first storm. Dis is gonna be a great winta. Who wants ta go outside layta and make snow angels?"

Everyone groaned in unison and Rick offered to make another pot of coffee. "Extra strong."

⁓

Kara rolled over in bed and looked at the alarm clock. She closed her eyes and waited until Stewart had finished his phone conversation.

"Who was that?" she asked, stifling a yawn.

"Gino. He wanted us to know he'd be by to plow us out as soon as he finished at his place and got Sophia to the hospital safely. Apparently there's over a foot of snow outside."

"Thank goodness it's Saturday and neither of us has anywhere to go. Maybe you should call him back? Tell him there's no hurry. I like the idea of being snowed in with you and Celia. Especially since it doesn't appear we've lost power."

"I'll let the dogs out for a run and make us breakfast. We can spend the rest of the morning entertaining the little one. I'm sure Sophia will want you to write a detailed account of 'Celia's First Snowstorm' in the ongoing biographical binder she organized before her goddaughter was even born."

Kara laughed. "We're fortunate to have them in our lives. I enjoyed dinner last night. So many changes have happened to us in the past few years."

Stewart gently touched her face. "Do you ever regret leaving the police force? I know the chief has told you a job will be there when you're ready to return."

She smiled and took hold of his hand. "I don't see that happening. Carl Sullivan is doing a great job and I'm perfectly happy with my decision. I get to spend time with you, watching Celia grow up and I love being able to consult and to go into the forensics lab whenever I'm called to help out on cases. It's the best of both worlds."

From the nursery they could hear the sound of their daughter babbling happily in her crib. "Well, I guess this is the start of 'Celia's Great Snow Adventure'. We'd better get out the camera to take pictures. You stay here. I'll turn up the thermostat and bring you breakfast in bed." He kissed her. "I love you."

"I love you more."

"I don't think that's even possible."

༄

Ruth set aside her laptop. "I've sent out emails to all of the workshop members. Today's session is canceled but we'll meet as scheduled on Monday evening. The parking lot should be plowed out by then. It will give me time to read their latest chapter submissions again. And what are you planning to do today?"

Rick returned to the table with another helping of scrambled eggs on his plate. "I think I'll go outside and help Gino for a while and then work in my studio. I'd like to have the triptych completed so I can hang it in the gallery next week. Did you ever figure out what that guy was calling you about?"

"I called an hour ago but no luck." She took the phone and pressed redial again. It rang three times and this time someone picked up. "Hello, Bartleby, it's Ruth Eddleman. I'm returning your call. It sounded urgent.

Hello? Are you there?" She was answered by a gasp. "Hello? Bartleby, are you still there?" The sound of a click ended the call "That's strange, I could swear I heard someone breathing. I hope he's okay."

"If you don't hear from him by tomorrow, we can take a drive to Westerly and see if he's home." Rick patted her hand. "Besides, I need to stop by the Savoy and pick you up a birthday present." He kept a running list of titles she wanted and was a regular customer at the local bookstores.

"You promised you wouldn't make a big thing of it."

"I don't see why you wouldn't want a grand celebration. It might be your forty-fifth, but you still look twenty-one to me."

"You didn't even know me when I was twenty-one."

"I've seen the pictures, Gorgeous. And you have the consolation of knowing you'll always be younger than me and Gino."

"Maybe younger than you, but everyone knows Gino will always be a teenager in his heart."

"And as long as he's around, he'll keep us all young."

Just at that moment, his brother came through the back door. "What a day! I made some huge snow piles wid da snow blowa. Who wants ta go sleddin?"

Ruth and Rick clicked their mugs together in a toast. "To Gino!"

And Ruth added, "May he stay forever young."

Ruth decided to spend the day working in her office on the second floor. It overlooked the front lawn where Gino and Rick were taking a break from gliding down snow mounds on large pieces of cardboard boxes and throwing snowballs at each other like two big kids. She took the manuscripts from her brief case and began to read each, adding comments in the margins. The sounds of laughter outside made her smile as she worked.

～

Carolynn Renzulli smirked as she sat in front of her laptop at the dining room table. She'd risen early and stolen quietly downstairs so as not to waken her husband Conrad. He hadn't arrived home until after midnight and since it was Saturday and the agency was closed, he was sleeping in. She reread the email from Professor Eddleman.

> Carolynn and Conrad,
>
> I've noted a marked change from the original story line which I thought was quite good. You'll need to concentrate on reworking the dialogue. Although the husband's voice seems like that of a seasoned detective, the wife's dialogue does not ring true. She's described as a clever woman in her early forties, yet sometimes she appears immature and overly compliant with whatever her husband suggests. I think the wife's role needs to be clearly defined and if she's an equal partner in solving the crime, as you have implied, reworking the conversations between the couple should be a priority. I can suggest specific examples of dialogue needing to be changed. Since today's workshop is canceled, you could begin rewrites before Monday's meeting."
>
> Ruth Eddleman

Carolynn squelched the urge to run upstairs and jump up and down on the bed yelling, "I told you so. I told you so." Conrad had been insistent on re-writing all of the dialogue and leaving the descriptive paragraphs (the info dumps) to her. She was becoming more and more resentful but did not know how to express her feelings rationally to her husband. Every time she tried, she ended up sounding like an irate teenager arguing with a parent because she wasn't getting her way. It originally had been her story Professor Eddleman liked which got them into the workshop in the first place. She was sorry she'd let Conrad convince her she needed a man to help make the male detective's character more realistic.

"I should know what I'm talking about since I'm already a published author," he'd boasted to her.

The only thing he'd ever written were two math texts when he taught at U Conn. And she knew for a fact his first wife had done most of the work he'd taken the credit for. She poured herself a second cup of coffee, turned up the thermostat, and then began reworking the first chapter as she sat waiting for her husband to get up.

Conrad lay awake with his eyes tightly closed against the morning sunlight pouring into their bedroom. He silently cursed his wife for not remembering to lower the shades the night before. He grabbed her pillow and thought how easy it would be to smother someone in their sleep. He covered his face, but the light crept in. He had no intention of getting up until he heard the front door close and the sound of her shoveling the walk. *A whole day stuck in the house with that woman.* She'd probably want to work together on the manuscript. Maybe he could slip a few sleeping pills into her coffee? Damn New England weather.

He tried to concentrate on remembering the courses he'd played while they were on vacation. Carolynn hated Arizona, New Mexico, California, and any place with a climate where he could golf most of the year. "I just love the change of seasons," she'd informed his parents when they visited them at The Villages last August. "I could never live in a place that was so hot all the time."

He grit his teeth. "It's not always this hot, Carolynn! Most of the year it's quite nice." They were all sitting around the pool and he'd jumped in to escape from her inane babble. She couldn't swim. A thought had entered his head at that moment. *Maybe I could coax her into the deep end?* He heaved a sigh remembering the golden sunlight that greeted them every morning in Florida – not like the harsh winter rays beating down on him this morning.

Conrad threw the pillow on the floor and opened the night table drawer. Underneath his neatly folded, monogrammed linen handkerchiefs was the amber container of *triazolam*. It was still half full. He tossed the pills back into the drawer and burrowed under the blankets. *Too damn hot. She must have the heat set at 90 degrees!* They'd need an oil delivery every week at this rate. *Maybe we should switch to gas? People died all the time from gas leaks.* He heard the front door slam and the sound of icicles dropping.

Sharp, pointy icicles. And frozen legs of lamb. Easily disposed of. Perfect murder weapons.

For the next half hour, the scraping of a shovel, like the screeching of fingernails drawn across a blackboard, kept him awake under the covers, grinding his teeth. *Too late for a sleeping pill … triazolam.* He swung his legs onto the floor pondering how long it would take for a person to freeze to death if she fell asleep in a snowdrift.

∾

They finished clearing the driveway in front of the garage. "If we lived in a condo, we wouldn't have to shovel this stuff," her Aunt Virginia declared, taking out a cigarette. Terry could picture her aunt selling the house and moving into an over fifty-five community. Then she would be on her own. *Probably for the best.* She swished at the smoke streaming her way. Terry was thankful to have lived here while she was attending school at URI, but now that she'd dropped out and had a job, she could afford her own place. Maybe something would become available closer to the center of town? A studio apartment near the bookstore where she was a barista in the café or a couple of rooms in one of the old houses around the Granite Theatre where she sometimes ushered. But whenever Terry thought about being on her own, she became anxious. Living near the beach in Misquamicut with her aunt made her feel safe.

Virginia threw the lit butt into the snow pile along the edge of the driveway. "Filthy habit! I'm going to quit for the new year. C'mon. Let's go in and I'll make us some hot chocolate."

Terry snuggled under the purple velvet throw on the couch and read the email on her iPad.

> Good morning, Terry,
>
> I hope you're safe and warm and taking advantage of the day off to work on your play. I think it's coming along fine. The characters you've created seem like real people. I particularly like the psychiatrist. I feel as though I know her. You've done your research well and the case study of the disturbed patient is intriguing because you've documented the progression of his behavioral issues and backed them up with factual data on his condition. You may want to limit the technical jargon in regard to the medications he's been prescribed over the years and excessive details on the treatments

he's undergone. I would put the emphasis on how well he disguises his present symptoms and behaviors. This will help build the tension especially when the audience realizes he's a killer and that the psychiatrist they've come to care about is in danger.

I'll see you on Monday.

Dr. Eddleman

Her aunt put the tray on the coffee table and handed Terry a cup. Virginia secretly worried about her niece who'd been living with her for over a year and had not once brought someone home. She couldn't remember even overhearing her having a conversation with a friend on the phone. "Skootch over and make room for me."

"Mm mm, peppermint marshmallows. Yum." Terry licked the stickiness from her fingertips.

"Wotcha doing?"

"Just checking my emails."

"Anything interesting?"

"No, tonight's performance was canceled."

"Not surprising. Everything's canceled. I called my client to make sure he didn't try to make it in for his appointment. I told him we'd be skyping instead. I'll be in my office most of the day. There's chicken salad for lunch."

"I think I'll spend the rest of the afternoon right here on the couch reading my book."

"Is it a mystery?"

"Yup. I just picked it up from the bookstore yesterday. It's the newest in that South County Series. *Last Castle in the Sand*. You can read it when I'm done. You'll love it, Auntie. Lots of beach scenes."

"Who doesn't love a good murder by the sea?"

Milton enjoyed the ocean view from the top floor of his home in Watch Hill. He'd just had a new window installed and the room was no longer drafty from the blustery weather that often gave the old cedar-shingled house a sound thrashing. The ocean scene across Bay Street was magnificent, but the cold air had chilled him. Now that the window was in place, he could sit comfortably in his favorite room on the third floor. Although it was part of the guest suite, he spent more time in it than any other room in the house. The sea was calm this morning. Blue and glistening in the sun. Yesterday, before the storm, he'd watched it leaping and crashing wildly, trying to break loose and flood the beachside community. He'd live through many Nor'easters.

He was a child when the famous 1938 hurricane hit Rhode Island bringing so much destruction in its wake. But today was beautiful and the room was cozy and warm. He settled into the white wicker rocking chair by the window and opened his manuscript to the first chapters. Ruth had called earlier to make sure he was safe and he assured her he was "Fine and dandy. My neighbor, Elaine, brought me a tuna casserole and I still have my electricity, so I'm warm and my stomach is full."

They'd had a nice long chat and she'd given him some advice on how to tighten up his writing. "You tend to spend too much time on settings, descriptions of the many racetracks you've traveled to around the country. Focus more on the thread of your main plot, the murder of the jockey," she advised. "And don't give away the motive too early in the book."

He took his pen and began crossing out sections which diverged too much from the real-life mystery he was documenting. He thought he might include some photos he'd taken on his travels. Opening the scrapbooks on the side table, Milton spent the rest of the afternoon lost in the memories of horses and stables and racetracks from a time long past.

"Ruthie, honey, you've been up here all afternoon. I thought you might like to take a break with me. I've made soup and sandwiches." Rick bent to kiss her.

"I just want to finish these notes. I need to go downstairs anyway, as I seem to have misplaced Bartleby's chapters."

"Did you ever reach him?"

"Not yet. I think we should take a ride tomorrow and see if he's home. We had tentative plans to meet so I could fill him in on what happened at Saturday's class. I'm sure he's okay, but I'd like to put my mind at ease."

A half hour later, Rick called up the stairs. "Campbell's tomato bisque and grilled cheese. Your favorites. And if you get down here in the next minute, warm butterscotch pudding with whipped cream for dessert."

Ruth's stomach growled. "I'll be right there."

∾

3

Keepers of books, keepers of print and paper on the shelves, librarians are keepers of the records of the human spirit.
Archibald MacLeish

Sunday, December 8

MISS FANNIE MACALISTER LEFT her apartment and walked along High Street toward the library, stopping at *Homespun Antiques* to see if Miss Lucy was occupying her regular spot in the store window. The orange tuxedo cat was curled up sound asleep in her bed. Although the roads and sidewalks had been cleared, nothing was open early on this bright Sunday morning. She went through the stone columns at the Serpa Gate. Walking past the skating pond and the bandstand, she followed the shoveled pathway until she reached the Wilcox Fountain where the bronze lady held up her scallop shell in greeting.

The library was closed, but she had a ring of keys which allowed her to come and go as she pleased. Miss Fannie often worked on Sundays when she had the marvelous stone structure all to herself. Sometimes she would just stroll through the building singing the old tunes she'd heard played on her grandfather's Victrola back when she was a child. Her voice bounced off the walls and ceilings, echoing around her as though she had an entire Greek chorus following in her wake.

The fragrance of lemon-scented furniture polish emanated from the neat and orderly desk in her comfortable office tucked away on the second floor. She devoted the first hour and a half answering correspondence left over from the previous week and then brewed herself a cup of jasmine tea. She spent the next two hours doing research and making copies of reference articles for Ruth Eddleman to hand out at the next workshop.

She was glad she'd referred Bartleby into the group. From what she'd overheard so far during the sessions, his book certainly had the most literary merit. Truth be told, she'd developed a bit of a crush on him since the loss of his wife. Fannie felt no loyalty to the dearly departed woman, although she would never speak ill of the dead. But the few times Mrs. Imogene Durst-Schnelling had graced the library with her presence could be counted on one hand. "Not much of a reader, that one," the librarian had mumbled under her breath in a brief moment of rare indiscretion.

Now, Bartleby Schnelling was made out of a different fabric. He was a true bibliophile and was exceedingly grateful for the many reading suggestions Fannie had offered over the years. Their subsequent discussions resulting from these readings were quite stimulating and she secretly nursed unrequited fantasies beneath the professional austere demeanor the prim librarian presented to the library staff and patrons.

Fannie stopped what she was doing. She heard footsteps. Surely the door had locked automatically when she'd let herself in. "Halooo! Hallooooo! Is anyone there?" Silence. *Just my imagination working overtime.* Checking the gold watch pinned to the lapel of her powder blue cashmere twin set, she stood up to stretch and then placed the pile of articles aside. In the bottom drawer of the antique file cabinet was a shoebox. Tucking it under her arm, she left her office to begin her noontime perambulation around the building.

The balcony of the third floor Terrace Room overlooked the expanse of the park, its gardens now asleep under the white blanket. In the distance, the bandstand always brought to mind the wonderful summer concerts Fannie had attended with her mother and father as a child. Snow covered much of the balcony reaching halfway up its copper-lined inner walls. On Sundays, it was her habit to go outside and reverently recite aloud the opening stanza of F. Frank Greenman's poem written in 1921. Today, she had to be content to look at the scene from the room's arched windows.

Of all the pretty spots around,
In daylight or in dark,
I find no spot in all the town,
That excels Wilcox Park.

Below, people were taking their afternoon strolls. Children were gleefully coasting down the slopes bordering the sides of the meadow on all manner of sleds and colorful discs. The skaters would have to wait until the temperature dropped low enough for the ice to freeze solid before the snow could be safely cleared off the surface of the pond. She entertained thoughts of asking Bartleby if he'd like to join her on a Saturday evening skating date. She'd make a thermos of hot cocoa and they would hold hands, hers chastely gloved, as they glided along together singing 'The Skater's Waltz'. She'd teach him the words if he didn't already know them.

A distinct thud interrupted her reverie. "Halooo. Is anyone there?" Silence. *Probably ice falling from the roof.* She walked back down the staircase, past her office, and on to the latest exhibit hung on the walls of the Hoxie Gallery. She strolled around the large room, moving from painting to painting, noting each artist and choosing her favorites. Then, setting the box on the baby grand piano, she sat on the piano bench to remove her shoes. She took a shiny pair of black patent leather Mary Janes from the box, placed them on the floor, and slid her size eleven feet into them. Striding to the middle of the room's brown and tan checker-patterned floor, sunlight streaming in from the vast skylight, she straightened the cap of her synthetic fiber almost-like-real-hair pageboy style wig before launching into the first verse of "Winter Wonderland". She adroitly warmed up her tap-dancing shoes through a medley of holiday tunes until they were ready to break loose, click clacking furiously to the strains of "Jingle Bell Rock". A pair of eyes, unobserved, watched her from the adjoining alcove above the main staircase to the first floor.

Breathless, Fannie finished with a grand flourish. She sat and removed the dancing shoes and placed them back into the box. Before returning to her office, she stood for a moment thinking just how much she cherished these Sundays alone inside her library.

Rick parked his car in the road outside of Bartleby's old Victorian house on Grove Avenue overlooking the park. The driveway and walks had not been shoveled. "No footprints in the snow around the house. I don't think anyone's around."

"I left a message on his cell telling him I'd be stopping by. I'm going to check," Ruth said. "You stay in the car." She trudged through the snow up the front stairs and onto the porch to ring the doorbell. When Bartleby didn't appear, she gave the brass pineapple doorknocker a few good raps. Peering into the parlor windows, she could detect no one inside. She went around to the back and banged on the kitchen door. No answer. She gave up.

"What do you want to do next?" Rick asked as she kicked off the snow from her boots before lifting her feet into the car.

"Let's see if the bookstore is open, Terry might be at work and they're good friends. Maybe she knows where he is?"

In the park, just below the slope leading up to Grove Avenue, a lone birdwatcher slowly turned the binoculars away from Bartleby's house to focus on the area near the bandstand. Children noisily chased each other up and down the snow piled along the edge of the paths while mothers sat conversing on a nearby bench. They took turns warning their little ones to be careful. A woman in a white ermine coat stood up suddenly when two of the older boys began shoving each other toward the pond. "Get away from there! The ice is still too thin. It'll crack and you'll fall in and drown." The children laughed at the ridiculousness of the thought and went off to race round and round the bandstand. They soon began pelting each other with snowballs. To anyone gazing down upon the wintery scene, it appeared perfectly idyllic.

The Savoy Bookshop and Cafe was closed. Ruth returned to the car. "I'll have to wait until tomorrow's meeting to find out what the call was about. Hopefully, he'll be there."

Rick patted her hand. "You're worrying for nothing. He was a spy. I'm sure he can take care of himself. As long as we're here, we should visit the park before we head for home."

"Brilliant idea," she agreed. "That reminds me of lines from an old poem about the park.

All strangers who come in to town,
With time to look about
Admire and praise this beauty spot,
Without a single doubt.

When light and shadow is just right,
And all the grass is green,
The grand old trees and winding paths,
Present a lovely scene.

I never can recall the poet or any of the other stanzas, but I've always loved those lines."

~

"Auntie, I wonder if there's skating at the park tonight?"

"I think it was too warm last week for the ice to set. The pond won't be cleared. But if you want to go over there later to take a walk, I could do with an airing out." Virginia began removing the dinner dishes from the kitchen table. "On the last day before summer vacation, when I was in grammar school, children were selected to read aloud a stanza from the poem 'Wilcox Park' at an assembly." She stood ramrod straight in front of the dishwasher and made a curtsy to her niece. "When I was in fourth grade, I was one of the chosen.

In winter, too, the many paths,
Are freed from ice and snow,
And we enjoy the various walks,
No matter where we go.

And our teachers would make us all stand with our hands on our hearts and recite the last stanza in unison.

> *May future generations, too,*
> *Ne'er fail to give due praise,*
> *For this grand gift to Westerly,*
> *Throughout all coming days."*

She bowed to her niece's appreciative applause. "And we'd be given little bags of cookies the principal had baked that morning. They were soft and warm and smelled delicious. Then we'd line up for a short walk and spend the rest of the day playing in the park."

"What a happy memory!"

"One of the best! It was when the family lived nearer the library in the North End before we moved closer to the beach. Lots of lovely memories here, too." Her aunt turned on the dishwasher and announced, "I'll pack the cookies if you'll get our coats."

⁓

"Today was fun. I'm not sure who enjoyed playing outside more, Celia or the puppies," Stewart said.

"I'm beginning to think Sophia's idea of keeping an account of Celia's first years is ingenious. I'm afraid I might not recall all of the memories we're making with her," Kara mused as she closed the binder on 'Celia's First Snowstorm'. "Do you remember any of your snow days when you were a child?"

"One day stands out. I made a blanket tent in my bedroom and read all day long. I heard the other kids playing outside, but I was content to loll the hours away among my book friends. My mother brought me Ovaltine and a bologna sandwich, crust cut off, with yellow mustard on Wonderbread for lunch. Oh, and a chocolate frosted cupcake for dessert."

"Didn't you want to go outside and make snow forts?"

"No, I think I enjoyed having time off all by myself. What about you?"

"There were lots of days when my sister, brother and I would wake up early and turn on the radio to listen to Salty Brine announce the cancellations. 'No school, Foster-Gloucester!' Other towns would trickle in to be added to the list and read in alphabetical order. On those mornings when we would finally hear him say 'No School South Kingstown', we'd jump up and down and run to the kitchen for breakfast so we could get our snowsuits on and spend the whole day outside with the neighborhood kids. Sometimes, if the lake was deemed safe, we'd take out our ice-skates and chase each other round and round until it got dark and we stumbled home exhausted."

"I skated once – not one of my favorite youthful experiences. It didn't end well. I remember falling and the other kids standing over me gaping at the blood on the ice." Stewart touched the back of his head. "I had to go to the emergency room for stitches."

"Well, then I guess we can both agree that Sophia will have the honor of taking Celia for her first ice skating lesson." Kara's hand gently brushed a strand of hair from her husband's forehead.

"No, I think I'd like to try it again when she's old enough. You and me and Celia."

Kara clapped her hands. "Sounds like a marvelous plan. Count me in."

"But right now, I believe I'll crawl into bed with a good book."

"I'll join you. I'm sorry to say we have no Ovaltine. But I can whip up a nice pot of Sleepytime Tea."

"I don't think I'll need it, I'm not sure I can stay awake for much longer. Snow days are exhausting."

There's no greater agony than bearing an untold story inside you.

Maya Angelou

Monday, December 9

JACOB'S BADGE IDENTIFIED HIM as a *Westerly Library Intern*. He opened the doors to a burst of frigid December air. "Come on, Nellie Belly. It's costing money to heat this place."

Nelson Belle took no heed of the teenager's insolence. He went straight to the circulation desk to return the books he'd signed out on Friday afternoon.

"Good morning, Mr. Belle. I see you braved the icy sidewalks to be with us today."

"Good morning, Miss MacAlister."

She handed Nelson his own official badge – DOCENT. It was a position the librarian had specially created for him. "We have two groups signed up at the moment and one cancellation due to the storm. The first tour won't be until later this morning, Mr. Belle."

"Thank you Miss MacAlister. I'll keep myself occupied and if you have need of any assistance, anything at all, you can find me at my usual post."

Nelson went directly to the rack where he took copies of the *Westerly Sun* and *The New York Times* and brought them into the Old Reading Room, his home away from home. This second home had a much cleaner bathroom and smelled of citrus furniture polish. None of the furniture in his squalid shack near the railroad tracks was ever polished or even dusted.

He sat down in the leather chair in front of the fireplace. Before opening the pages of the local newspaper, he imagined a conversation he would like to have had with Miss Fannie MacAlister, the kindly librarian who greeted him each morning.

"Mr. Belle, I hope your weekend was a good one."

"It certainly was, Miss MacAlister. And yours?"

"Highly uneventful days – just as I prefer. Snuggled up with Lady Winklemere, a cup of hot milk, a good book, and asleep by nine each night."

"Sounds quite cozy, I must say. And I trust Lady Winklemere is doing well?"

"She's such a finicky little tabby who really doesn't like the cold weather. She's begun to complain a lot. I think she's trying to tell me we need to move to Florida."

"Oh you can't do that, Miss MacAlister. This library would certainly fall apart if you weren't here to keep everything in perfect order."

"Why thank you, Mr. Belle. And I see you're returning the Nathaniel Hawthorne books. 'Bartleby the Scrivener' happens to be one of my very favorite characters in American Literature.

"Mine, too, Miss MacAlister. With every conversation, I'm delighted to find we both have so much in common."

"You're a man after my own heart, Mr. Belle. One who appreciates the vast world existing inside the covers of books."

"Indeed I do, Miss MacAlister. And now I must continue my literary journey through all of the immense wealth of knowledge contained in this marvelous library."

"And what will it be today? Perhaps you might venture with me into the Romance Section?" At this point in his Walter Mittyish daydream, the discrete librarian suppressed a giggle. He pictured Fannie catching herself before it was too late, coyishly pressing dainty fingers against her pursed lips.

"To quote Bartleby, our scrivener friend, 'I would prefer not to'." He chuckled and then gave her a wink.

"Oh, Mr. Belle, you are quite a card! Here's your newspaper. Have a pleasant day."

Nelson looked forward to a future time when they would be on a first name basis and he could call her Fannie. He made himself comfortable, and turned to the obituaries. *Lots of dead people out there.* He scanned the names. *Nobody I know.* By the time others had ventured into the room, he'd made it to the sports section. He'd never been interested in sports of any kind and the pages were filled with football and hockey. He particularly didn't like football. And he'd never stoop to be part of the rabble of fans that identified with "their" teams. The players themselves did not appear to have any loyalty to their fans except for the fact that they allowed them to pay big bucks to wear clothes that were essentially walking billboards.

"Hey, Nellie Belly, wotcha thinking about?"

He could feel the presence of the pimply-faced teenager towering over him and consciously chose to ignore him, pulling the newspaper higher to block the sight of the young punk.

"Hey, I'm talkin to ya, old man." Jacob flicked at the paper with his thumb and index finger making a loud snap. He laughed loudly bringing the librarian into the room. He jumped at the sound of her voice.

"Aren't you supposed to be unpacking boxes in the gallery?"

"Sorry, Miz MacAlister. I was just discussing sports with Nel… with Mr. Belle." Nelson glared up at him. "Go Pats!" Jake announced as he exited the room.

"And it's Miss MacAlister," the librarian corrected him. He didn't bother to turn, but gave a curt salute outside the door. "That young man's skating on thin ice," she murmured under her breath, but loud enough for Nelson to hear. It made him feel warm and tingly, knowing she had stood up for him and he made a silent promise that he would always be there for her, should she ever need a knight in shining armor. This brought to mind his all-time favorite movie, *The Princess Bride*, which the children's librarian had chosen for one of the family film nights. He had no family, but he tried to blend in with the parents in the back of the room while pretending his make-believe children were up front with the other youngsters.

Nelson opened the *New York Times* settling in comfortably behind the obituary pages and soon lapsed into another series of daydreams, which kept him occupied throughout the morning until Miss MacAlister came to tell him his first tour group was waiting.

Terry arrived early to prepare the coffee, tea, and pastries she served in the café. Entering the double doors of the bookshop, she bent to pick up the mail and went over to the couch, dropping the envelopes and flyers on the steamer trunk. She sat sorting the pile that had accumulated during the past few days. The large manila envelope gave her reason to pause. She opened it up and found another envelope bearing the name and address of Ruth Eddleman. *How did this get here?* She turned it over but found no clue as to why something for the professor would be left on the floor of the bookstore. It wasn't properly sealed and bore no stamp. She suppressed the urge to peek inside the envelope to find out its contents, but instead decided she would personally deliver it at tonight's workshop. She placed it in her bag and rose to begin her day.

Later in the afternoon, Greg stopped by the café. Terry looked forward to seeing him and waited to take her break so they could sit together at a table by the back window with their cups of coffee. He was a few years older, but really bashful and awkward, so, he seemed younger. Greg, who'd been on the police force less than a year, had explained to her that rookies usually drew the night shift. Terry spent her days at the bookshop and weekends at the theatre, leaving little opportunity in their lives to consider taking the relationship up a notch to the dating level. The afternoon coffee break had to suffice for now.

He often purchased the same book she currently was reading and they would spend their time together discussing the characters or plots. She'd told him a little about the play she was writing and that her friend Bartleby was going to show it to his publisher. Greg seemed interested in hearing about it. But she wasn't ready to share it with anyone except for Bartleby and Dr. Eddleman. Terry had even been hesitant for the others in the workshop to read certain sections of the three-act drama, carefully choosing which scenes in the first and second acts they'd discuss. She wanted to insure nobody would be able to discern the source she'd used as the basis for her story. If the play were ever performed, she'd deal with the problem then.

She left the cafe earlier than usual and promised the other barista she'd return to help with clean up. Terry was looking forward to seeing Bartleby and spending some time talking about his recent trip before the others arrived. He came into the bookshop every day. She'd missed his visits during the past week and was eagerly anticipating hearing about New York and the meeting with his publisher at GreenTree. She walked up Canal Street turning right on High Street, not realizing her old friend had turned left for the last time at that same corner just three nights ago. The wind blew down from the surrounding brick buildings and Terry pulled her scarf up around her chin to keep out the chill she suddenly felt in her bones.

∽

Conrad left his insurance agency early, as he did every Monday. When he arrived home, his wife was still dawdling upstairs in the bedroom. "Let's get a move on Carolynn. I want to make sure we get a chance to talk about the latest chapter in our book. I don't want Schnelling taking over with his spy saga if we're not on time. He jumps in every opportunity he gets."

"I thought you were friends?"

"Why would you think I'd be friends with that pompous prig?"

"You were pretty chummy with him when you tried to sell him that insurance policy."

"There's a line between business and friendship that I don't cross, Carolynn."

"Well, I think Dr. Eddleman plans to spend some of this session on Bartleby's book. He's still having problems with the final chapters, so try to be patient with him. Help me look for the keys to my car."

"We'll take mine. You probably don't even have gas in yours."

"Last time I checked, the little red warning light wasn't on. So, there's plenty of gas to take us to the library and back."

"Grab your coat. If you're not outside by the time I open the garage door, I'm leaving."

Conrad would have preferred attending the group without his wife. He suspected she was purposely undermining him with this ridiculous piece of fiction he'd agreed to do with her. His first wife had helped him write two books. Non-fiction. Everyone knows non-fiction has much more status than a dumb little cozy mystery. And unlike Carolynn, his first wife never tried to upstage him. She let him take full credit for those textbooks, thankful for a mere mention in the acknowledgments.

To put it mildly, Carolynn was a major disappointment. Granted, it was her initial book draft which had gotten them into the workshop, but now he was having to re-do everything she'd written. But, she was great at editing. Finding errors was definitely her forte. She was one of those people who was good at pointing out mistakes. Mistress of the red pencil. Although her perky personality and self-confidence were what had attracted her to him at first, now that he had to live with her, the combination was simply annoying.

Conrad pushed the button and the garage door began to slide upwards. He looked into the rear view mirror and saw her standing behind the car. He weighed his options and then decided running her over was probably not the prudent way to go. At least not until she'd edited his final draft.

∽

In his chair in front of the reading room fireplace, eyes slightly closed, Nelson tuned his ears in on the conversation at the oak conference table nearby. He liked the woman who ran the group. Dr. Ruth Eddleman. He loved the name Ruth – a character straight from the Bible. If he could have named himself, he would have chosen Moses or Abraham or Soloman. Maybe Noah. Definitely not Jesus. Nelson considered himself to be a humble man. The person he identified with most in the Bible was Job. Not the rich Job. Nelson had never had much money. But the unfortunate man upon whom misfortune visited later in life. Yes, his mother should have named him Job.

Ruth's voice brought him back into the present. It was patient and soothing. She was telling Milton and Terry they needed to wait a few more minutes for Bartleby and the Renzullis, the couple writing the romance mystery with the dumb title, *More Than Just a Simple Hello*. In Nelson's opinion, from the plot summaries presented during the earlier meetings, this was the weakest book in the group. It was a lot of drivel about a woman's infatuation with a college professor. Bored with being a mother and housewife, she'd returned to college and became embroiled in a sordid affair. The underlying drama of her inner turmoil in having to choose between her family and her dreams of living a more exciting life in the world of academia was particularly nauseating to him. And it reminded him of *The Bridges of Madison County*. He'd hated that movie, although he could totally understand someone wanting to run away with Clint Eastwood.

Nelson had decided, after listening to the opening chapters, this adulterous housewife was a one-dimensional narcissist with no redeeming qualities. He sincerely hoped, since this was a murder mystery, that her husband would discover the affair and kill her off as soon as possible. A crime of passion. He'd certainly be given a light sentence. Probably home confinement where he could bring up his motherless children.

The Renzullis were well into the fifth chapter with apparently no dead bodies on the horizon, although they'd managed to fit in an overabundance of romance. Nelson wished he was part of the group so he could offer his two cents. *Everyone knows if a novel is going to grab and keep a reader, you have to capture that reader's attention immediately. If a writer doesn't kill off someone in the first chapter, the book is probably going to end up on a scrap heap.* And in his humble opinion, from the direction this plot was moving, Nelson feared the victim might end up being her husband, the guy who worked two jobs so that his boring wife could attend college, their kids could go to private schools, and they could afford designer clothes and nice vacations. *What a schmuck!* To quote the Impressive Clergyman in *The Princess Bride*, "Mawiage, that bwessed awangement, that dweam wifin a dweam..." Nelson chuckled to himself. He was glad he'd stayed single. He had never dated a woman he'd even considered marrying and he wasn't really that fond of kids. Yup, he'd made the right decision. *Married life sucked.*

As if to prove his point, the Renzullis entered the room looking like they'd just had a spat. Nelson whispered to himself, *"And wuv, twu wuv, will fowow you foweva..."* Peeking over the top of his newspaper, he noted that this Casanova didn't bother to help his Princess Buttercup remove her coat as she struggled getting her arms out of the sleeves. Instead, Prince Charming went to the side table Jacob had set up for the group and poured himself a cup of coffee. Nelson smirked. *None for you, little wifey.*

Carolynn flounced into her seat. Milton sensed her mood and asked if he could get her something.

"Thank you. A hot chocolate, please."

Nelson thought Milton was one of the nicest guys he'd ever met. He always came early and took the time to sit and have a chat. Unfortunately Fannie liked him, too, and spent a lot of time finding reading material for the old guy. He often wondered just how many books on horses and racetracks there were in the library. He thought Milton's book held a lot of promise. Even though he was not a fan of sports, horse racing was different. He loved horses. If he could live in a stable, he would. It would be a step up from his place. But Nelson comforted himself with the knowledge that she certainly must look upon him as a father figure. Grandfather, even. He couldn't deny Milton was spry for his age, but he was much too old for her.

Now Schnelling was another kettle of fish. Although his favorite manuscript was the spy thriller Bartleby was writing, Nelson sometimes viewed him as a rival for Fannie's affections. He'd noticed a sparkle lit up Fannie's eyes whenever Bartleby came into the library. He wasn't sure what she saw in him. He was short and had no meat on his bones. A slight wisp of a man who would probably fall over in a strong wind. His long, pointy, grey goatee always needed trimming and was a repository for crumbs from the Ritz Crackers he pulled from the cellophane packets he kept stored in his pockets. Nelson vividly recalled an incident recently, when, to his utter dismay, Fannie grabbed a paper napkin decorated with pilgrims and Indians to blot the hot chocolate that had coated the top of the man's pale, thin, upper lip. This caused Nelson to cringe each time his mind wandered back to the scene on that awful November day.

He often listened in on their conversations of the latest books she'd chosen for Bartleby to read. One particular discussion was seared into his brain where they'd both agreed *The Spy Who Came in From the Cold* was an all-time favorite. Fannie's eyes had filled with tears while reliving the end of the book when Alec Leamas, the spy, chooses to remain and die with Liz Gold, rather than continue over the Berlin Wall to freedom. Bartleby made it a point to emphasize that the two doomed lovers had met when Leamis was working in a library and that Liz Gold was a librarian. Nelson connected the dots and understood why this book, in addition to its *Silver Dagger Award*, would have special appeal to Fannie.

And, as if the topic of illicit love affairs wasn't inappropriate enough, Schnelling once ventured to teasingly ask if she'd seen the James Bond movie, *The Spy Who Loved Me,* causing Fannie to giggle. Nelson felt this an unseemly discussion to be having in a library reading room. He was shaking his head in stern disapproval and to rid his mind of the vivid pictures he'd been painting when Ruth's voice made an announcement.

"I think we should start without Bartleby. Terry, have you heard anything from him lately?"

"He came into the store on Tuesday and had his usual mug of herbal tea. He told me he was on his way to catch the train to New York. I thought he'd be back by now."

Ruth took out her folders and began the meeting. "I sent you all assignments on Saturday. Carolynn, do you want to discuss the changes you made this weekend?"

Conrad flashed a puzzled look at his wife. "What changes?" She hadn't mentioned any assignment to him.

Nelson sensed the tension building. He lowered the paper slightly for a better view.

Carolynn jumped in. "I followed your directions and reworked the female detective's dialogue so that she seems more professional." All she'd really done was to take the chapters she'd originally written and tossed out the ones Conrad had substituted.

"Would you read aloud the edited version? You take the part of the woman detective and Conrad, will you read the male detective's lines?" Ruth requested. "And then we can discuss the edits you've decided to make."

Nelson perked up behind the cover of the newspaper which he lowered even more so as not to miss anything. *This could be fun.*

Conrad begrudgingly read the dialogue his wife had written without his permission. He was not pleased and Carolynn knew they would have an uncomfortable ride home. Her husband loved using the silent treatment on her. Sometimes it had lasted for days. When they'd finished the chapter, the others spent the next hour giving their feedback.

"I think you have the right idea. I'd like to make one more suggestion. You should get to the actual crime before you go any further or your readers will lose interest." Ruth added. "And maybe you should space the love scenes farther apart?"

Nelson ducked back behind the cover of the newspaper and gave himself a pat on the back. Even he knew you had to kill off someone right away or there goes your audience. But he was pretty sure twenty corpses on the first page wasn't going to help save this book. *What a snoozer!* He made a snoring noise which must have come out louder than he'd meant it to because suddenly there was dead silence in the room. He turned a page, rustling the paper to fill the quiet.

Ruth focused the group back to the task at hand. "Have you decided who your victim will be? You need to give your detectives a murder to solve sooner rather than later."

"No, we have a slight difference of opinion whether it would make the most sense to kill off the husband or the wife," Conrad answered, knowing it would definitely not be the husband as Carolynn had planned in her original version of the story.

"We'll work on that this week," Carolynn assured the group.

"Who wants to go next?" Ruth asked. "Terry?"

"I'd like to wait until Saturday's meeting, if you don't mind. I'm making some major revisions and need more time."

"Okay then, Milton, you now have the floor."

"I took your advice and got rid of the excess words. And I've done some more writing and tried to focus on the main plot. Listening to Carolynn and Conrad, I realized I need some help with my dialogue, keeping in mind there'll be some racetrack jargon. And I think I should kill off the jockey earlier in the story."

"Good plan. We'll start from your rewrites and then discuss where it might make sense for the murder to happen," Ruth said.

Nelson folded up the newspaper and sat back to let his mind wander as the group helped Milton improve upon his work. He thought he should be able to write a book himself if he had people to help him. He had plenty of great ideas from all the stuff he'd read, but a lot of them had been over-used. *How many people can you poison with strychnine, bash over the head with an andiron, impale on a sword, or electrocute with a hairdryer in a bathtub before it gets old?* He'd need to search his own life experiences to find something nobody had ever written about. He made up his mind to check out that book on exotic poisons he noticed mixed in with the non fiction he'd re-shelved last week. Maybe he'd even discover a mystery to solve right in his own back yard? Human beings were always dropping dead. He read the obituaries every day. They couldn't all be from natural causes or accidents. And there were lots of people he'd fantasized about snuffing out. His cheap landlord; corrupt politicians; damned old biddies who held up the supermarket checkout lane fishing around in their handbags for the right change; wise-ass teenagers. *I'll bet I can come up with a spectacular plot by next week. A mass murder.*

The sounds of people preparing to leave snapped him back into the moment. The meeting was over. He began to clean up and return the leftover refreshments and plates to the Coy Café across the hall in the room that had once been the office of one of the town's revered and much loved librarians, Sallie Coy. She'd served the library in various capacities for fifty-two years. Nelson hoped Miss MacAlister would be around for that many years and he made a commitment to be right by her side, every day.

Ruth had ended the session by assigning them the task of making their introductory chapters more riveting and distributing articles she'd chosen on the topic. She asked Terry to stay behind as the others prepared to leave. Jacob was nowhere to be seen, so Nelson began tidying up the area while keeping an ear tuned in on their conversation.

"Did Bartleby tell you anything about his trip to New York?"

"Just that he wanted to meet with his publisher about finding him another editor. He doesn't get along with the one he's been working with. I asked him what the problem was and he said, 'I'll never get the final chapters completed. She's always finding problems. Things she wants me to correct.' When I mentioned that was her job, his answer was, 'But she takes particular enjoyment in pointing out my mistakes. It makes her feel superior.' He told me if he weren't assigned someone else, he'd tear up the contract. He finished his tea and gave me a ten dollar tip. That's the last I saw of him."

"So, he took the morning train and you haven't heard from him since?"

"Uh huh. He was supposed to return by Sunday. I know he planned on being here for tonight's meeting. He thought you'd be pleased because he'd finished the last chapters."

"If he gets in touch, please tell him to call me. I'm worried."

"His housekeeper, Mrs. Mayfair, also cleans the bookshop. I'll look up her number and call you with it. Maybe she knows something?"

"I'd appreciate that, Terry. I'm allotting you the whole first hour at next Saturday's session, so work on your script this week."

Miss MacAlister walked with Ruth to the door leading out onto the Columbus Terrace and wished her a good evening. "If you forward the articles you want to use for the next class, I'll make copies for everyone."

"Thanks, Fannie. I'm happy to report the group is making progress."

"You're a great teacher. I love to listen in on your sessions. I'm glad you agreed to do this workshop."

She left Ruth standing alone on the terrace inhaling the crisp night air, the sound of the door locking behind her. A shadow flickered. *Was someone lurking behind the Columbus Statue?* Pulling her wool scarf up closer to her chin, she moved quickly down the stairs to the fountain and along the path to the parking lot. Behind her, the sound of crunching snow. She removed her mitten, fumbling to find the keys she thought were in her coat pocket. They were at the bottom of her handbag. She unlocked the car door and glanced over her shoulder. A dark figure slowly emerged from between the two stone columns of the park's entrance.

Suddenly, Terry came rushing into the lot from the sidewalk. "Dr. Eddleman, I almost forgot to give you this." She handed Ruth the manila envelope. "It was left at the bookshop. Mixed in with the mail from over the weekend."

"Oh! You startled me. Where did you come from?"

"I was on my way to the store. I parked my car there, in the lot. I'm going back to help close up."

"Do you want a ride?"

"No, it's right down the street. I'm perfectly safe. See you next Saturday."

Ruth looked back to the entrance, but the figure had disappeared. She locked her door, then drove from the lot and waited on the street, watching until she saw Terry enter the store. She sat for a few minutes until her heart stopped pounding. *Too many murder plots. You're letting your imagination get the better of you.*

When she arrived home, she opened the envelope. Inside was a copy of Bartleby's manuscript. She read it through. Not much had changed from the original draft he'd shown her. And, in spite of what he'd told Terry, the last chapter was still missing. In its place was a note.

> Ruth,
>
> Here's the book. It is my only final draft copy. I've decided not to proceed with plans to publish at this time. Keep this in a safe place. Show it to no one until I can meet with you and explain.
>
> Bartleby

Now she was curious. It was time to enlist Kara's help to get to the bottom of this.

Some editors are failed writers, but so are most writers."

T. S. Eliot

Tuesday, December 10

"Good morning. It's Ruth. I was wondering if you would be around today?"

"Celia and I weren't planning on going anywhere and Stewart will be at the college."

"I'd like to stop by. I need to talk to you about Bartleby Schnelling."

"The spy guy?"

"Yes. It appears he's dropped off the face of the earth."

"I'll be here."

"Sophia says she wants to come along." Ruth whispered into the phone, "I suspect she's going to check your assignment on 'Celia's First Snowstorm'."

"Stewart and I did it together last night."

"Sophia wants to know if you took pictures."

"We did one better. A video."

"Great! I'll pass that information on. We'll be by around ten."

Kara lifted Celia from her bouncy seat. "Come on, little one. We need to choose a special outfit for today. Aunt Sophia is coming to visit."

As she carried the baby cooing and babbling to the nursery, she could have sworn she heard her say, "Auntie".

Ruth showed Kara the manuscript and the note. "I don't care what he wants. I'm worried and I need your help."

"When was the last time anyone saw or spoke with him?"

"Terry said he stopped by on Tuesday before catching the train to New York. I spoke with his housekeeper this morning before I called you and she told me she only cleans on the first Monday of each month. She has a key and lets herself in. She said she didn't see him in December but he was home when she was there in November. She agreed to meet me at the house and let us inside. My imagination is running rampant. He could be lying somewhere hurt and unable to contact anyone."

"That's a good place to start. Call and tell her we'll be there at noon today."

While Ruth phoned, Kara went into the nursery where Sophia and Celia were busy reading a book. Pierre and Marie Curie, the labradoodles, sat with their ears perked up on either side of the rocking chair listening to every word and hoping patiently that Celia would share a piece of the page she was studiously gnawing on.

"Should she be chewing that?" Kara asked.

"Don't worry, these books are totally edible. The ink is made from vegetable coloring. I thought Stewart would appreciate them."

"There may be nothing left for him to nibble on at the rate she's going," Kara observed. Sophia gave her a frosty look. "Ruth and I are taking a drive to Westerly. You two seem settled in. Do you want to go with us?"

Sophia conferred with her niece who stopped licking the book's cover to babble a moment. Her aunt translated. "We prefer the comfort of the nursery to a ride in the car."

"Then we'll leave you two here. Ruth and I shouldn't be long. And if you feel hungry, there's milk and actual real food in the refrigerator. Have fun."

The cleaning woman was waiting at the front door to let them in when they arrived.

"We appreciate your taking time to help us, Mrs. Mayfair. I'm Ruth Eddleman. We spoke on the phone. And this is my friend, Kara Langley."

"The private detective lady. How'd you do?"

"Fine, thank you." Kara shook the outstretched hand.

"We'd like to see if we can find something that will give us an idea where Mr. Schnelling might be. As I told you, he wasn't at last evening's workshop and I'm worried. I've left messages on his cell phone but he hasn't answered them."

"That is quite unlike the Mr. I've always known him to be extremely dependable." She escorted them through the downstairs rooms talking all the while. "This is the spare bedroom. It's where guests stayed when his parents were alive and he was off working for the government. They left him the house when they passed. It was within a few months of each other. By that time he'd gotten married to the Mrs. I don't think his parents approved of the age difference. She was a few years older than him. I heard them calling her Methuselah once. He seldom came to visit, but they moved in after his parents passed on. I helped keep the place clean through it all," she said proudly.

"You've worked for the family a long time?"

"Since I was a girl. I would come with my grandmother. She kept house for his parents until I took over. I came every day back then. This place sparkled. I'll take you to see his room. It's on the second floor in the back."

They followed her. At the top of the stairs was a large bedroom. "This was where the Mr. and the Mrs. slept. After his wife died, he instructed me to move all of his belongings into the room he had as a boy." She led them down the hall into a sparsely furnished space. A twin bed with a black iron headboard, a night table, a small lamp, and a child's bureau gave it a cell-like feel.

The bed had not been slept in. Kara moved around the room. She was struck with the scarcity of belongings she found in the drawers and closet.

"And where does this door lead?" Ruth asked.

"That would be his office. It's locked. I was never allowed to clean in there." Mrs. Mayfair jiggled the glass doorknob in case they doubted her.

"I think it would be wise for us to see if we can find the key." Kara looked at the two women who nodded in agreement. "If you'll go through his clothes in the dresser, Mrs. Mayfair. Ruth, check the closet. Shoes and pockets. And the gift box on the shelf."

Kara ran her hand over the tops of the window and doorframes and lifted the lamp. *Not even a speck of dust.* She took out the *Gideon's Bible* and fanned through the pages. Taped to the inside back cover, she found the key. Inserting it into the lock, she opened the door and stepped into an office with bookcases on all sides. A chair and a desk were the only furnishings. No couch, no carpet, no curtains, no pictures on the walls, and thankfully, no dead body. But it was filled from floor to ceiling with books.

"Mrs. Mayfair, we're going to be in here for an hour or so. If you'd like to go downstairs and brew yourself a cup of tea, we'll make sure the room is locked and the key put back when we leave."

"I think I'll do that, Detective. I'll just prepare the kettle in case you might want to wet your whistles when you're done."

Ruth looked around the room. "Kara, what are we looking for?"

"Information on his publisher. I'd like to talk with him. And maybe we can find the last pages of his manuscript. I'm curious why he didn't include it in the copy he left for you. I think it might shed some light on the reason for his disappearance. If you'll look over those books while I check the desk."

Within a few minutes, Kara had found the business card she needed in a folder of correspondence. She made a call while Ruth continued to scan through the books on the shelves.

"Hello, my name is Detective Kara Langley. I work with the Rhode Island Forensics Department and would like to speak with Mr. Pinkham. It concerns one of his clients ... If you could have him call me." Kara gave the secretary her number. "Please tell him it's urgent."

"Have you found anything interesting?" she asked Ruth who was reading a book she'd removed from a top shelf.

"Actually, I have. Most of the books are fiction – mysteries or novels. But this entire wall contains non-fiction. History books, biographies, memoirs, and a section on famous spies, double-agents, and code breakers."

"I watched the *Bletchley Circle* about the four women code breakers who reunited to help solve mysteries after the war. Imagine being bound to silence by the Secrets Act. Not to be able to share such an important part of your past life with anyone. Not even your own husband. These women did top secret work for the government. To return from doing such a critical job to live the life of a housewife or a secretary ... I could never have accepted that."

"I totally agree with you. It isn't my personality, either. But look, Kara, these books belonged to his wife." She opened to one of the back covers.

Property of Imogene Durst. "I'm wondering if she might have been the real secret agent in the family?"

"Why do you say that? She was too young to be a code breaker during the war."

"The writing style in his book, the voice, it's not like him at all."

"Do you think it could be her work?"

"Or the work of someone she knew. He told me they both had jobs with the government. He led me to believe he held an important, top-secret position and that she was an office clerk."

"Maybe he was the clerk and she was the spy? If it was someone else's unfinished memoir, it would explain why he needed my help with the final chapter."

At the sound of footsteps in the hall, they stopped talking. Mrs. Mayfair stood in the adjoining bedroom. "There's a pot of tea waiting for you in the kitchen."

"We're almost done here. We'll be down in a minute."

"No hurry, Dearies. I've nowhere else to be today."

On the kitchen table was large teapot nestled inside a red gingham cozy with a plate of warm gingerbread beside it. Mrs. Mayfair served them generous slices with dollops of fresh whipped cream. "I've always believed the aroma of something baking in the oven makes a house feel more like a home."

"Thank you, Mrs. Mayfair. This is such a nice treat," Ruth said.

"I've been wanting to ask you – do you think the Mr. is … safe?"

"We haven't found anything to lead us to believe he's in danger. Detective Langley and I will do our best to find out what has happened to him," she assured the woman.

"Has anyone ever visited him while you were in the house?" Kara asked.

"I've met the young lady from the Savoy. Terry's her name. She comes by sometimes. She was visiting when I was here in November. They like to talk about books and writing. I caught some of their conversation. She was telling him all about the play she wanted to publish and said he should try to get into the workshop with his spy novel and maybe Dr. Eddleman would help him to finish it which would make his publisher happy."

"I noticed there's a landline. Has anyone else called on the days you're cleaning?"

"I don't answer the phone. I just let it go to the machine. It seldom rings. The Mr. uses his cell. One of those smart phones, don't you know. Carries it with him everywhere. There's no messages. I checked while you were upstairs."

"What about workmen?"

"The Mr. hired someone to do jobs around the yard, but to my knowledge, almost no one has come to stay in this house since the Mrs. passed away and her son slept in the guest room for a night."

"They have a son?" Ruth glanced at Kara.

"Mrs. Schnelling had grown children. Deighton and a daughter Miranda by her first marriage. I don't think the girl ever came by. Lives in another country, I believe. She didn't attend the funeral. A bit of a mystery, that one."

"And Deighton? Where does he live?"

"I don't know. The Mr. didn't have much to do with him. The children were on their own when the Mr. and Mrs. got married. Deighton stayed here the night of the wake. I didn't meet him. The Mr. had instructed me to make up the bed with fresh linen. I guess he came from out of town."

"There was no address book in the desk. Do you know how I could reach the son?" Kata asked.

"The Mr. kept important numbers in his head. Did his own taxes, he did. I always thought he'd have made a good accountant."

"Do you know if Mr. Schnelling had a lawyer? There must have been someone to take care of legal matters when his wife died."

"That would be young Mr. Whitcomb. He has an office downtown. His father, old Mr. Whitcomb, was the family lawyer as far back as I can remember."

Mrs. Mayfair rose and brought her cup and saucer to the sink signaling that teatime was over.

"Can we help you clear the table?" Ruth asked.

"No, Dearies. I'm sure you have things you need to do to find the Mr. and get him home safe and sound."

She brought them their coats.

"Well, thank you, Mrs. Mayfair, and here's my card. Please call any time if you think of something that might help us," Kara said as they left the house.

"It's been more than forty-eight hours. Time to visit the Westerly police and file a missing person's report," Kara declared as she snapped in her seat belt. "And we should call the lawyer's office to make an appointment as soon as possible. I'd like to find out about the stepson and see if I can get contact information on him."

Kara's phone rang as they sat in the waiting room at the police station. It was Mr. Pinkham from GreenTree Press. After she explained her reason for the call, he apologized because he only had a small window of time to talk but would try to be of help. She put the call on conference mode and Ruth leaned in to listen.

"When did you last see Mr. Schnelling?"

"He met with me on Thursday morning. Let's see … that would have been the sixth of December at 11:30. He left at approximately 11:45."

"And what did you discuss, if I might ask?"

"If it will help to discover where Bartleby is, I'm happy to tell you what I know. We'd had a rather heated exchange in regard to Ms. Albright, his editor. He wanted me to assign him someone else. He even suggested he use a person from Rhode Island. I'm looking at my notes … a Dr. Ruth Eddleman."

"Mr. Pinkham, Dr. Eddleman is here with me. She's the person who asked for my help in locating Mr. Schnelling. He left a message for her on Friday night and she's not been able to reach him since then. He had a meeting scheduled with her on Sunday and a workshop on Monday which he did not attend."

"Well, that doesn't sound at all like Bartleby. He sets great store in keeping his appointments."

"Do you know where he was going when he left your office?"

"His departure was quite abrupt after I refused to acquiesce to his demands. I told him I felt Ms. Albright was the perfect choice for his book, and I certainly had no intention of allowing someone, not in my employ, to edit any book my agency intends to publish. We have the highest standards, uh, no offense to Dr. Eddleman."

"Did he tell why he was displeased with Ms. Albright?"

"He stated that Ms. Albright was too picky – constantly finding fault with his writing. I informed him I was pleased to hear it since it was precisely what she was paid to do. That's when he grabbed the manuscript from my desk and demanded I rip up his contract. 'Our business relationship is hereby officially terminated and you will never see any of the chapters I've written,' were his exact words, according to my notes, before he stormed from my office."

"We'd like to speak with Ms. Albright."

"Of course. I'll transfer this call back to my secretary and she'll provide a contact number for you. I hope I've been of assistance and if you would tell Bartleby to get in touch with us when you find him. Please inform him that ripping up a contract is not the proper way to terminate a business agreement."

The secretary offered to make the connection to Ms. Albright's office. Kara took the number and said she would call the editor at a later time because the dispatcher had entered and told them they could go in to see the desk sergeant.

Kara handed the sergeant her business card and introduced Ruth. "We're not family but it appears he has no relatives nearby and I've become concerned about his well-being."

He placed some forms on his desk. "Do you have an idea when Mr. Schnelling was last seen here in Westerly?"

"He stopped into the Savoy Bookshop before taking the 10:46 AM train to Penn Station last Tuesday and spoke with a friend who works there. Terry Ricitelli. We believe he returned Friday night. At around 6:40 PM." Ruth told him about the manuscript and her attempts to return Bartleby's phone call. "I kept his message." She took out her phone and played it for him.

"And when you returned his call, you left him a message?"

"Yes."

"Tell me, Dr. Eddleman, has Mr. Schnelling been showing any sign of forgetfulness or disorientation?"

"No, quite the opposite. He's very much in charge of his faculties. Sharp as a tack," Ruth assured the sergeant.

"Does he drive?"

"I know he has a small motor bike, but mostly, Bartleby prefers to walk. He takes the train when he ventures out of town," Ruth said.

"If you would fill out this form with as much information as you can. We'll start with that. I'll have a patrolman speak with the young lady at Savoy to get confirmation on the time and a description of what he was wearing on Tuesday. I'll issue an official 'Be on the lookout for' in case he's somewhere else in the state. We can check with Amtrak to see if he bought a ticket on line or if anyone might have recognized him on the train back to Westerly on Friday night. There is also the chance he never left the city."

"That's remotely possible, Kara said. "I served on the police force in New York. I still have connections and may be able to get some help finding out more about Bartleby's movements from my old partner, Sergeant Perez. Dr. Eddleman and I have been able to piece together some of the places Schnelling went while he was in the city."

"That would be helpful, if you could contact your partner. Get back to me with anything you find out. I'll assign the case to one of our detectives. If you'll excuse me, I have a meeting. Just give the forms to the dispatcher when you're finished filling them out."

It was beginning to rain and they rushed to the car.

"So, what next?" Ruth asked.

"I'll call the editor, if you'll take care of making an appointment to speak with the lawyer. I'm not sure how much he can tell us, since we're not family. But we should at least try," Kara said. "And I'll contact Sergeant Perez and see what he can do to help us."

"We don't seem to have much to go on. We know Bartleby took the train from Westerly to Penn Station on Tuesday morning. He met with his publisher on Thursday. Possibly, he dropped the manuscript into the Savoy mail slot and then called you on Friday night. When did he meet with his editor? What did he do all day on Wednesday? Lots of holes to fill in."

"Well, the police have been notified and they'll be on the lookout. Hopefully, Ms. Albright will be able to give us additional information?" She turned on the wipers.

Ruth looked out the car window. "Kara, where in the world could he be?"

"Don't worry, we'll keep searching. And once we figure out where he's been, you'll have material to write your own mystery."

~

Milton waved to his neighbor, Elaine, as he crossed Plimpton Street on his daily walk to the flying carousel. She spent every afternoon reading on the enclosed sun porch of her home in Watch Hill. At the same time every day, Milton began his jog to the beach where he'd spent many days during his youth.

His father had owned the local taxi service. In summertime, taxis drove many of the well-to-do tourists with their large steamer trunks from the Westerly train station to private homes that dotted the cliffs. And some visitors were dropped off at the front door of the famous Ocean House Hotel that sat up on the hill in all its regal splendor.

He recalled memories of a time when their own simple house had been surrounded by cow pastures and laughed when he thought about the cannons installed along the coastline during World War II. Whenever they were going to be set off, a call would come in to the house to caution them to open the windows and avoid the panes cracking. He recalled his mother telling him about having to evacuate the area during the 1938 Hurricane and upon their return, discovering though much had been destroyed, their house miraculously remained in place.

Memories flooded back as he turned left on Bay Street toward the business section and the beach. Most of the out-of-staters had closed up their houses in the fall until their return on Memorial Day, so some sidewalks weren't shoveled. He hadn't jogged since Friday's storm, but today, he'd decided to get out for a while. There was little danger since few vehicles were on the road.

When he arrived at the carousel, he was reminded about the tale of the circus that had come to town and had left a week later without its merry-go-round. His mother would give him a dime on Sundays so he could swirl around on the flying steeds and dream of riding real horses some day. And at fifteen, he'd gotten a job at the nearby stables which eventually led to the years he'd spent traveling the racing circuit.

It was an exciting time for him with many happy memories, except for the murder of that young jockey which wasn't such a pleasant experience. He shook his head to clear away the cobwebs and breathed in the fresh salt air. The carousel was boarded up for the winter and the beach was empty, the waves much calmer than the past week. The smell of rain as the sun moved behind the clouds told him it was time to start back home.

He returned to the roadway and chose an easier pace, walking briskly along, thinking about the famous people he'd driven around town those many years gone by. From somewhere in the distance, he heard an engine revving. As it grew closer, he moved to an opening between the snow piled along the roadside in front of the Olympia Tea Room. He turned to see a motorcycle bearing down on him and in his rush to get to the sidewalk, he tripped on the curb and fell in a heap.

Elaine looked out just as he was limping up to his front gate. She yanked open the door and called to him. "Milton, what happened? Are you okay?"

He sensed the concern in her voice and waved at her. "Just a little spill. I'll be fine," he hollered from the steps.

Safe inside, he stiffly removed his coat and gloves and dialed the phone in his kitchen. "Hello, Westerly Police Station?.... With whom am I speaking?... This is Milton Stafford out in Watch Hill. I'd like to file a report. Some idiot on a motor scooter just tried to run me down."

*If I had a bookstore,
I'd make all the mystery novels hard to find.*
Demetri Martin

WEDNESDAY, DECEMBER 11

DR. VIRGINIA WALDEN HAD only one client scheduled on Wednesday morning. She'd planned on using the rest of the day to transcribe tapes of case histories she'd begun compiling while practicing at a prestigious Connecticut institute specializing in clients with severe neurotic disorders. The book would center on her work with the worst cases. Although Walden achieved much recognition and success during her twenty years at the institute, the dedication to her patients and the long hours she spent at work eventually took a toll. This resulted in the breakup of her marriage followed by a bout of severe depression. She decided to make a change and devote time to getting her own life in order. *Physician heal thyself.*

After the divorce, Virginia returned to her childhood home in Misquamicut, a popular beach area in Westerly. She had a two-room addition built to be used as her office and set up a small practice for well-to-do clients willing to pay the exorbitant sum she charged because of the reputation she'd established with her successes at the institute.

Today's session with her patient started poorly. She heard the door slam in the outer office, and entered the room to find him looking out the front window. "Good morning. You're early."

He turned quickly. His face was flushed. "Don't ever sneak up on me like that again!"

He rushed by her into the inner office and grabbed a Kleenex from an end table to dab at the sweat above his upper lip. He began nervously pacing the length of the room as she settled quietly in her desk chair.

"Why don't you take a seat?"

"I'd rather keep moving. I can talk and walk at the same time, you know." He gave her a defiant look as he circled around to the side of her desk.

She turned on a small tape recorder, stood, and moved to one of the chairs against the far wall in the sitting area. "You seem anxious. Have you taken your medicine this morning?"

"I've told you a thousand times, I don't like the way those drugs make me feel. Don't you ever listen to me?"

"What you say is important to me. We've discussed your treatment and decided to try this new medication for a few months. You agreed."

"I didn't know I'd end up feeling like a zombie."

"I can see about modifying the dosage, but it will still make you feel differently. Do you like the way you act when you aren't taking the drugs?"

"I hate the way I feel and I know how I act. I've acted this way all my life. I don't see the problem."

"Let's talk about that, then."

"I don't want to talk."

"Then why are you here today?"

"If you're going to sit there asking stupid questions, maybe I'll just go."

Walden remained silent looking intently at the belligerent figure now standing in the middle of the room.

"You know why I'm here. We've discussed it all a million times."

"You've told me you're afraid of what will happen to you, what you'll do if you don't come to these sessions. We've talked about your fears." She watched as he moved forward and then slumped into the seat opposite her." Has something happened? I know you've been upset about not getting the job you applied for but you were doing better during our last few meetings."

He grabbed at the sides of the chair and squeezed them until his knuckles turned white and his arms shook. His face was pallid. And then, to her surprise, his lips began to quiver and he put his head down and wept.

She'd often seen him angry and anxious but he'd never cried during any of their sessions. She wondered if he were acting. "I'm not getting better. I'll never get better. This is all a waste of time. A hoax. I want to go back to the institute where it's safe for me and everyone else." He blew his nose into the crumpled Kleenex and threw it on the floor.

"You think you're in danger? What would make you feel that way?"

"How can you be so stupid? You have no idea the danger we're in." He bounded from his seat and went to peer out the side window, then pulled down the shade and whispered. "I'm being followed." He moved suddenly to the far wall.

Walden went to the window and raised the shade. Someone was next door in her neighbor's yard with a snow shovel. Before she could calm her patient and assure him no one was watching, he opened the door and ran from the room. She grabbed her coat from the closet, but by the time she was outside, she found she was alone. She came back into the office and sat thinking for a long time finally deciding it was best to make arrangements for this patient to be readmitted. She sighed and then made a call to the institute to speak with her ex-husband.

Ruth called Kara to tell her about the conversation with Mr. Whitcomb's secretary. "I requested an appointment, but was informed he's at a conference out of town and would be unavailable until the end of the week. When I mentioned Bartleby, the secretary asked if it was about Mr. Schnelling's meeting in regard to his will. I said I needed to speak with Mr. Whitcomb personally. She wouldn't give me his cell phone number but did say she'd fit me in to see him at 1:15 next Friday."

"A will? That could be helpful, especially if he was planning on making changes," Kara noted. "My phone call with Ms. Albright was interesting. Bartleby was at her office early Thursday morning, around 9:15 to discuss his manuscript. She'd returned it to him with lots of comments, particularly on the final chapters. He became irate when she suggested the writing style was uneven. She tried to point out specific examples, but he wasn't hearing any of it, so she asked him if he'd written most of the memoir in his early years, as the later chapters were not as lucid. He demanded to know if she was suggesting he'd gone senile? When she didn't answer him, he grabbed the manuscript, and told her he was going directly to Mr. Pinkham and have her fired. He left her office around 9:30 and she hasn't heard from him since."

"Well, fifteen more minutes accounted for," Ruth said.

"I was curious about Wednesday and phoned the hotel where Pinkham said he was registered. The woman remembered him because she was a fan of Hawthorne and said she'd never met a Bartleby before. She didn't recall anyone coming to the desk to inquire about him."

"He said he planned to meet someone regarding the book. If we find out more about this person, maybe it will give us a lead." Ruth began to speculate. "Was there something about his manuscript they didn't want published? Was Bartleby followed back to RI?"

"Without more information, I'm afraid we're jumping to conclusions and we've reached a dead end," Kara said.

"I think I need to look at that manuscript more closely and see if I can dig up a clue or two. Did you find out anything else?" Ruth asked.

"I called my old partner, who proudly told me he'd been recently reassigned and was now Detective Sergeant Perez, NYPD. He's glad to help. I told him I'd be in touch when I knew better what I was looking for."

Ruth shook her head. "Well, my friend, it appears this has suddenly become an official missing persons investigation."

The bookshop was busy with people doing their Christmas shopping. Terry was afraid the cafe might run out of pastries, but they got through the lunch hour without a problem. She was disappointed when Greg didn't stop by. She'd decided to show him the script and run some ideas by him for set designs. He'd mentioned improvements he'd made around his apartment and gave her the impression he had better than average carpenter skills. She could use some help.

The first and second acts of her play were revised and she had an outline of how it was all going to end in Act Three. She was beginning to visualize the way she wanted her set to look. She imagined a revolving platform on one side of the stage, which would provide the best way to handle scene changes between the house and the office. She wasn't sure if it would be cost prohibitive and wanted Greg's advice. She could always use a scrim to open up a wall for the audience to view the action on the other side.

When Greg hadn't arrived by three, Terry left the cafe in the hands of the other barista. She went downstairs and stepped outside to sit in one of the wrought iron chairs on the patio. Closing her eyes, she breathed in the cold air slowly exhaling thin clouds of white until she couldn't feel the tip of her nose. *Time to go in.*

She went to the back of the store and peeked into the children's nook. She would have liked to spend her break inside the little log cabin cuddled up reading a book with her aunt. She stopped to scan the latest mail left for the faeries who lived behind the tiny doors built into the baseboard. She loved everything about this store. The white tin ceilings, the green glass prisms embedded in the wood floors, the sunshine pouring in from the massive windows. She imagined it when it had been the old Savoy Hotel back in the 1800s. She hoped someday to meet Chuck Royce, the developer who'd taken the old building and created this wonderful oasis she got to come to every day. She'd buy him a coffee, thank him for all the work he does to make the town an awesome place, and then tell him to come back any time. The drinks were on her. She stopped to help a customer in the mystery section choose some books with local settings and then returned to the café.

∽

It had been tense around the house since their silent ride home on Monday night. Conrad had taken to leaving for work early each morning and returning home late every night after his wife had gone to bed. He wasn't happy Carolynn had kept the changes from him and had decided he'd punish her by not working on the book. *Let's see how much she can get done without me.* He was even considering not attending Saturday's workshop.

On Wednesday, he closed the office at six and went to the Knickerbocker Cafe for a beer and to listen to the music. There was a flirty young waitress there he liked. He inquired what time she got off work and offered to give her a ride if she was in need. He handed her his business card along with a large tip.

Back at the office, Conrad poured himself a glass of Scotch and lifted it in a toast to himself. He had cause to celebrate. November had been a good month. He'd written a record amount of policies and December was shaping up to be even better.

He began jotting notes on a yellow legal pad. He'd decided to write his own book. In his mystery, the handsome, bachelor detective worked alone. He dated a pair of identical twins, which would make for some pretty steamy romantic scenes to spice up the action. Conrad kept some of Carolynn's original plot line. But in his version, he had the wife running off with a math professor and the heartbroken husband hiring a private detective to track her down so he could convince her to return to him and their two children. The twist was that the hubby secretly wanted her found so he could kill her.

At the end of the hour, Conrad was satisfied with the pages he'd completed and was particularly pleased that the cheating spouse and her lover were both dead by the end of chapter two. He'd decided to use flashbacks to unfold the story for his readers but was having problems keeping the time sequencing straight. He blamed it on the Scotch and decided to take a rest. He was beginning to doze off on the couch in the break room when the phone rang. It was the cute, little waitress and she needed a ride home. The night wasn't over yet.

Carolynn was enjoying her time alone. She took a frozen lasagna from the fridge and popped it in the microwave, then poured herself a glass of Chianti. The early evening was spent correcting students' term papers and later, after a warm, lavender bubble bath, she snuggled under the covers. Sipping the wine, she continued working on her romantic mystery the way she'd first planned it out. The main character was a woman detective, Jasmine, the brains behind a detective duo. She was happily single and her young, hunky, Swedish partner, Lars, was great in bed but useless in tracking down clues.

In her original plot outline, the private detectives were investigating the disappearance of a high school chemistry teacher who'd abandoned her family to run off with a professor. Conrad had wanted to murder the wife, making her husband the obvious suspect. He intended to have a few twists and turns with the killer ending up being the professor's young teaching assistant with whom he was also having an affair. This wasn't in keeping with Carolynn's story line, which Conrad had felt was too complicated. He insisted they keep it simple. A lover's triangle or in this case, rectangle.

She tried to explain the basic attraction of a mystery. "It's a complicated puzzle and must present a challenge for the reader to solve." They were at an impasse. The book was a total mess and she was sorry she'd ever agreed to let him help her. Carolynn opened the manuscript on her laptop, and began to type. The words flowed smoothly onto the page. She was confident it would be in good shape for Saturday's workshop. And she was taking Dr. Eddleman's advice by making sure the husband was dead before the end of the first chapter.

*There's no better teacher for writing than reading ...
Get a library card. That's the best investment.*
Alisa Valdes

Friday, December 13

GINO WAS SUPERSTITIOUS. AT the beginning of each New Year, he took out the wall calendar the oil company had mailed to its customers and counted out every Friday the 13th placing a large X in black magic marker in the squares for those days. Nothing good ever happened to him on Friday the 13th. In his mind, he relived some of the worst ones – when his father had died; when he'd fallen from the scaffolding outside Saks; and just last April, Kara had almost been killed in the cellar of the library where Ruth was directing a play. He shuddered to think what was in store for him today and considered not getting out of bed or, at least, not leaving the house. He had enough indoor chores to keep him busy without having to venture outside.

Ruth's office needed a fresh coat of paint and she'd chosen a soothing rose pastel. He gathered drop cloths, rollers, and brushes, then climbed up the ladder, which he'd been careful not to walk underneath. By midmorning, he had the first coat on the walls. He thought he might take the powder blue paint he had left over from one of the guest bedrooms and coat the ceiling. Then he'd add some white, fluffy clouds. Ruth would love it.

He brought another ladder into the room and made a scaffolding with a thick plank of wood balanced on the top rungs. He repositioned the drop cloth underneath the first section he would paint, but before he could begin, he heard a phone ringing and followed the sound to a pile of file folders. Rick was always reminding Ruth to take the phone when she went out, but today she'd left it charging on her desk. Gino looked at the caller ID. *Bartleby Schnelling. The missing spy guy!* He answered. Before he could identify himself, a raspy voice whispered, threateningly, "Stay away from the library. I'm watching you."

Gino looked around the room. He flew to the window to check the yard but no one was there. "Ay! Why you watchin me? Wadda ya want?" On hearing his voice, the caller abruptly ended the call. Gino put the phone back on the desk and leaned against one of the ladders thinking about what the person on the other end of the line had said. It suddenly dawned on him the message had been meant for Ruth and she could be in danger. He had to find Rick and tell him. Just then he realized he was under the scaffolding and in his haste to get out from beneath the ladder, he tripped on the cloth. As the bucket of blue paint came crashing to the floor, Gino cried out, "I know I shoulda stayed in bed!"

༄

Sophia had decided it would be a good day to get Celia her first library card.

Ruth whispered to Kara, "I can't wait to visit the section entitled *Edible Kitty Lit*."

"I heard that," Sophia said from the back seat of the car. "Don't pay any attention, Celia. Your Aunt Ruth underestimates how advanced you are. We'll be through the classics before you're in kindergarten." The baby cooed and appeared to lift her hand to give Sophia a high-five.

Kara turned to Ruth, quickly changing the subject. "When we're done at the lawyer's office, maybe we can shop a bit and then get lunch?"

"I like that idea. I want to buy some flavored vinegar and lemon stuffed olives at Capizanno's. If we go to the Savoy, I can get that new photo book, *Shade: A Tale of Two Presidents*. Rick admires Pete Souza's work."

"And I need to pick up a pair of ice skates for Stewart."

Ruth looked at her in disbelief. "I should have warned you before I introduced you two that the Stewart Langley we've all come to know and love is a total klutz."

Kara agreed, but then related the story he'd shared with her of his childhood snow day.

"That is so sweet. I'll make him some pompoms to tie on the laces," Sophia said.

"I think my gift to him this year will be a first aid kit," Ruth declared. "With a tourniquet," she added.

"What are you getting for Gino?"

"All of my presents have been wrapped for months," Sophia informed them. "I may start on next year's Christmas shopping, but the first thing we need to do is sign Celia up for a library card."

Ruth left them at the circulation desk and went in search of Fannie. She met Nelson Belle coming out of her office.

"If you're looking for Miss MacAlister, she's at a board meeting. I don't expect her back any time soon. They can last a while. Can I help you with something?"

"I wanted to give her this article to make copies for the next workshop."

"Oh, I can do that for you." He took the edition of the *Writer's Digest* from her.

"I appreciate that. I've marked the pages."

"I'll have them for you on Saturday. I expect Bartleby will be back from his trip by then, so I'll run off five copies."

"Thank you. Um, Nelson, did Bartleby happen to tell you where he was going or when he'd be returning?"

"Oh, no, but I overheard him talking about his trip to New York. I thought he said he'd be back last weekend, but I could be wrong. I'll leave Miss MacAlister a note that you were here." Nelson went into the office and closed the door.

She found Kara in the Children's Room gazing out a window. "Make yourself comfortable. Sophia insists on walking up and down the stacks to familiarize Celia with all of the books she'll be reading in the next few years. She's even spoken to the children's librarian about building an entire section devoted to black literature. She presented her with a list of authors and titles along with their appropriate age categories."

"I imagine she'll be arranging a fundraiser for the project in the near future," Kara said.

"I'm sure she will. Have you ever seen such a beautiful park? We'll have to come back for the annual concert and fireworks display this summer. It is truly spectacular. When Harriet Wilcox announced 'The people shall have their park', she couldn't possibly have realized the lasting legacy she'd be leaving."

Sophia brought Celia to her mother and announced, "We're ready to go window shopping. But first I want to take Celia's picture next to the *Runaway Bunny* sculpture in the park. It's inspired by one of Margaret Wise Brown's books. See." She took it from her bag and held it up.

"Is it the edible edition?" Ruth asked.

Sophia ignored her friend's attempt at sarcasm. They went upstairs to the second floor and Sophia waved goodbye to the librarian behind the circulation desk. A young man joined them. "I'll help you get the stroller outside to the patio." He opened the door onto the Centennial stairs leading to the terrace and flashed her a smile. "I'm Jake."

"I think Sophia has an admirer," Kara whispered to Ruth.

"Yes, Jacob's acting very gallant. That's quite out of character for him."

He set the stroller down, then pointed to the statue in honor of Christoforo Colombo. "We got lots of Italians in this town," he informed them. "It took four guys to carve this monument out of Sullivan blue granite."

"Yes, immigrants came from Italy and other places in Europe to work in the quarries here." Ruth said.

Lots of their monuments were shipped all over the country. But you can see some of their work right here in the park. The fountain, the balustrade, the war memorial, the urns." He pivoted, pointing as he spoke in the direction where each could be found.

"And of course the red granite used in building the library," Ruth added. "Italians brought their culture with them when they left the old country."

"I couldn't get through a week without an Italian meal with wine," Sophia added.

"Then make sure you buy some pasta and a bottle of tomato basil sauce from Capizzano's over on the other side of the river in Pawcatuck. Their olive oil will unclog your arteries. And you have to get the suppis from Westerly Packing on Springbrook Road. It's my favorite. The recipe comes from Roman times when they dried meat to take with them on their journeys. Those Italians know how to make great sausage. I go there every week to shop."

"Gino loves to shop there. He especially likes their soppressata. He gets the XXXHot," Sophia chimed in.

"The Trombino's are famous and if you're lucky, you'll get to meet one of the family. It's a fifth generation business. There are pictures of grandparents and great grandparents up on the walls." He was happy to have an audience to show off his knowledge. "Bruno or Medoro can tell you all about the history of soppressata or as it's known here in Westerly, suppis. But don't ask him for their recipe. Everyone here in Westerly has a different blend of spices they add into the meat. The Trombino recipe is the best," Jake declared.

"You should give tours. People appreciate learning about the history of places they visit," Sophia said. Her encouraging words made him blush and he continued.

"We're in the spot where the old high school stood until it was taken down to make way for the park. During the '38 Hurricane, dead bodies were brought to the gym so people could come and identify them." He stopped and looked at them to see if he was impressing them with his recitation. "Lots of interesting things happened here. I've been reading stuff they keep in the reference rooms. I could take a picture of you down below on the Ruth Buzzi Bench. She was a famous comedian. She played a crotchety old lady." He stared directly at Ruth when he said this making her wonder exactly how old he thought she was. "You'd probably remember the show. *Laugh-In*. It was on TV way back in the 70s." Sophia giggled but didn't make eye contact with her friend. "When she lived here in Westerly she was known as Gladys Ormphby." He led them across the slate patio and down the cement stairs to the bench where he put his foot next to the plaque in honor of the hometown celebrity.

"Okay, everyone scrunch together while Jake takes our picture." Sophia handed him her cell phone and he snapped a few photos to show to her for approval. "They're perfect. Thank you, Jake."

He smiled at her. "Just call inside to the desk and ask for me if there's anything else you need. I could take another photo of you around the fountain even though they drained the water out for the winter." They turned to admire the sculpture in the Wilcox Fountain.

"We're fine. I don't want to keep you any longer from your work," Sophia said.

"Such a shame Stephen and Harriet Wilcox didn't live to enjoy all of this beauty," Ruth sighed.

"Life's a bitch. We all gotta go sometime," the teenager called out to them as he climbed the steps of the patio and disappeared into the library.

"Now that's the Jake we've come to know and love," commented Ruth.

∼

"Rick, where are ya, Bro? Ansa ya phone." Gino had been calling Rick every five minutes leaving voice messages for the past half hour. Finally, his brother answered.

"Gino, what's up?"

"I been tryin to get ya."

"I'm at the Artisans' Gallery in the Westerly train station. We were hanging the triptych. This sounds important."

"I answered Ruth's phone and someone told me he was watchin me."

"Why would they call Ruth to give you a message? Where are you?"

"I'm at home."

"I thought Ruth was going out with Sophia."

"Ruth's not here. She left her phone chargin and I picked it up and when I answered it an evil voice told me he was watchin me but I figured out it must be Ruth he's watchin even though we don't look alike at all and she could be in danger and it's Friday the thirteenth and I don't understand why she has to hang around wid all dose killers."

"Whoa, let me see if I understand what you're saying. Ruth's phone is at home but she's not there. You answered it when it rang and someone said he was watching you because he thought Ruth had picked up. You're afraid she's in danger and you think it might have something to do with the murder mystery writers."

"Zactly. You shoulda heard da voice. I'm not even sure if it was a guy. It didn't sound human. I'm gettin chills thinkin about it."

"They must be someplace close by. Ruth said they planned on shopping in town. I'll call Kara and find out where they are right now."

"If dare with Kara, den I feel better."

"Don't worry. I'm sure they're safe. I'll call you back when I have more information."

"Okay. I'll be here. I'm not leavin da house. I may even go back to bed after I clean up dis mess."

"Mess? What? Never mind. I'll call you."

"Bro, be careful. Stay away from any laddas or black cats."

"I'll do that. Thanks for the warning. I'd forgotten. It's Friday the 13th."

As soon as he hung up, he dialed Kara. "It's Rick. Are Ruth and Sophia with you?"

"Hi. We're all together taking photos in the park. Is something wrong?"

Rick summarized his conversation with Gino.

Kara looked around cautiously. A small child bundled up in a blue snowsuit was in the bandstand. A few people were strolling or sitting on benches. Piles of melting snow surrounded the paths and pond. She moved away from her friends.

"I don't see anyone suspicious. Ruth and I are going to Bartleby's lawyer's office at 1:15. Then we're planning to do some Christmas shopping. We'll make a stop at the bookshop. I'll call you when we're ready for lunch and we can meet at The *Brazen Hen*. Call Gino and reassure him we're all safe."

"Thanks, Kara. I'm sure he'll be relieved you're with them. See you at lunch."

She decided not to share the conversation she'd just had with Rick.

"Kara, come get your picture taken next to *The Runaway Bunny* with your daughter," Sophia called to her.

Kara's eyes swept across the expanse of meadow and paths. A few children were at the top of the slope near Grove Avenue with their sleds. A mother watched her toddler dance in the middle of the bandstand, clapping and singing along. Figures passed like shadows inside the library, their forms moving behind the second floor windows. A man came out to the balcony over the patio and opened a ladder, placing it against the yellow brick. The bell in the church steeple across the street chimed, sending a sudden chill over her as she remembered Jake's tale of the bodies lined up in the high school. She made up her mind they would all return in the spring when the perennial gardens and foliage began to bloom. The thought of new beginnings gave her solace.

"Kara, are you waiting for the bunny to run to you?" Sophia asked.

She moved toward the bronze statue, its hind legs high in the air, her daughter and two friends looking expectantly at her, but for some reason she could not escape the ominous feeling she was having. She sensed something was seriously wrong and they were being caught up in it. Putting a smile on her face, she glanced around one more time to check and see if someone was watching, remembering at that moment it was Friday the 13th. She took Celia in her arms and rubbed her tiny hand over the runaway bunny's foot for good luck.

They went in and out of the shops together, stopping by *Homespun Antiques* to introduce Miss Lucy to Celia. The orange cat was in a sociable mood and even came out of the front window to have her picture taken, much to the child's delight.

"Now, wouldn't you love to have a soft kitty of your own?" Sophia asked as she took the delicate fingers and guided them along the cat's furry back.

"I think we have our hands full with the two puppies we recently inherited. I'm not sure Marie and Pierre Curie would appreciate another animal stealing any attention from them."

She was well aware of Sophia's view that children should have pets in order to "truly grasp the full concept of responsibility". But at the moment, it was the parents who were learning the lessons and Kara couldn't imagine the chaos that would reign around the house when Celia and the pups reached their terrible twos together.

When they left the store, Kara and Ruth continued on to their appointment with Bartleby's lawyer. Sophia and Celia had more stores to visit and they agreed to meet up at the Savoy in an hour.

They didn't have long to wait. Young Mr. Whitcomb was prompt and after brief introductions, he led them into his office.

"My secretary gives me to understand you are concerned with the whereabouts of one of my clients, Bartleby Schnelling."

"Yes, Mr. Whitcomb. He was supposed to meet with me last Sunday. I went by his house and spoke with Mrs. Mayfair who gave us your contact information. She has not seen nor heard from him either. I believe he called me last Friday night and left a message. It wasn't clear and although I've tried to reach him, I've not been successful. We understand he has a stepson and we're hoping you could help us to contact him. We think he should be apprised of the situation, as I've been told he's next of kin." Kara waited for his reply.

After a long pause, Whitcomb responded. "Yes, Deighton Durst is Bartleby's next of kin, although they have never been close. I'm not sure he will be of much help to you, but I agree he needs to be aware of what has happened. He works in New York City. You can contact him at this number."

Kara took the sheet of paper and noted the information. She handed it to Ruth.

"Do you know anything about his sister?" Ruth asked.

"The last I'd heard was at the reading of Imogene Schnelling's will three years ago. Her husband was given the bulk of her estate. She left her stock portfolio to her son and to her daughter, her books. Miranda has never returned to collect her inheritance. I believe it is still in the upstairs' library at the house."

"You've never met Miranda?"

"No, she hasn't contacted me and Deighton was unsure of her whereabouts. The last he'd heard, she moved to New Zealand. Or, as he put it, 'As far away from us as she could get'." The lawyer consulted his watch signaling to them their fifteen minutes were up.

"Then, I will attempt to find Deighton to tell him of his stepfather's disappearance and place it in his hands to notify his sister," Kara said.

"Might I ask if Mr. Schnelling has a will? It would make it all the more imperative should we find out the worst." Ruth tried not to sound pessimistic."

Whitcomb seemed surprised at the question. "Yes, I often advised him over the past three years to come into the office and make revisions on the original will. His wife was the one who always took care of business matters, but I reminded him, this was something he needed to deal with, as he wasn't getting any younger. Under the present circumstances, I'm relieved he finally took my advice. I thought that might be why you'd asked to meet with me, as you were recently named his executrix."

"Bartleby never mentioned it to me," Ruth said.

"He sat with me last Monday to finalize the changes. Perhaps with his trip to New York the next day, he didn't have time to discuss it with you? But this is most irregular, I must say." Whitcomb began to straighten items on his desk, lining them up in an orderly row.

"He'd asked to meet with me on Sunday. Maybe that was when he intended to tell me. And then there was the phone call on Friday when he returned. It appears now that he was in the middle of making changes in his life. All the more reason to find out what has happened to him," Ruth said.

"Yes, I quite agree."

"We thank you for your time, Mr. Whitcomb and will certainly let you know of any information we might gather." Kara stood up and shook his hand. She gave him her card. "We'd appreciate it if you could reciprocate and keep us informed should you learn anything of Mr. Schnelling's whereabouts."

Outside, Ruth took a deep breath. "Well, I have to say, I wasn't prepared for that news. We really have to find Deighton Durst. He works in New York. I wonder if he's the person Bartleby was planning on meeting?"

"I thought the same thing. I'm going to contact Detective Perez and pass on this information. Maybe he can track things down faster than we would be able to?"

Ruth looked in her pocketbook. "I'll call Rick and see if he wants to get together with us for lunch. That's funny, I don't have my cell phone. It must be on my desk charging."

"About that. We need to talk," Kara said.

⚜

It had been busy all day and Terry had yet to stop for a break. She was glad she'd waited because Milton and Greg came into the store at the same time. She introduced them and brought tea and scones to the round table at the window. They listened as Milton told her about his encounter with the cyclist. She patted his hand gently, noticing it was bruised.

Greg said, "It was wise of you to call the police. Have they been able to trace the bike?"

"No one has contacted me to follow up. I wasn't able to give them a license plate number, so it will probably be difficult to find the scalawag."

"Were you able to give them a description?"

"He was wearing a helmet. I only caught a brief glimpse of the motorbike. It reminded me of our friend Bartleby's. He keeps it in the backyard shed. It sounded like it, too. He drove it to the library during that warm spell in November. I told the policeman that and he thanked me. I don't think I was much help."

"I'll see what I can do when I go in to the station," Greg offered.

"I would be much obliged." He turned to Terry. "Speaking of Bartleby, have you heard from him?"

"No, I haven't. I've called his cell phone and left messages, but he never got back to me. I know he wouldn't want me to be worried and he'd contact me if he could. It's not like him at all."

"I think Dr. Eddleman is concerned, too. I remember she told me her friend Kara is a detective and I'm hoping they're looking into his disappearance."

"Wow, there's a lot going on with your little writing group," Greg said. "Maybe you should switch genres? A nice romance would seem safer." He winked at Terry.

"We already have a married couple who are writing a mystery romance. I don't think they'd appreciate Milton or me stealing their idea," Terry told him.

"Carolynn seems nice enough, but that husband of hers is something else. Lots of tension there." Milton shook his head. "My wife and I never argued like those two do. And certainly not in public. Young people today! Present company excluded," he added apologetically to his friend. "You have lovely manners, my dear. You'd be a great catch for any young man." He looked directly at Greg.

"Well, I have to get home and change for my shift," Greg stood up and shook Milton's hand.

She blushed. "And I have to get back to work. Milton, I'll see you tomorrow at the library." And to Greg she said, "Stay safe."

∽

Kara found Sophia and Celia in the little log cabin room. Whatever book they were reading had the baby enthralled and she clapped her hands and laughed whenever Sophia would stop, point to a page, and ask her a question.

"I won't disturb you. When you're done, you can find me upstairs. I'll be in the mystery and true crime section," Kara whispered to them.

Ruth was speaking with Terry, filling her in on what had been done to find Bartleby.

"I'm really worried, Dr. Eddleman. I gave the police a description of what he was wearing last Tuesday. He's so responsible. It isn't like him to up and disappear."

"I agree. I'm afraid I've begun to think the worst, Terry. I'm looking for any glimmer of hope."

"Milton was here and he said he'd almost been run over by a motorbike. And it reminded him of Bartleby's. Maybe you could check in the shed behind his house and see if it's still there?"

"I'll have Rick stop by on his way home. And we need to find out the whereabouts of his cell phone. There are lots of things we should investigate. Terry, did Bartleby ever talk about his stepchildren?"

"He has stepchildren?"

"Yes, his wife was married before they met. She had a son and a daughter."

"That's the first I've heard of any relatives. He told me once he'd been considering leaving his books and an endowment to the library foundation. I think he's sweet on Miss MacAlister."

Kara came to the register and waved to them.

"We're going next door for lunch. You're welcome to come with us," Ruth offered.

"Thanks, but I took a late break and I'm leaving early to go to the Granite Theatre. I'm ushering tonight," Terry said.

"Okay, I'll see you tomorrow. Be ready to report on what you've accomplished with your play."

∼

Rick was waiting for them at *The Brazen Hen*. He was sipping on a Guinness and looking over the menu.

"I don't know why you bother. You know you're going to order the meat loaf. The waitress has probably already put in your order." Ruth said as they settled around the table. They took turns telling him about their day and Ruth informed them of the meeting with the lawyer.

"You would think the man would have at least asked you if you wanted to take on the responsibility," Sophia muttered indignantly.

"He may have intended to but things obviously didn't fall in place as he'd expected," Ruth said although she agreed she'd been taken aback at the news. When they mentioned Gino and the phone call, Sophia's attention was immediately diverted from trying to get Celia to drink from her bottle.

"Someone's watching you? Ruth, this is getting out of hand. Kara, if she's going to continue working with that group, you need to go with her to the meetings."

"Sophia, I'm sure I'm not in any danger. I just walk from the parking lot to the library and back. What could happen?"

"For someone mentoring murder mystery writers, you have a limited capacity to imagine the worst, Ruth. First thing, on the way home, we are stopping at *Job Lot* and getting you a burner phone. That cell of yours is going to get shut down. Until we find out who's at the other end of those calls."

"Sophia, I don't ..."

Kara jumped in. "I think that's a perfectly wise idea. I'm going to speak with Professor Hill at the forensics lab and see about tracking down Bartleby's cell and I'll need your phone. I should have been on that from the start of all this."

"Rick, could you stop by Bartleby's today and see if there's a motorbike in the shed?" Ruth asked.

A smiling young waitress stood at the edge of their booth and placed glasses of water in front of them before taking out a pad and pencil. "We've done what we can at the moment. Katya is here to take our orders so let's all agree to take a break and have a nice, relaxing lunch." Kara hoped her tone helped to give them a feeling of calm. Or at least calmer than the ominous feelings she'd had earlier while standing in the middle of Wilcox Park.

∽

I write to give myself strength.
I write to be the characters I am not.
I write to explore all the things I'm afraid of.
Joss Whedon

Saturday, December 14

"THIS IS REALLY BEAUTIFUL, Gino. I can sit at my desk and look up at the sky. I'm sure it will inspire me."

"I don't think you woulda thought it was beautiful yestaday when I was cleanin up blue paint all ova everything."

"You wouldn't even know there'd been an accident."

"I'm just glad for turpentine and dat Friday da thirteenth doesn't come around til next March and den November.

"You already have them on your calendar?"

"Yup an I'm plannin on sleepin in both days. I'm just glad you all got home safe. Dat voice creeped me out, I tell ya."

"I won't be using my cell until Kara finds out who's making the calls. She's at the lab this morning."

"I feel betta already. If anyone kin figure it out, it's Kara." He began to leave, then turned. "You're not still plannin on going to meet wid dem mystery writers, are ya?"

"Rick is going to take me. He'll drop me off and do some volunteer time at the Artisan's Gallery, then I'll phone and he can come and get me."

"Dats good."

She called after him, "But I really don't understand the fuss."

He returned for a moment to add, "Yours is not ta reason why."

Ruth was impressed that he'd remembered the lines from the Tennyson poem. But she was pretty sure he didn't know the next line. "Theirs but to do and die. Into the Valley of Death …." And she wasn't going to be the one to tell him.

∽

For the past two months, Professor Hill had been working with Kara on a hit and run case. The evidence was ready to go to court and she'd taken a few days off, so he was surprised to see her in the lab when he arrived on Saturday morning. "Housework getting you down?"

"I gave up the good life and am now dreaming the dreams of an everyday housewife."

"Ahhh, Glen Campbell. I know you're not into country music. I'm impressed."

"I thought you would be and no, I'm not bored. Actually, I'm working on something for Ruth." She explained the situation.

"I have to tell you, it doesn't look good. I think this Bartleby might be dead," Hill said.

"Unfortunately, that's the most likely explanation. If I can find out who has the cell phone, I could get down to the bottom of it once and for all. I'm going to refer to the person who now has it as *he*, keeping in mind that hasn't been determined. Ruth heard breathing but not a voice and Gino said it was too raspy for him to distinguish. Let's analyze this. If we believe Bartleby is alive and has the phone then why won't he communicate during Ruth's calls? Why hasn't he answered the messages left by Ruth and Terry? And why would he warn Ruth he's watching her, then hang up? The more reasonable theory is that someone else has the phone. If it were a kidnapper, he'd have made his demands already. If not, why keep the phone if Bartleby is dead?"

"And there's the possibility it could be someone who simply found the phone and knows nothing about Bartleby," Hill suggested.

"But the last call was too threatening to make me think that. Find the phone, find the answers," Kara told him.

"Well, let's figure out where the calls are originating from."

"I have Ruth's phone with me. Sophia bought her a burner phone and we shut this one down last evening. Both Bartleby's and Ruth's cells are smart phones."

"The battery in them is hard to remove. They're pretty tough to break, so, if it's on, it can be tracked if the battery still has a charge. Keep in mind, it's been a week."

"This could futile, but I still want to try," Kara told him.

"Okay. We'll rule out driving around Westerly with devices that can monitor a phone's broadcasts. Doing that would be akin to playing the game "You're getting hotter. You're getting colder."

"I could have suggested the Westerly police request a judge to issue a warrant to Bartleby's service provider to use data to determine which tower the phone is connected to. But, I know pinging a cell phone can take days to get the results back and judges are not likely to grant this type of warrant because of privacy issues. What other options do we have left?"

"It's a long shot, but cell phone companies can report on the last tower a phone was connected to when it was powered off or the battery dies. A tower has a radius of 6-12 miles so we'll only get a general location where the phone was when it was connected to the network."

"Let's try that. I have a hunch the phone is somewhere in the area around downtown. The police confirmed he was on the train that got into the Westerly Station on Friday night. He purchased his ticket on line with a charge card. The train arrived at 6:40. He left the depot and apparently crossed Canal Street and stopped at the Savoy on his way home to leave his manuscript at the bookstore around 6:50 when the call to Ruth was made. Also, the voice warned Ruth she was being watched and she was at the library when that call was made. The caller would have assumed she had the phone on her and not charging in her office. I think it's our best bet. If we can't find the phone, we can confirm the person who has it could live or work around that area," Kara said.

"If we find it, we'll still have to get a warrant to access the data. I'll contact some people who owe me favors and start the process rolling," Hill told her as he picked up the office phone and dialed.

Terry went to the reading room in the library to work on her play. Her aunt was unaware she was in a writing group. She assumed her niece was spending her spare time at the Granite Theatre. If Dr. Virginia Walden ever found out her niece had used one of her case studies as the basis for her play, there would be hell to pay, so Terry was trying to re-work the plot to make it less obvious. Maybe she could change the man into a neurotic teenage girl? Or an old man with a history of insanity in his family? As she concocted and then discarded the changes, she realized Dr. Eddleman was expecting her to read portions of the play and discuss character development and plot issues at today's class. *If only she knew!*

Late morning turned into afternoon and soon the group would be arriving. Jake came by to place a red plastic rose on the table in front of Terry. He then proceeded to slouch in the chair across from her and stare. He raised his shirt sleeve so she could see his tattoo of a wolf, hoping he was piquing her interest, but she held a completely different perspective. To her, he was just plain annoying, although good manners wouldn't allow her to tell him how she really felt.

He finally broke the silence. "Hey, I bet I know what you're writing about."

"She didn't look up."

"I'm psychic, ya know."

Still no reaction from her

"So this psychiatrist is treating a little boy who gets real angry. He's a bully. Uncontrollable. His parents threaten to put him away to keep the rest of the family safe. Then, his mother falls down the cellar stairs and breaks her neck. It looks like it might not be an accident and the father has the son locked up. How am I doing so far?"

Everyone in the group knew all of that from the summary of Act I she'd given at the first meetings. She wasn't impressed.

"But the real problems start happening during Act II, when the father gets the son released cuz he thinks the kid is no longer dangerous. They bring him home and Oops! the father falls off a ladder and ends up dead. Another unfortunate accident and the boy disappears. Act III. Time has passed. The guy is older now and he's done some really bad stuff."

He cocked his head. She glared at him. "Now I can see you're impressed."

"How do you know about this?"

"I told you, I'm psychic. I know lots of things. I could write a gigantic book with the things I know. A tome." Jake stood up. Placing the rose behind his ear, he hummed a tune. With an imaginary partner in his arms, he tangoed out of the room, tripped into the hall, and grabbed the carved newel post at the base of the staircase to regain his balance. He glanced back sheepishly into the reading room where Terry was trying her best to pretend she hadn't seen him almost fall on his face.

"Goofball," she muttered to herself. She packed up her papers and left out the front door.

∽

Milton was the first to arrive and he spread his notebook and papers out on the table in front of him. When Carolynn came in, she sat next to him and they began talking about the work they'd been doing on their manuscripts. He hesitated to ask where her husband was and she didn't volunteer the information. Nelson began setting up a table with refreshments he'd taken from the coffee shop. When he was done, he sat down to chat.

"Any news of Bartleby?"

They shook their heads no.

"Miss MacAlister is really on edge. I think she's worried he's dead somewhere. That would be awful."

"Let's hope he met a nice woman in a bookstore while he was in New York and they ran off together," Carolynn offered.

"Now that's a great idea. I like it. It's optimistic. We certainly can use more optimism nowadays," Milton said. He stood up as Ruth entered and helped her off with her coat.

They waited for Conrad and Terry, but after ten minutes, they began without them. Milton had made major changes in the past week. "Killing off the jockey in the first chapter made me use that flashback technique you explained to us. I think it fits into the story well."

Ruth agreed. "You can keep developing the character of the jockey even though he's dead. Flashbacks open up endless possibilities in a plot. You need to know when to use them and how to keep your readers aware of the elapsed time. Placing dates at the beginning of each section or chapter has been used in a number of popular books today."

Carolynn was excited about all of her changes. When she finished reading the portions she felt were the best, Ruth praised her. "I like the fact you're getting back to the plot you'd outlined for me at first. It was solid and had potential. Keep working at it."

"I think Conrad has decided to gather his ideas into another book rather than for us to continue together."

"How do you feel about that?" Ruth was curious.

Carolynn raised her hands high into the air. "I feel free!"

Milton applauded.

"Then I would suggest you both continue on your own," Ruth advised.

Miss MacAlister came in to see what the commotion was all about. "I assume today's session has gone well in spite of the sparse attendance. I hope I'm not being intrusive but I was wondering if anyone has heard news about Mr. Schnelling?"

"My friend Kara, the detective you met on Friday, is going to try and track where his cell phone is. She's working on that today," Ruth said.

"I'm relieved someone is at least attempting to find out that poor man's fate. He's quite wealthy, you know. He might be helpless. In the clutches of a kidnapper."

"Could that be a possibility? Who would they even contact for the ransom?"

"If he hasn't been kidnapped then the only other possibility is, he's dead. And I can't bear to think we'll never see him again." The distraught librarian ran from the room holding back tears.

"I'll see if there's anything I can do," Nelson said.

They straightened the room in silence. Ruth reminded them of their next meeting on Monday night and went in search of her friend. The librarian was not in the office nor at the circulation desk. Ruth wrote a note on a piece of scrap paper. "Fannie, here's my new number in case you'd like to talk. Call any time." She placed it on the counter.

Outside, alone on the terrace, the sun had set and the air was cool and still. She rested on a bench in front of the Columbus monument for a while, then called Rick to tell him she was ready to go home. People filed out of the church and crossed the street to enter the park. It seemed so peaceful to her. Surely, everything would end up fine. Happily ever after. Bartleby would be discovered wandering somewhere across the bridge in Pawcatuck with temporary amnesia. Gino's over-active imagination may have gotten the best of him - the phone call a harmless prank. Nelson came out to sit beside her.

"In all the years I've known her, Miss MacAlister has never cried. She's really upset and I don't know what I can do to help."

"You are a help to her. I think she knows she can rely on you as a friend." She saw Rick's car pull up to the curb. "Goodnight, Nelson."

When she was safely inside, he returned to the library. He went down into the basement as he did every Saturday evening and listened until it was quiet overhead and he was sure the building had been safely locked up for the night. He took out his bedroll and the old couch cushion he used for a pillow. It had been a long day and soon he was sound asleep.

∽

*After nourishment, shelter and companionship,
stories are the things we need most in the world.*
Phillip Pullman

Sunday, December 15

NELSON WOKE AROUND SIX in the morning and packed his gear, stowing it in an unused cupboard. He gathered his overcoat and backpack and went upstairs to the men's room on the first floor to attend to what he liked to call "his morning ablutions". After washing as best he could with paper towels, he brushed his teeth and shaved.

He took the flashlight from his backpack and rode the elevator up to the third floor Terrace Room. In the kitchenette, he prepared himself a cup of instant coffee and warmed a leftover blueberry muffin in the microwave. Looking out the window into the darkness, he envisioned Fannie MacAlister making her way up the park path toward the library as she had every Sunday since he'd known her. He finished his breakfast and returned to the reading room on the main floor.

Settled comfortably in his leather chair in front of the fireplace, he imagined the heat of blazing logs against his feet. Outside, a fierce wind was blowing. But inside the sturdy granite building, this was the one morning of the week he felt safe from the harshness of the winter weather. His shack, on the other side of the railroad tracks, was drafty and damp even on the best of days.

The sound of footsteps caused him to sit up straight. He checked his watch. Seven forty-five. Fannie usually arrived promptly at nine. This was much too early for it to be her. His senses were on high alert. He closed the book he'd been reading, turned off his flashlight, and stuffed them into his backpack, moving swiftly from the larger room into the smaller alcove where the stained glass window of Chief Ninigret stood guard. He ducked behind the half wall and waited.

Someone was walking around the reading room. He closed his eyes and said a prayer, fearing he'd be found out and probably arrested for trespassing. After a few moments he heard stomping up the main staircase. He left his hiding spot to cautiously peek into the hallway in time to catch a glimpse of a hooded figure at the top of the landing holding a penlight and turning toward the Hoxie Gallery.

He waited, listening expectantly for what might happen next. From upstairs came the sound of someone testing the keys on the baby grand. A familiar tune. *Chopsticks* played softly and slowly at first but on each succeeding rendition it became faster and louder eventually bordering on maniacal banging until it ended in a thunderous cacophony of notes and loud, guttural roars. An eerie silence followed. He sensed this wasn't the custodian. This was someone choosing not to abide by the rules of quiet demeanor posted in every library.

Nelson wiped the sweat from his forehead and upper lip. Not a sound. After a long interval, he weighed his options and decided to leave by the Centennial door. He would go into the park and wait to intercept Miss MacAlister when she entered from the gate down by the pond. As he ran from the building, he didn't notice the dark figure watching from a second floor window.

An hour passed. It felt like an eternity. Crouching down inside the bandstand, Nelson looked up to the Terrace Room where a thin beam of light made its way in front of the arched windows, then disappeared. A few minutes later, a door opened and a beam shone from the balcony above, darting back and forth across the park. Nelson imagined its light resting on him as he huddled in the cold, a loyal sentinel, waiting to save Miss Fannie MacAlister from walking straight into certain danger. The wind howled around him.

At nine fifteen, the interloper came from the side of the building heading away from the park toward the church across the street, disappearing from sight. Nelson rose stiffly, stretching his legs to get the circulation going. A set of fairy lights dangled from one of the trees, barely touching the icy surface of the skating pond. He left the park through the Serpa Gate and started for home down Canal Street.

At the corner of Railroad Avenue a sudden bout of dizziness caused him to lean against the lamppost to steady himself. Numb with cold, stomping his feet, he swiped at his runny nose with a coat sleeve. He felt as though he was about to pass out and looked around for help but the only sound he heard was an engine revving. He looked back toward High Street and saw a van rounding the corner on to Canal. Nelson stuck out his thumb, but the driver raced past him without slowing down. He watched it travel in the direction of his place. He could have used a lift.

∞

Her aunt had left for the nine o'clock Mass at St. Clare's and Terry used the time to let herself into the office to return the folder she'd "borrowed" to the locked cabinet behind the desk. She knew where to find the key because she'd been helping with filing the previous week. Her aunt offered to pay her for the work she did around the office, but under the circumstances, guilt would not allow her to accept it. She now had all the information she would need to finish the play. Although her main character in real life was living outside the grounds of the institution, in her fictional version, the character of Andrew remained psychologically unbalanced and dangerous. She planned to kill him off at the end of Act III, which she hoped to complete before tomorrow's meeting at the library.

Terry had written a brief email to Dr. Eddleman apologizing for not attending Saturday's session explaining she'd been called in to usher for the matinee at the theatre. In reality, she wasn't ready to unveil her completed script and still was unsure of how much she wanted the group to know.

On Thursday, she'd confided in Greg and he'd given her some ideas on how to be evasive without appearing to be devious. He'd had a lot of experience with suspects he'd grilled, he said and could always tell when someone was lying to him. "It's a sixth sense I have."

Terry had nervously handed him the play. "You're the only person I've shared this with except for Bartleby. He thought it was good enough to show it to his publisher. Even Dr. Eddleman has only read Act I and the beginning of Act II. She assured me it has real promise and I may even get to see it performed on stage some day. That would be so fantastic!"

After reading it through, he declared. "It's a real spellbinder. I think Dr. Eddleman could be right. You'll be famous."

She sat across from him drinking her tea and hoped her face was not as red as it felt.

"I have to do a lot of polishing and Dr. Eddleman will give me advice on that."

"I only could find one thing I'd change."

She looked up curiously.

"I think you should have the young policeman and the girl hook up in her hospital room in the end."

She laughed. "I'll take that into consideration."

Right now the main thing she had to take into consideration was how her aunt would react if she found out about the play. She'd been able to keep her in the dark but if it really did get published and maybe even performed, she would have to come clean with what she'd done. It could mean a potential rift between the two and that was something Terry didn't want to think about.

She heard someone in the waiting room. It couldn't be her aunt. She usually went out for breakfast with friends after church on Sunday. "Hello. I'm in here."

A man entered the office. He pushed back the hood which had been partially covering his face.

"Where's Doctor Walden?"

"She's not here. She's at church."

"Do you know when she'll be back?"

"Not until much later. The office isn't open on Sundays."

"The door was unlocked," he said fluffing a throw pillow and making himself comfortable on the couch.

Terry moved from behind the desk then realized she hadn't locked the file cabinet. She couldn't leave this stranger in the office with the files open.

"I was just cleaning the office."

"Don't let me stop you."

"I'm done and now I'm going to lock up." She waited for him to leave but it appeared he had no intention of moving from his spot. He put his head back and closed his eyes. "You'll have to leave." Her voice sounded more like a pleading than a command.

"Why don't you stay awhile? We can have a little chat."

Her hands were shaking and sweaty. She looked down at the desk. Seeing her aunt's silver letter opener, she moved closer to it. He seemed to sense her thoughts and a chuckle, which sounded more like a low growl, came from between his closed lips.

"I don't think Dr. Walden would appreciate us using her office to socialize. Why don't I take your name and number and leave her a note to contact you when she returns?" Terry suggested. An interminable silence permeated the room.

Unexpectedly, he bolted from the couch, his eyes still closed. His face was red and his fists balled up menacingly by his sides. Terry was startled. She cringed, her hand reached out for the letter opener. And then, as suddenly as he'd appeared, he left the room, slamming the door behind him. She sat down on the desk chair wanting to get up and lock the doors but knowing her legs would not support her. It occurred to her, at that moment, this was the type of person her aunt had worked with every day for twenty-four years. Terry had cast someone like him as the main character in her drama. Maybe her aunt wasn't the only one she had to worry about if the play was ever staged?

***

"Ruth, Professor Hill called to say the police had tracked the last ping from Bartleby's phone from a tower near downtown Westerly. They're getting no more signals, so it must have run out of charge or been turned off," Kara informed her friend.

"Then, you were right. Now, when can I get my phone back? All my contacts are in it. Unfortunately, I haven't memorized any of them."

"Not until I'm sure you're safe. It simply could be someone who found his phone and is prank calling the numbers in it, but until we figure out what has become of Bartleby, your cell stays with me. That's why I'm calling. Can I come by to get your charger later this afternoon?"

"Plan on staying for dinner. Sophia and Gino are in the kitchen making individual pizzas. The counters are crowded with bowls filled with assorted toppings. They're planning on having Rick and me choose the winner for the most unique concoction. Bring Stewart. This is something he can get his teeth into, literally." Ruth laughed.

"Sounds like fun. We'll be there."

The table was set with platters of colorful pizzas. Assorted bottles of wine from WinterHawk Vineyards were on the table and Gino's stereo was on the sideboard playing Frank Sinatra and Perry Como tunes. The first selection was called *English Breakfast* with toppings of cheddar cheese, poached egg, fried tomato, and bacon bits. Sophia would not let them continue to the next selection until they had written comments about texture, taste, ingredients, and overall presentation on the note pads at their places. There were plenty more with an array of crusts and toppings. *The Calamari*, a thick crust filled with Rhode Island's favorite appetizer; The Blushing Tipsy Bride, a thin white crust with pink vodka sauce and chicken; *The Some Spicy Meatball* with the infamous Mayor's homemade sauce; *The Lobsta Pot*, a deep dish pizza filled with lobster and covered in warm butter; *The Soupie Sales*, featuring Gino's favorite Italian sausage and melted mozzarella; *Hawaiian Luau* with ham and pineapple chunks layered with poi and coconut; *A Holiday Mash* covered in marshmallow peeps, candy corn, and peppermint patties.

Gino got up to place his favorite album on the turntable. Grabbing a wooden spoon, he stood at the head of the table like a conductor in front of a symphony orchestra. He sang the first line of the tune as a solo and then signaled them with a broad swish of the spoon to join in.

"When the moon hits your eye like a big pizza pie, it's amore.

When the world seems to shine like you've had too much wine"

At the word *wine* they lifted their glasses in a toast before joining in with "That's amore."

As the song continued, much to Celia's delight, Gino picked her up and danced with her while the grownups drank and sang along with Dean Martin until they all ended with one final "That's amore".

Gino returned the baby to her seat and bent to give Sophia a kiss. "Dey don't make songs like day yous ta," he declared as he sat down and they soldiered on with the feast of pies set before them.

As usual, they couldn't come to consensus on a winner. They finally agreed that Celia should choose and Stewart held her up, walking her the length of the table until she pointed to the colorful, soft, doughy crust pizza entitled *Fruit Loopy* which combined mashed banana, cherry, peach, and blueberry toppings. Sophia informed them, she'd made that one especially for her niece. "I know what the girl likes!" She declared, giving Celia a messy high five and then offering to bring the baby into the kitchen to clean her up.

The table was cleared and Rick brought the silver service with coffee and tea and china cups into the library where a large Norway spruce stood lit with twinkling white lights and covered with hand-made silken cobwebs. Ruth lit the candles on the fireplace and window ledges. Stewart added a log on the fire and the room took on a golden glow.

When they were all settled, Sophia announced she was going to tell her special Christmas story. "I know you've all heard it before, but this will be Celia's first time." The adults in the room loved all of the trees Sophia had decorated throughout the house. But the fragrant fir tree Gino brought to her every December was their favorite and they never tired of her telling the story she'd first heard when she was a child. She began the old folk tale by reminding them that in Germany, finding a spider or a web in a tree was good luck.

"Once upon a time a poor widow and her children awoke to find a pine cone wedged into the dirt floor of their hut. They decided to let it grow and when it became a tree, they enjoyed it every Christmas, although they could never afford decorations. But one magic Christmas they awoke to find the morning sun reflecting beams of gold and silver from all of the webs that had covered the tree while they slept. And on the top branch sat a simple house spider looking down upon them. And they marveled at the beauty she had created."

Carrying her niece to the tree, she held her up to see the delicate glass spider perched high above them. "My Tia Sophia told me this story every year at Christmas and now your Auntie Sophia is sharing it with you."

They took turns having their pictures taken with Celia in front of the tree. "Make sure you record this in her book when you get home. Here's a copy of the folk tale I made for her." Sophia presented Kara and Stewart with the story written out in calligraphy on ivory linen paper encased in a hand-made, leather bound cover of deep blue. They were overcome by the thoughtfulness of such a precious gift.

"Sophia. It must have taken you weeks to do this," Stewart said as he looked through the pages.

"Dat's my Sophia. No Bik pens and spiral notebooks for her!" Gino announced proudly.

Kara hugged her friend and whispered in her ear, "You're the best gift our family could ever wish for."

Hours later, the friends stood on the porch saying their goodbyes. They waved until the Langley's car disappeared down the long drive and then went inside. Sophia announced she was off to get her beauty sleep. Gino began putting out the candles and turning off lights. "I'll take care a things down here. You two hit da sack."

Before going to bed, Ruth discussed her plans for the next day. Rick wanted to be sure his wife was safe from the "crazy person on the other end of the phone".

"Kara said she was going to come over tomorrow to read the manuscript drafts. She's convinced Bartleby's disappearance is tied in with the writers' workshop."

"Kara's instinct is always right on."

"And she's accompanying me to the library for tomorrow's session."

"Then you won't be needing me. I was going to cancel my afternoon tutorial and now I won't have to. I'll sleep better tonight knowing she'll be with you." He turned off the lamp.

"Tonight was fun. I hope this mystery is solved soon so we can enjoy Christmas without all this worry," Ruth leaned over to kiss him goodnight.

"I know Kara will do her best to figure it all out. She always does."

༄

*The profession of book writing
makes horse racing seem like a solid, stable business.*
John Steinbeck

Monday, December 16

SOPHIA LEFT FOR WORK the next morning and Gino went to the hardware store to buy supplies for a special project he was working on. Rick headed to the college to teach his art classes, leaving Ruth with the mansion all to herself. She walked through the downstairs' rooms in her pajamas and slippers munching on leftover pizza and admiring the Christmas trees Sophia had decorated and placed around the house. In the middle of the dining room table, on an Irish linen tablecloth, was a white embossed bowl holding a blue-grey plant covered in scarlet velvet bows. On the top perched two white porcelain turtledoves. She ran her fingers along the stems and the heady herb's scent filled the room.

In front of the bow window in the formal parlor was the silver aluminum tree. Sophia's mother's tree that she loved so much. Ruth pushed a button on a revolving color wheel, which threw its light on the metal branches changing them from red to blue to yellow, and green. The doorbell rang and she opened it to find Kara on the front porch.

"You're early. You should have just stayed here last night."

"I thought we could start by reading Bartleby's manuscript to see if there's some clue to his whereabouts."

"The folders are on the sideboard. We can work at the dining room table. There's coffee and tea in the kitchen and cold pizza."

"I think I've had enough pizza to last me through next year. But I could use a cup of coffee." She took the folder labeled *B. Schnelling – Spy Novel* and sat down at the table, leaning over to stroke the plant's branches. "Rosemary, that's for remembrance," she whispered.

Ruth returned from the kitchen with two steaming mugs and sat next to her friend.

"I want to go through this together carefully, line by line," Kara said. "You can analyze it from a literary perspective – writing style, point of view, characters, settings – and I'll read it as though it were a piece of forensic evidence in a crime."

They'd spent an hour taking notes when the phone rang and Ruth left to answer it. She returned, and took the folder entitled *T. Ricitelli – Psychological Drama*. "That was Terry. She wants to meet with me at the library before the rest of the group arrives. She says she needs to discuss her play because she may not be able to continue with it."

"What's it about?"

"It involves a psychiatrist and one of her institutionalized patients – a young boy being treated for serious psychological problems. It's believed he may have been the cause of his mother's death. After years of treatment, the boy's father signs for his release against the psychiatrist's advice. He's convinced his son is cured but the doctor feels he's cleverly learned to project a facade of normalcy and once outside of the confines of the institution, she fears he'll be a danger to himself and others. Not long after his release, the father is found dead under similar circumstances to the mother's death. The boy disappears before the police can bring him in for questioning."

"You've grabbed my attention. How does it end?"

"I don't know. Terry never submitted the last act. Come to think of it, she's been extremely evasive. I'll find out more today."

"How much of the play has she presented to the group?"

"The first act. And she's shared some ideas on where she's going with character development and plot."

"But didn't Mrs. Mayfair tell us she let Bartleby read the script? She said they worked together at his house."

"Kara, do you think we could be looking in the wrong place for a motive?"

"I've felt from the beginning his disappearance was tied in some way to the library."

"It might explain why that call was made from his cell. It could have been to intimidate me into not continuing with the workshop," Ruth said.

"I think we need to keep our minds open. Bartleby's disappearance could be totally unrelated to his book. If something's happened to him, we need to get to the bottom of it sooner rather than later."

"What if others in the group are in danger? They've all discussed their plots."

"Do you know if any of them have received phone calls from his cell?"

"No, I'm the only one. But Milton said he'd almost been run down by a motorbike that looked like the one Bartleby owned. Rick checked and it wasn't in the shed. We need to find out how much Milton knows about Bartleby's and Terry's drafts. Conrad and Carolynn haven't mentioned anything unusual happening to them, but we should definitely ask them today."

"When we finish comparing notes on Bartleby's novel, we should look more carefully at the two acts Terry's submitted."

"You don't believe we'll find Bartleby alive, do you, Kara?"

"It doesn't look good. But, until we find a body, there's always hope."

Fannie spent most of the day working alone in her office. Usually she began Monday with an uncluttered desktop, but she'd stayed home on Sunday. Now there was more work than usual to begin her week. Around noontime, it occurred to her she hadn't seen Nelson. He'd never missed stopping by to have a short conversation with her first thing in the morning, so she went in search of him during her lunch break.

She found Jake in the terrace room on the third floor. He was seated at the end of a long table partially hidden behind a pile of books. He ducked his head down to avoid acknowledging her presence, hoping she'd go away.

"Jacob, have you seen Mr. Belle?" She waited for him to answer.

He thought for a minute and decided it might be fun to send her on a wild goose chase. "Yeah. I saw him going into the cellar."

"How long ago was that?"

"About fifteen minutes. Just before I came up here to eat my lunch in peace."

"When you're done eating, please go down and tell him I'd like to speak with him." She entered the kitchenette to retrieve a Tupperware container of tossed salad from the refrigerator, then poured herself a glass of water and went to a table in the corner of the room by the window looking out on the Columbus monument. She took a book from her bag to read while she ate.

Jake chewed slowly. He felt her eyes on his back. When he was done with his sandwich, he blew into the paper bag, popped it, and threw it down on the table next to an empty soda can. He crushed the can with his fist, got up, and strolled toward the door.

"I believe you're forgetting something, Jacob," she said in that stern voice mothers and teachers use to warn children they've gone too far.

He slapped his palm against his forehead. "Oops. My bad! I was in such a hurry to go find Nellie … Mr. Belle, I forgot …"

"Never mind the excuses. Please, clean up your mess and get back to work."

From the corner of her eye, she saw him salute her before leaving the room. She made a conscious note to call his probation officer and tell him the internship wasn't working out. His bad attitude wasn't improving and since he'd begun at the library, things had been disappearing. She'd made a list with dates and times but was hesitant to confront the boy. It was possible he wasn't the culprit – that it simply was a coincidence things went missing from her office and the circulation desk during the hours he worked.

Fannie wished she could ask Bartleby for his help in solving this mystery. But Bartleby hadn't been seen in over a week and now Nelson couldn't be found. She'd intended to call Ruth on Sunday, but hadn't felt well. She wasn't in the mood for singing and dancing. Fannie looked for the number Ruth had left for her on Saturday, but after searching around the counter, she concluded she'd misplaced it. She decided to confide in her friend tonight after the workshop.

Jake sat on the discarded library table in a storage section of the cellar and took out a joint. Using a silver lighter he'd found in the old biddy's top desk drawer, he lit up, inhaled deeply, then blew the smoke toward the window he'd just opened. He felt comfortable in the basement. It was dark with lots of secret spaces to spend time alone. He had to admit this job wasn't bad. The pay sucked but it was quiet and nobody bothered him except good ole Fannie, his supervisor. And he admitted to himself she wasn't that bad, considering he made it his business to give her a hard time.

He closed his eyes and smoked half of the joint before pinching the end and placing it in his pocket, he stood and stretched. It would have been nice to stay and take a nap, but he had books to put back on the shelves. And it was Monday. *The hot babe from the bookstore should be coming in later. Maybe I'll make her day and ask her out?* The thought made him smile as he headed up the stairs to deliver the news to the old broad that Nellie Belly was missing in action.

∽

Carolynn placed the draft into her new Louis Vuitton briefcase, an early Christmas present to herself. She was confident the group would appreciate the latest revised chapters of her romance mystery. She'd decided to write under a pen name. The love scenes between Lars and Jasmine were pretty steamy and she didn't want to risk losing her teaching position.

Conrad would be surprised when she presented her chapters for discussion. He'd informed her this morning that they were no longer working together on the same book. He'd been writing his own potboiler. "More manly," he'd informed her. He seemed to think he could get along fine without her. She doubted he'd get more than two chapters written before giving up. She couldn't wait to see the look on his face when she brought out her own manuscript at the workshop.

"Carolynn, let's get going," he shouted to her.

She was driving. His Corvette was at the shop being serviced and he didn't like driving the company van.

"I'm looking for my keys!" She had them in her hand but was enjoying making him wait. The door slammed. She counted to ten before going downstairs. She wondered how long it would take for him to notice the briefcase.

∽

Milton was satisfied with his revisions. He'd even written the blurb for the back cover. "The victim, a seasoned jockey, is found dead hours after a race in which his horse had been favored but lost. His head is bashed in. In the stall with him – a champion racehorse still saddled. The dead jockey is dressed in his colors. But something's not right. The position of the body. The head wound. Officials declared it an accident, but the young trainer knew it was murder."

During his first year on the racing circuit, Milton had heard of jockeys who'd colluded to throw a race by banding together and "riding herd on one horse" in order to help another horse coming down the stretch. He'd overheard an argument about it in the locker room. In spite of the danger he found himself in, Milton gathered evidence to prove the death was not an accident but murder because the jockey knew too much and was going to rat on the others. This had happened a long time ago, but Milton remembered it as though it were yesterday. His testimony at the trial resulted in long jail sentences for the guilty parties. By now, all of the people directly involved in the scandal were long gone.

Throughout the years, he'd received veiled threats from embittered friends or family, but that was all in the past. He often thought, if he had to do it again, he'd have been less likely to become involved. He was more cautious in his old age. But right now, it made a great story. His first draft was ready to hand in at today's meeting. Ruth would be pleased.

They sat in the small alcove off the reading room. A backlight shone through the stained glass window of Chief Ninigret standing silently by as Terry explained the predicament in which she'd found herself to Ruth and Kara.

"No matter what you choose to do with your play, you need to sit down as soon as possible with your aunt," Ruth advised.

"Unless I decide to rip it up and start something as far removed from psychiatry as possible," Terry offered as an alternative.

"What I've read so far is quite good and I wouldn't suggest you do that," Ruth told her.

"Do you think a few revisions to cover up the facts would be acceptable?"

"Obviously, your aunt feels the case is valuable enough to be the source of her book and it will help others to understand this disorder better. I don't believe it's too far-fetched to think she could help you with her knowledge about psychiatry. It would make a great drama that could be presented and reach more people. Maybe you could suggest collaborating on it? But I don't feel you should continue with this until you speak honestly with her."

"Aunt Virginia is very open-minded. I'll get up the courage to have a serious discussion with her this week."

"I won't expect you to read any more of your play today until you've made a decision to finish it or start on a different project."

"Um, there is something else I should share with you. Yesterday morning, I was in my aunt's office while she was at church. I clean and straighten up and sometimes help with the filing … bills and such. A man came in looking for her. He appeared to be upset and wouldn't leave when I asked. His behavior bordered on threatening. It was a frightening experience. After he left, it occurred to me he might be the subject of my aunt's book. If so, I don't want anything to do with him."

Kara had been silent up to this point but suddenly moved forward in her chair. "Is your aunt aware of this?"

"I mentioned that someone had stopped by, but I didn't go into detail with her."

Kara asked Terry for a description of the man and to explain exactly what had transpired. When she'd finished, Kara said, "You need to tell her about this as soon as possible."

Their conversation ended when Conrad and Carolynn arrived and they moved to the long oak table to begin work. Milton came in soon after. Ruth introduced Kara who gave them her card and looked at each one closely. "Has anyone heard anything that can help us in finding Bartleby?" They shook their heads. "Please contact me should you find out anything related to his disappearance. The police are involved and we are working together to find out what has happened to him."

The Renzullis were scheduled to present the rough drafts of their book and Conrad began by announcing that because of artistic differences, they were now working on separate mysteries. "My new title is *Never Too Hot to Handle.*"

Ruth avoided making eye contact with Kara who managed to maintain a straight face while he summarized his potboiler and read some of the dialogue. When he finished, he looked around the table expectantly.

Milton was the first to critique. "It's certainly different!"

Terry didn't say it out loud, but she felt the plot was very similar to a *Magnum, P.I.* she'd recently seen on the channel that specialized in reruns from the past. She preferred *Colombo* or *Murder She Wrote* but searched for something positive to say so as not to discourage Conrad from continuing with his book. "I think your main character is very macho. I can picture him having a humorous side and wearing Hawaiian shirts."

"That's exactly the vibe I'm going for!" Conrad announced.

Ruth stepped in with advice on staying with one point of view and not changing from third to first person, as it may confuse the readers.

"I'll keep that in mind, but I want my book to be different than other stuff out there."

"It's always refreshing to listen to new ideas," Ruth said.

When it was Carolynn's time, she explained she was keeping the same title and plot as the original mystery she and her husband had been writing. "I have made modifications, especially in respect to the main characters." She described Jasmine and Lars and the potential they presented for writing steamier encounters. "And I've decided to use a pen name. Trixie Belden. Trixie was my first pet and Belden was the name of the street we lived on when I was younger."

Conrad burst out laughing. "Carolynn, I think that's the method for choosing a stripper name. I'm sure I saw it somewhere on social media."

In the hope of keeping the peace, Terry and Milton immediately voiced their opinions in favor of her choice.

"It's very catchy," Ruth agreed.

At this point, Kara whispered to Ruth, "I'll let you continue with your class. I'm going to speak with Miss MacAlister."

Conrad jumped up and handed her his card. "In your line of business, you never know when you'll need insurance," he informed her.

Fannie was across the hall. When she saw Kara, she looked up expectantly, but Kara had no news to report. "Could you give these copies to Ruth? I haven't seen her, yet. I'm the only one working the circulation desk at the moment. My assistant's out sick with a cold and Nelson isn't here either."

"And where is Mr. Belle?"

"That's the strangest thing. He seems to be among the missing. Jake said he saw him earlier, but the boy may have been fibbing. I'm sure if Nelson were in the building, he'd have checked in with me by now. He's extremely dependable and has never been late or absent in all the years he's been with us. I was under the weather, myself, yesterday. I hope he hasn't caught anything from me. I left a message on his cell but still no response."

"Can I have his contact information, Fannie?"

"Oh, dear. You don't think he's disappeared like Bartleby?"

"I may need to speak with him to find out what he knows. He could have information we can use in the investigation."

"It's against library policy to hand out staff's telephone numbers, but under the circumstances, since you're a detective, I believe we can consider this an exception to the rule." She looked him up in the files and wrote the number on a slip of notepaper, which she handed to Kara.

"Thank you, Fannie."

"Please keep me apprised. This has all been very unsettling. I've never been sick a day in my life. But yesterday, I got up to feed Lady Winklemere, then went directly back to bed. It's all most upsetting. And this crazy weather isn't helping matters at all. Blizzards, gale-force winds, branches strewn willy-nilly all over the park. What is the world coming to?"

Jake walked into the room and went behind the counter to pick up the books to be re-shelved. "Sounds like Armageddon to me," he said under his breath.

At that moment, the sound of sirens could be heard. "Kara left the folder on the counter and went outside to the veranda. Lights were flashing down near the bandstand. "You stay here and take care of the desk. I'll see what it's about," she called in to the librarian.

"I told you. It's Armageddon," Jake declared.

She walked swiftly toward the emergency vehicles. Yellow caution tape was being strung along the paths around the pond. This wasn't a good sign. She caught a glimpse of what appeared to be a body where the pond was closest to the entrance of the park. *Bartleby? Nelson?* Taking out her identification, she pushed through the people who had gathered and asked a sergeant standing guard to be allowed on the other side of the tape. He took the ID to the detective in charge who waved her in. She recognized two members of the forensics team. She explained to them that she was working on a local missing person's case and asked if they'd found any information on the body.

"Nothing on him. Looks like he's been in the water for at least a week."

"Who discovered him?" she asked.

"The maintenance crew." He pointed to two men. "They were cleaning up the branches that came down overnight."

She walked over and identified herself. "Forensics seems to think he's been in the water for some time."

"Until Saturday's rain storm, there was a layer of snow. He must have fallen in before the snow started and was covered up," the bearded man told her.

"We probably wouldn't have discovered him this soon if those faerie lights hadn't been dislodged. They were hanging over the pond, so we went out to get them, and there he was, under the ice," the other man offered.

"We pulled him out, but he was frozen stiff as a board. Big gash on his head," the bearded man added. "Not much we could do for him but call the police."

"Do you know who he is?" She looked from one man to the other.

"I told the cops he looked kind of like the old guy who lives over on Grove Avenue. I've spoken to him a few times. Wanted to know about some of the trees around the Arboretum. Had a weird name. He spends … spent a lot of time out here in the spring and fall roaming around, looking at the plants and flowers."

"Bartleby?" she asked.

"That's it. Bartleby." He shook his head. "Poor guy. Must have slipped and fallen in some time last week before the storm."

"Thanks for your help. I'll give the name to the police."

After speaking with the detective in charge, Kara stood quietly taking in the scene around her and making mental notes of anything that may prove to be important later on. Then she gave a slight wave to the forensics team and went back to the library to share the bad news. Fannie had left

Jake inside to watch over the circulation desk and was waiting for her on the stone steps above the fountain.

"What's happening? Has a tree limb fallen on someone? Is anyone hurt?" Kara took her by the arm and sat her on a bench. "I'm afraid they've found a body in the pond. It hasn't been officially identified. All they can tell me is it's been in the water for over a week."

"Is it Bartleby?" The librarian's voice quivered slightly.

"I think you should prepare yourself for the worst, Fannie."

"Oh, no. I can't bear to think he's been right here all this to time and no one knew. It's too awful to imagine." She placed her head on Kara's shoulder and cried softly.

Jake came out to tell Fannie someone was on the phone and needed to talk to her. He jumped on a bench to get a better view. "Hey, what's that all about?" He jumped down and started to walk toward the commotion, but Kara stood in his way telling him to go back inside to watch the desk. She and Fannie followed him in.

"Are you going to be all right?" Kara asked.

Fannie nodded, then wiped her nose with a lace handkerchief and straightened her wig before answering the phone.

Kara went into the reading room and sat listening to the writers discuss their work with each other. At the end of the session she requested they stay a minute longer because she had something important to tell them. She took Ruth aside and explained what had happened, then went back to the table to deliver the news. Jake had begun to straighten the room. He stopped to listen.

"The police are outside in the park. A body was found in the skating pond. There's been no official identification yet, but from what I've been told, it's possible it's Bartleby Schnelling." She watched their faces as the news registered.

Conrad was the first to talk. "Was it an accident? Did he fall in?"

"I don't have any further information. Professor Eddleman will email you should we learn more this coming week."

They filed quietly from the room, leaving the library through the main door. Ruth and Kara sat on the couch in front of the fireplace. When Jake had finished, he left without a word.

"We need to inform Mrs. Mayfair. It wasn't an accident, was it Kara?" She looked into her friend's eyes.

"I doubt it. We'll have to wait for the coroner's report."

Fannie came to announce she was locking up early.

"Please call if you need to talk." Ruth gave her a hug and she and Kara left to deliver the sad news to Mrs. Wayfair.

∽

The job of the artist is always to deepen the Mystery.
Francis Bacon

Tuesday, December 17

EARLY THE NEXT DAY, Kara spoke with the Westerly police chief who told her what the detective assigned to the case had found out so far. "I'll keep you informed of anything else we uncover," Chief Baker said.

She told him she'd do the same. "I plan on working with the forensics lab on the case. *Whitcomb and Son* is the law firm Bartleby used. They gave me the contact information for his stepson, Deighton Durst. His business is centered in New York City." She handed him the number.

When Kara came into the lab, Professor Hill informed her he'd been on the phone with the Medical Examiner, Harry Henderson. "The stepson confirmed the body to be Bartleby Schnelling,"

"Did he give you any idea of what may have been the cause of death?"

"Harry's doing the autopsy today and will call when he has more information. He mentioned that he didn't believe it was the head wound. I've examined the photos and can concur with that. He said the most probable cause is drowning, but he has to rule out other possibilities."

"He'll determine if there was a seizure prior to his falling in the pond," she said.

"You don't seem convinced it was an accident. Why is that?" He gave her a questioning look.

"The incidents with Bartleby's phone," she answered

"How did you get mixed up in this case?" Hill asked her when they returned to his office.

"Ruth asked me to help find one of the writers she was mentoring at the Westerly Library. Her friend, Fannie MacAlister, the librarian, had asked her to conduct the workshop as a favor. She's trying to encourage local authors to publish. It's a select group of mystery writers."

"Just a bunch of harmless people figuring out ingenious ways to kill people on paper," he noted. "Sounds to me like a good starting place to find a murder suspect."

"It's this whole thing with the phone. I listened to the message he left for Ruth the night he disappeared. From the little I could understand, it sounded urgent to me. He was trying to warn her about something. And now I'm afraid she may be in danger. And Rick, Gino, and Sophia are worried, too." She related the call made to Ruth's phone a week after Bartleby disappeared. The one Gino had answered by mistake.

"What about Ruth? How does she feel about all this?"

"Ruth is one of those people who remains calm while everyone else is running around screaming the sky is falling. I sense she's nervous but trying to hide her feelings. She doesn't like to worry anyone."

"So what do you intend to do next?"

"I'll wait for the autopsy results, but in the meantime I'll assume he was murdered and pursue the leads."

"Putting the puzzle together piece by piece. If this is a homicide investigation, I'm sure you'll get to the bottom of it."

"Means, motive and opportunity. I'll be talking with members of the writers' workshop and people connected with the library. The cell was tracked to that specific area during the past week, which narrows things down. And the threatening message to Ruth tells me it wasn't someone who happened on the phone and used it for pranks. My instincts say there's a more sinister motive underlying it all."

Her phone rang. It was Mr. Whitcomb, Bartleby's lawyer, thanking her for notifying him the previous evening that the body had been found. "I've spoken with Deighton Durst. He arrived late last night and is staying at the Ocean House in Watch Hill. He's agreed to meet with you."

"I'll call and make plans to see him as soon as possible."

"One more thing. Deighton has asked for the key to the house and a meeting with me on Thursday afternoon. He has the right of access to his stepfather's property as he is next of kin, but I will be sending someone from my office with him to make sure nothing is removed from the premises until the will is read. I'll be informing him he is no longer executor of the Schnelling estate at that time. I'd like Professor Eddleman to be there. As you may well understand, I prefer to tell him of the change in person rather than on the phone."

"Thank you, Mr. Whitcomb. I appreciate your help in this matter."

Kara told Professor Hill about the latest news. "If Bartleby's murder has anything to do with his book, it could mean his stepson or someone from the publishing company is somehow involved. I need to consider the possibility that something happened while he was in New York which may have led to his death."

"It's always a good idea to keep an open mind in any investigation," Hill advised.

They spent the rest of the morning examining clothing, photos, and trace evidence.

"The wound leads me to believe he fell forward landing face first. Possibly pushed from behind. The autopsy will tell us if any other marks were found on the body and if he died from the injury or from drowning." Hill looked closer at the pictures he'd laid out on the table. "Considering the thickness of the jacket and the leather gloves and boots, I don't expect they'll find other wounds unless there was a violent struggle. The middle of the pond is the deepest. Six feet. But the body was lying in the shallow end and had been covered by the snowfall and the mounds formed when paths were cleared."

"We need to consider the possibility he got up, was dazed, or had some kind of seizure, then walked forward and fell in by accident. But, I believe, if he were only dazed, he would have been shocked by the icy water and would have crawled his way back out onto the path," she commented.

"These statements by the men who found him said he was lying face down. He could have been shoved in and held under. The easiest way to drown someone, even in shallow water, is to get them into a prone position, then pull from their ankles," Hill said.

She examined the jacket, turning it over. "The back is in good condition but the front is frayed as though he crawled or was dragged at some point."

They went through the witness interviews and the photos together and agreed if it were found he died of drowning, it most likely was murder, not an accident.

"Ruth said he always carried his papers in a portfolio. He was coming from a meeting in New York with his publisher, Mr. Pinkham. So where is it? Pinkham said he left the office with his copy of the manuscript. And he obviously put the envelope with that manuscript addressed to Ruth through the mail slot of the bookstore. But where is the portfolio?"

"There's nothing about it in the statements or the photos at the scene," Hill said. "My guess is it was taken by the killer who later found the manuscript was not inside."

"And there's the phone to consider. If the killer took it, he or she must have heard Ruth's message to Bartleby indicating he'd called her that night. Not knowing what he told her could place the killer on alert. And the cell was later used to contact Ruth and attempt to intimidate her into staying away from the library for some reason we have yet to figure out. I've always connected his disappearance to the workshop," she said.

"Have you met the other writers?"

"Briefly. I intend to question all of them in the next few days. I need to keep in mind the motive to Bartleby's murder may not be centered around his book. They're all writing about crimes, some of which seem to be based on actual events. And they discuss their work with each other during the class sessions. One of the writers, Milton, said he was almost run down by a motorcycle last week. He thought it looked like Bartleby's bike and when Rick went to check out the shed, it wasn't there."

"What's Milton's book about?"

"A memoir centered around a murdered racetrack jockey and a cheating scheme Milton uncovered when he was younger. He gathered evidence and testified against the people involved. They all served time."

"Could one of them be seeking revenge?"

"It was decades ago. They'd all be dead now, although the families might harbor resentment and want to make him pay. It seems far-fetched someone from that time in his past would be connected with Bartleby and also know about where to find the bike."

"What about the others?"

"Carolynn, the English teacher, seems harmless. Her husband is a real lady's man from what Ruth tells me. Conrad Renzulli owns an insurance agency. He gave me his card. Ruth assured me it wasn't an attempt to flirt. He hits everyone up to buy a policy from him. And then there's Terry, the young woman who's writing a play based on a psychiatric patient her aunt was treating. She related a disturbing event that I may need to look into."

"I think you should keep a close eye on Ruth. Whether or not she knows something related to Bartleby's death, the killer seems to have assumed she does."

"I agree. There's an underlying evil and Ruth is unknowingly involved. For her safety, I need to gather the pieces together as soon as possible. I'm going to start with the stepson." She took out her phone and made a call.

~

Deighton Durst looked out on the breaking waves from his suite at the Ocean House. He'd been in Rhode Island for more than a week. This was where he often came to get away from his hectic life in the city. Most of his work could be done on-line and sitting in a room overlooking the ocean was much better for his well-being than a crowded office in Manhattan. He'd just spoken to the woman detective. What could she want from him? His stepfather had been found. He'd made the identification. A tragic accident. He was arranging for a small service once the body was released. On Thursday, he would ask for a copy of the will and prepare to settle the estate. He was efficient. Nothing more to do. Case closed. But the woman was persistent and requested a meeting as soon as possible. It seemed the world was spinning around like a whirligig. Everyone was in such a hurry.

Deighton inhaled deeply, then exhaled slowly, imagining himself on the tippity top of the white crests surrounded by the sea mist. He pressed fingertips to his temples. He was feeling unusually tense and called to make a reservation at the hotel's spa for his usual - a facial and an aromatherapy massage.

"Of course Mr. Durst. We can accommodate you immediately."

His phone rang again. He looked at the caller ID and declined the call. He turned off his cell and left it in a drawer before he went to his appointment. *Lavender. That would calm his nerves.*

Terry was anxious to get this over with. She knocked on the office door. Her aunt usually spent Tuesday afternoon and evening working on the draft of her book. Terry had stopped to get takeout on the way home. Chicken fried rice and egg rolls. Her aunt's favorite.

"Come on in."

"Have you been here all day?" Terry set the bag on the coffee table.

"Pretty much. Ummm. That smells delicious." Virginia moved to the couch and helped unpack the food.

"How was your day? I think you were brave to go to work."

Terry had come home upset the night before and she'd decided to tell her aunt about Bartleby.

"Everyone was curious. I couldn't tell them anything because the police haven't released a name yet. I'm still hoping it isn't him. A friend came in and we spoke for a while. He's a policeman, so I could talk to him about it. He knew about Bartleby. It helped to talk with someone who knew what had happened. I felt like I was going to burst all day."

"I'm glad you're home. And thanks for bringing me food. It means I won't have to cook tonight and I can spend more time on this book."

"Look, I have something else on my mind that's been bothering me."

"Do you want to tell me about it?"

"Yes, I do. I haven't been honest with you about where I go on Saturday afternoons and Monday nights."

Her aunt stopped eating and listened as Terry began her story.

"I've been writing a play and I'm part of the workshop at the library..."

Milton had spent a sleepless night. He couldn't stop thinking about his friend. He had known him before the workshop. They'd met one summer afternoon in the park. Bartleby was sitting on a bench munching on crackers and invited Milton to sit down and share. They had quite a lot in common. Favorite foods, flowers, books, and of course, they each admired Miss MacAlister. She knew their life stories which they'd often discussed with her and she had encouraged them to be part of the writer's workshop she was forming.

Bartleby's spy thriller was way more exciting than his recollections of the scandal he'd unearthed when he was a young man first hired to run the photo-finish equipment used in the horse racing business. More than once, his pictures at the finish line decided a winner or a loser by the tip of a horse's nose. Lots of money riding on those photos. Bartleby assured Milton his story was worthy of writing about and so he'd agreed to be part of the group. He wondered if it would continue now that his friend was gone. He wasn't sure what he'd do if Ruth decided to stop working with them. He wasn't like the others. Writing didn't come natural to him and he'd need help finishing his book.

The sun was shining outside the window on the third floor where he'd sat all morning. He'd thought about dressing and taking a walk but was still nervous since his accident. And he kept hearing the sound of a motorcycle engine whenever he would leave the house. No, today he'd stay inside. Maybe he'd go back to bed, under the covers where he'd be safe and warm. Yes, that's what he'd do. He'd go back to bed.

Carolynn arrived home from school to find a note on the kitchen table.

I have appointments tonight so don't bother with dinner. I'll be home late. Don't wait up.

She hadn't planned to make dinner. She'd been invited to a Christmas party at the Babcock-Smith Homestead. She was still upset about Bartleby and was glad to have an excuse to be out with friends rather than home alone.

She had a few hours to spare and decided to correct some papers. Moving folders aside on the desk, she noticed one with *Bartleby Schnelling* stamped on the top. Inside was the life insurance policy Conrad had sold him. They'd made some kind of a deal. She read through it carefully and found her husband was named as beneficiary. It was dated November of the previous year, but she distinctly remembered he'd bought it this year. She recalled the embarrassing scene. Conrad handing out his business cards to everyone at the first workshop. It had been so inappropriate and they'd argued about it on the way home.

She looked through the other folders, then picked up her cell phone and snapped some photos. Before leaving the study, she returned the documents to the folders, making sure to put everything back on the desk exactly as she'd found it.

⁓

Nelson jolted awake when he heard his phone ringing. *Strange. No one ever called him.* It was dark in the room and he had no idea of the time. The ringing stopped. He was cold. He struggled to the door and turned the knob. Something was jammed against it on the other side. His knees buckled and he stopped himself from falling to the floor. *How long had he been out?* He tried to concentrate. His last memory was coming home from the library on Sunday morning. A white van was parked at the end of the dirt road. He'd felt tired and sick, had taken some pills, then went to bed.

What day was it? His head throbbed, his eyelids felt crusty, and his nose was runny. It was hard to breathe. He called out, but no one came to his rescue. He could use a glass of water. His throat was sore. A bitter taste in his mouth made him swallow hard. A racking cough took hold sending searing pain into his chest. Outside, a train went by causing the house to shake and drowned out his weak pleas for someone to rescue him. *Help! Please help me!* This brought on another painful bout of coughing.

He sat back on the bed and closed his eyes, trying to imagine he was far away from this place. Somewhere in a movie. *The Princess Bride.* Surely someone would come along to save him? He wanted someone to throw a blanket over him to keep him warm. He wished for a happy ending. Every movie he'd ever watched had a happy ending. Nelson would wait for his. People would notice he wasn't at work. He never missed work. Fannie always told him he was the most dependable person she'd ever hired. She would notice he wasn't there. Help was probably on the way. He hoped it would come soon.

The detective isn't your main character, and neither is your villain. The detective's job is to find justice for the corpse. It's the corpse's story first and foremost.
Ross MacDonald

Wednesday, December 18

KARA HAD MADE APPOINTMENTS with Deighton Durst and some of the members of Ruth's writing group. She wanted to find out as much as she could from the people who could provide her with information she needed to solve Bartleby's murder.

The medical examiner had concluded death by drowning. The head injury was not fatal. There was no sign of prior seizure and all evidence was pointing away from it being an accident. Someone had murdered Bartleby Schnelling. He'd been followed into the park, shoved, and ended up face down in the pond. His body would have been discovered sooner had it not been lying under a thin layer of ice and covered in snow for over a week. Kara was convinced this wasn't a random crime. It was tied to the authors' workshop in some way and she had to ask the questions which would lead her to the killer.

Deighton Durst was first on her list. He'd invited her for a late breakfast at the Ocean House where he was staying. Stewart had taken her there for their anniversary in November. It had a five-star rating. The food and service were excellent and sitting at a candlelit table overlooking the Atlantic Ocean was one of the most romantic evenings they'd shared since they'd become parents the previous spring.

Kara was waiting in the lounge when Durst came to meet her. He hesitated, visibly uncomfortable for a moment before offering his hand.

She gave him her card, wondering if he was surprised to see he was about to have breakfast with a woman of color.

The hostess escorted them into the dining room. He seemed quite at home in the elegant surroundings and she noted the maître d' and waiters treated him deferentially. They were led to a table by the window where a bottle of Dom Perignon was cooling in a silver ice bucket on a stand. A basket of warm rolls tucked under a blue linen cloth was on the table. Whipped butter, the texture of freshly churned cream, sat nestled in a delicate porcelain bowl. Crisp white napkins were placed across their laps and menus opened in front of them for their perusal. Kara was glad she'd chosen to leave her mommy jeans at home and had dressed up for the occasion. After they'd ordered, Deighton disposed of civilities and asked pointedly about her interest in his stepfather's death.

"Although I work for the state forensics' department, this began because of a personal connection. My friend, Professor Ruth Eddleman, is mentoring a group of writers and your stepfather was one of those authors. She became concerned and asked for my help when Bartleby stopped attending the meetings." Kara purposely didn't mention the cell phone.

"I must admit it surprises me that he was attempting to write a book. I always felt he had a limited vocabulary. Bartleby was not known to be proficient with the written word. He wasn't even a good conversationalist from the few times I was in his company. Now, my mother was the clever one of the pair."

"Was she a writer?"

"Writing was part of her work, but she was reticent to speak of what her job entailed. As you must be aware, the rules are rigid when you're dealing with federal agencies and classified documents. Everyone is expected to comply with the regulations. But Mother was well versed in many topics when she chose to converse. She was a charming lady from an upperclass family. I never understood what she saw in Bartleby."

Kara broke off a piece of roll, placed it in her mouth without buttering it, and chewed twenty times before responding. "I believe they met while in government service."

"He was my father's friend. I would think more likely an acquaintance. After Papa's death, Bartleby didn't waste much time. Mother was a wealthy widow and I don't believe he came into the marriage with much to offer."

"They settled here in Westerly in his family's home."

"Yes, there was that. The simple life." Kara noted he was about to put his nose in the air before he caught himself. He carefully buttered and placed a small portion of a roll delicately between his pursed lips. "She seemed to be comfortable enough, with their life style," he added with a swish of his hand.

Warmed plates were delivered to the table. "The Eggs Benedict is marvelous. I haven't found a better recipe in any of the fine dining establishments we have in The City."

She tasted her champagne before digging in to her omelet. Neither spoke for a while until Kara stated, "I worked in New York when I first began my career."

He looked up and seemed interested.

"I was a member of the police force."

He stopped for a brief moment before continuing with his breakfast.

"I still have friends working there. I spoke with my partner just last week. He's a detective now. I was trying to find out what your stepfather had been doing in New York before he went missing."

Deighton poured himself more champagne.

"Did you know he was in the city?" She tested him.

He sipped from the flute, then placed it on the table. "Yes, I was aware he was meeting with his editor."

"He had a contract with GreenTree to publish a book. A spy thriller. Were you aware of that?"

"In fact, I was. You see, when my mother died, she left me her stock portfolio. My sister Miranda inherited her library. Most of the books are first editions and therefore extremely valuable."

"What does this have to do with the book your stepfather was writing?"

"Miranda hasn't claimed her inheritance. Apparently, she's chosen not to return to this country and has made no arrangements to have the books shipped to her. As the executor of Mother's will, I am responsible for them."

"And Bartleby's novel? Are you insinuating it's part of your mother's collection?'

"I'm not insinuating anything. I'm convinced it is my mother's book. It may be his story, but I assure you, she wrote it for him. I can tell you, they were involved in high-level government work, therefore it most likely contains highly confidential information, which shouldn't see the light of day. He does not have the right to publish it. I told him I could tie him up in legal red tape for years. He would never see that book published."

"I'm not a lawyer, but I think he may have had a strong case."

"It's a moot point, now that he's dead."

"That's assuming the rights didn't revert back to him." She let that hang in the air for a minute.

Deighton's placed his fork on the table and wiped his mouth. "Why ever would it revert back to him?"

"Your sister never claimed her inheritance and was not at her mother's funeral. That strikes me as strange and I have to ask myself if she's still alive. You admit you've not heard from her in years."

"I think I'd have been contacted if she died." He dabbed again at his lips before placing the napkin on his lap. He emptied the flute and refilled it to the brim.

"Do you come here often?"

"Rarely. I do little business in Rhode Island and have absolutely no reason to spend time with my stepfather."

They ate in silence for a few minutes. He appeared to have lost his appetite and he pushed the half-empty plate away from him, tossing his napkin on the table.

When Kara had finished, the waiters came to clear the dishes. "Would you like coffee or tea, Madam?" one of them asked.

"Neither, thank you." She sensed the conversation had almost reached its end. "When did you last speak with your stepfather?"

He looked over the table at her knowing she already had the answer to that question.

"We met on Tuesday for dinner. He came to the Plaza where I was attending a conference."

"Did you see or speak with him after Tuesday?"

"No, I've been busy with a major international project and haven't had much time to think further about our conversation. I wanted to make sure he understood my position on the book."

"Do you know of any reason why someone would want to kill your stepfather?"

"Seriously, I know nothing about his private affairs or the people with whom he chooses to associate. The circumstances surrounding his death have nothing to do with me, I assure you." He stood up, not so subtly signifying their time together had ended.

He walked her to the hotel lobby. "Thank you for breakfast and for answering some of the questions about Bartleby while he was in New York. Will you be staying here much longer?" she asked.

"No, I'm meeting with his lawyer on Thursday and hopefully the service will be held on Friday. I'll be leaving right after that. As I said, I have a busy schedule. I left immediately when I was notified by the police last night. It's been terribly inconvenient to get these four days free."

She stared into his eyes. After a moment, he abruptly turned away leaving her standing alone. The hostess brought her coat, handing her a sheet of stationary from the sign-in desk.

Mr. Deighton Durst – reservations beginning Thursday, December 5h

"I also included the license plate number of his car. It's a rental. Is there anything else I can help you with, Detective Langley?"

Kara folded the paper and put it into her coat pocket. "No, I'm all set. Thank you, Marilynn. Give your mom and dad my regards."

She walked slowly out to the front portico and turned to gaze at the beautiful structure. She was leaving with more questions needing to be answered than when she'd arrived.

When Deighton was safely back in his suite, he wrapped ice cubes in one of the facecloths and held it against his forehead. He was feeling woozy and sat on the end of the bed. His cell phone vibrated in his jacket pocket and he checked the caller ID before pressing *Accept*. "I just met with that detective woman. Pack a bag. I'm going to need you."

Milton had baked a cake for his guest. He rarely had visitors and was honored that Dr. Eddleman's detective friend was making time for him. He suspected she must be incredibly busy now that Bartleby's body had been found and it was no longer a missing person's investigation. This brought forth memories of his own investigation into the racetrack cheating incident leading to a jockey's murder. You didn't see as much scandal nowadays. He intended to help her as much as he could. Maybe she would even ask him to be her partner in crime?

He opened the front door, "Well, hello." He looked past her to the street. "Where's your car?"

"I just came from the Ocean House and decided to leave it in the lower parking lot. It was easier to walk down the hill from there."

He was curious about what she'd been doing at the hotel but it was not his business to ask. He helped her off with her coat. "Please make yourself comfortable. I'll just be a minute."

She settled into the feather-cushioned couch and picked up a thin, brown 1947 telephone directory from a side table. She laughed at the instructions for dialing rotary phones and placing long distance calls with an operator. Cell phones made life more convenient nowadays but tracing calls was much more difficult when an operator wasn't involved. She was browsing the booklet when Milton returned with a tea tray.

"I was looking through that this morning to see if I could find Bartleby's parents listed. I found them. He grew up on Grove Avenue. In those days we had party lines and we didn't have numbers on our houses. The postmen knew all the names. Lots of memories lying around this house. Here's something interesting." He handed her a copy of *Sports Illustrated* from 1962 and opened it to a section entitled *A Nose Is a Nose*. "Those are three of my finish line photos taken at a race track in British Colombia on Vancouver Island. I've got scrapbooks filled with interesting stuff from back then."

He poured a fragrant liquid into delicate china cups and cut two large slices of angel food cake with chocolate frosting. He handed her a napkin embroidered with purple dragonflies.

"How exquisite."

"My wife loved to do needlework. I've kept everything she made. It's nice to have a reason to show it off."

Kara placed the delicate cloth over her lap but was careful not to let any crumbs fall. "This is delicious. Thank you for going to all this trouble for me."

"No bother at all. My wife's favorite dessert. I learned to make it for her from one of my mother's recipes."

"You must have traveled a lot with your job."

"Yes, we did, during the racing season. But we spent our summers here and this is where I retired. It's where I'll breathe my last and where they'll bury me in the family plot at River Bend next to my wife."

"Certainly that won't be for a long time. You're very robust for your age. Ruth mentioned you jog around the neighborhood every day."

"At times it's more like a fast walk. I try to stay healthy."

"You said someone almost ran you down on a motorbike last week. Did you get a good look at the driver?"

"No, I jumped to the sidewalk and fell. I just remember the sound. Bartleby had a muffler issue he was always intending to have fixed. His bike made that same noise when he let me take it out for a spin." He put his cup down and took a handkerchief from his pocket. "I'm going to miss him." He swiped at his eyes.

"Do you think someone tried to hit you on purpose?"

"I can't imagine anyone who would want to run me down. I thought about it and then realized all of the jockeys and trainers I testified against are dead or out of commission."

"Did any of their family or friends threaten you during or after the trial?"

"One young man assaulted me outside the courthouse the day the verdict came in. And I received some pretty nasty letters. I even bought an insurance policy at the time, so if anything happened to me, my wife would be able to pay the bills. I'd saved up a nice bundle to retire on. No worries about where the next dime would come from. We cashed in the policy to buy a car. Insurance was a lot cheaper back then, I can tell you."

"Did you keep the letters?"

"Oh, I save everything." He left the room and returned with a large shirt box. It was filled with notes and papers dated around that time. She briefly scanned some of the letters.

"May I take these with me?" she asked.

"Why would you want them? I thought you were investigating Bartleby's death."

"Your recent accident makes me want to see if there's a connection. I don't believe in coincidence and Bartleby's bike is missing."

"Oh, I see. Of course. I'm not sure if they'll be of any help to you, but keep them as long as you like."

Kara got up to leave. "I'm going to the library now to speak with Fannie MacAlister."

Milton helped her on with her coat. "I believe this must be hitting her hard. She and Bartleby spent hours talking about spy mysteries and thrillers. I think she formed the mystery writer's group just for him. She always felt that book of his had promise. Send her my regards. And thanks you for the visit. Please come again any time."

He stood on the steps and watched her walk up the hill, then stepped back inside the house. He sliced himself another piece of cake and poured out the remains of the tea. After he finished cleaning up, he put on his track suit and running shoes and went outside into the afternoon sunlight. He took a deep breath of the salty air and thought how good it was to be alive.

∽

Fannie was working in her office and she jumped up to greet Kara. "I'm so relieved you're looking into this. Have you learned anything else since Monday?"

"Bartleby's stepson has come in from New York to take care of details. I spoke with him earlier today. He's planning a small service on Friday. When I find out more, I'll let you know. Is Nelson here? I'd like to speak with him."

"He phoned yesterday to say he was ill and wouldn't be in for the rest of the week. I could hardly understand what he was saying. I even looked at the caller ID to be sure it was him. I asked if he needed anything but he'd already hung up."

"I have to speak with him. Do you know where he lives?"

"I have his cell phone number. He never gave us an address. It's somewhere near the train station. Behind the tracks off Friendship Street. I heard him complain to Milton once about the house shaking whenever the high speed Acela goes by."

"Fannie, how are you doing?"

"I think I'm still in shock. I'd really hoped he was on another top-secret mission and he'd return with an adventure to tell me. To think I won't ever see him again ..." Her eyes watered as she stared straight ahead lost in her thoughts. "I must ask Ruth what will become of his book. I knew it was going to be a success. He just needed to get it finished. He said Ruth was a big help and had given him some good ideas. He was having problems with his editor. She was a real fussbudget, that one."

"So, he shared the book with you."

"Yes, he kept a copy here in my office."

"Did you have any idea how it was going to end?"

"Oh, no. He didn't want to spoil the surprise for me. He said I'd never guess who the killer was. Someone good at hiding their real character. Maybe they'll find the missing chapters and Ruth and I can work to get the book published? I imagine being a detective, you have a lot of stories to tell."

"I'm not a writer. But I do love to read. I have a bookcase filled with books by black authors for Celia to explore when she's older. Maybe she'll become the writer in the family? At the moment, her Auntie Sophia is helping her discover a taste for children's literature. Literally."

"Thank you for coming by, Kara, and for being interested in my dear friend, Bartleby."

Kara decided to leave her car in the parking lot and walk to the bookshop following the same route Bartleby must have taken the night he died. She crossed the park to the bandstand and then down the path to the skating pond where she gathered up a strip of yellow police tape left from the other night. She stood where the body had been taken from the water, then walked toward the exit and through the stone pillars out on to High Street. Across the road was a mural of Wilcox Park painted on the side of a brick building. In the top corner was a picture of Harriet Wilcox and across the mural was the quote "The people shall have their park".

At the intersection, she turned right to walk down Canal Street toward the bookstore. A scaffolding was in place at the entrance of the United Theatre. She wondered when the work would be completed and the people would have their cultural center. She crossed over to the Savoy and stood under the cover of the entrance, imagining Bartleby taking out his phone and calling Ruth, leaving a message, and then pushing the envelope through the mail slot.

Terry was working in the café. "I'll take my break as soon as the other barista gets back from his," she said.

Kara went to the front windows and looked outside toward the train station. She sat on the couch and waited.

Terry brought them each a hot chocolate. "Which do you prefer? Whipped cream or no cream?"

"I'll take mine straight. Thanks."

"How have you been?" Kara asked.

"I was a mess for the past two days. But my aunt was a help. She's a psychiatrist."

"Yes, I've been curious if you've followed the advice Dr. Eddleman gave last Monday?"

"I did have a discussion with my aunt about my play. She wasn't aware I'd been attending the workshop at the library. We talked mostly about Bartleby. I never got around to telling her about the plot and the fact I've used one of her files as a source. I intended to, really, but I couldn't bring myself to tell her."

"So, she's not aware of the man who confronted you in her office on Sunday?"

"No, she'll really freak out if she thinks I put myself in danger. Especially now with Bartleby's murder. I don't know how I'm going to explain it all to her."

"Would you like me to help?"

"I think I need someone to mediate on my behalf. I'm not sure how Auntie will take all of this."

"If you want, I can go with you to speak with her?"

"I'm off work in an hour. I'm not scheduled for tonight."

"One more thing – close your eyes. Now tell me what Bartleby was wearing when you saw him on Tuesday before he went to the train station."

"He had on that brown suede coat he always wears. The one with the fur around the hood. And those olive colored rubber-soled duck boots and thick black leather gloves."

"Good. And did he have his portfolio with him?"

She thought for a minute then grimaced. "I don't remember it. But he had a dark blue valise. More like a small suitcase. I gave him my script and he opened the case and slipped it in He'd offered to show it to his publisher for me. Maybe his portfolio was inside, too?"

"Thanks, Terry. I'm going over to the depot for a bit. I'll be outside on the bench when you get off work."

Kara walked across the street to take some photos before going into the building. She spoke with Lora, one of the artists who volunteered at the Artisans' Gallery now housed inside what once was the station's entrance area and waiting rooms. Lora unlocked the bathroom and Kara examined the stalls, but did not find what she was looking for. She left the building to explore for other potential hiding places.

Somewhere across the tracks was Nelson's house. She felt he was a key person to interview. He was the one who knew all that went on in every crevice of the library. A train pulled into the station and she imagined Bartleby getting off and heading toward home. Kara walked the route he may have taken from the tracks back to the bookshop and she stood on the sidewalk looking in the window as he must have done on that stormy Friday night. Terry saw her and waved, holding up her index finger to signal she'd be out in a minute.

Kara sat on the bench noting everything she could see from that vantage point. *Did someone follow him from the depot? Someone who had been on the train from New York? Or was his killer lying in wait for him to return and take his usual short cut across the park to the safety of his home? Considering the inclement weather conditions, he may not have noticed he was being shadowed.*

Terry sat down next to her, interrupting her thoughts. "Are you thinking of Bartleby?"

"Yes, I just came from the train station and was trying to imagine what occurred that night." She turned to Terry. "Do you know where Nelson Belle lives?"

"I often see him walking down the street toward one of the neighborhoods on the other side of the tracks. He was passing by the store one evening when I was leaving and I offered to give him a ride home. It was raining. He said it wasn't that far, but thanked me for asking. I gave him my umbrella. He came into the store and returned it to me with a thank you note the next day."

"I left my car at the library. Can you give me a ride?"

"Sure thing."

"If you don't mind, I'd like to make a slight detour and check out the area where you think Nelson lives. Miss MacAlister told me he hasn't been to work. He called her to say he's sick. She's concerned and I think she has reason to be."

Terry drove down Canal Street and turned right on Friendship Street. Kara directed her to make another right on to a dirt road running parallel to the tracks. At the end of a row of houses in various stages of dilapidation was a small structure separated from the others by a stockade fence.

"Stop the car here, please." Kara got out and walked to the back of the shack where she spied a bright blue tarp. It was new and weighted down with cinderblocks on all four ends. Kara kicked two aside and pulled up an edge to reveal the rear end of a motorbike. She threw off the tarp and snapped a picture with her cell, then continued on her circuit around the house, stopping to look into a window. She banged on the front door. No one came out to greet her or to tell her she was trespassing. Winter darkness was creeping up, but no lights shone from within. Still, Kara could feel the presence of someone watching.

Terry called out to her from the car, but Kara held up her right hand for the girl to stay where she was. She called the police station and asked to speak with Chief. Baker. "It's urgent. Please tell him it's Detective Kara Langley."

He came on the line immediately.

"I'm on a dirt road off Friendship Street behind the railroad station. Could you send back up? I'm outside one of the houses and I've just uncovered what I believe to be Bartleby Schnelling's stolen motorbike. There may be someone in the building. I'll wait until a patrol car arrives to go inside. Please ask them not to use their sirens."

She walked around the house again, taking more photos. She went to the car to show Terry the picture of the motorbike.

"It's Bartleby's. He kept it in the shed in his back yard."

Before long, two policemen arrived. Kara flashed her ID and explained the situation.

"I need to get inside."

The older cop banged on the front door but there was no answer. It was unlocked. He called out Nelson's name and identified they were the police before they entered the open space. The younger cop found a switch. An overhead bulb cast a faint light. Kitchen cabinets and appliances stood against one wall and on the other, a tattered couch, a battered chair, and a coffee table like the discarded furniture sometimes left on corners around town.

A door on the back wall led into a tiny room. It was the size of a closet and had no windows. Her eyes adjusted to the dark. A coverlet was thrown over a mound in the center of a twin bed. Kara carefully moved it. At first, she thought she'd uncovered a corpse. Its skin was freezing cold. She felt for a pulse, then instructed one of the men to call for an ambulance. She'd found Nelson Belle, but he was barely alive.

Kara spent the rest of the night in the intensive care unit at the Westerly Hospital where Nelson was hooked up to intravenous tubes and monitors. The resident on duty had told her she should go home and rest. He didn't expect the patient to wake any time soon. But she chose to remain, keeping watch by Nelson's bedside.

The police chief had come to the hospital and she'd shown him the photos she'd taken. He told her that the motorbike was registered to Bartleby Schnelling and had been placed in police storage. The house had been searched and Bartleby's wallet and a smart phone were found inside a leather portfolio hidden in a pillowcase under Nelson's bed. The phone had been smashed. They were also being held as evidence.

"It all points directly to him as Schnelling's murderer. Open and shut case," the chief stated. "He certainly had the opportunity. We don't know, as yet, what his motive was. It may have been connected to the theft of the vehicle."

"We'll find out more when he regains consciousness," she said.

"If he regains consciousness. He's in pretty bad shape. Looks like he'd been lying there sick with no food or water for some time. Do you know if he has any next of kin we should contact?"

"No, I called Fannie MacAlister and broke the news. She wasn't aware of any relatives. Most of the people he had known were people from the library. Fannie had hired Nelson as a docent and helper years ago when she noticed he was spending most of his time in the reading room in front of the fireplace. She thought he may have been homeless, but he told her he had a place nearby. He gave her his number but not his address. Did your detectives happen to come across another phone belonging to Nelson?"

"No land line, no other cell."

"Now, that's strange because Fannie said he'd called to say he was ill and wouldn't be in work for the rest of the week. The voice was hard to distinguish but the caller ID was his." Kara said. "Are there people living in the houses on his street?"

"No, they're in pretty bad condition. I can't even imagine anyone living in his shack, although it had electricity. The others didn't. We contacted the landlord and he's coming into the station tomorrow. I'm heading out. You should go home and get some rest."

"I'll stay a bit longer."

"I've arranged for a police guard outside the room."

"I don't think he's going anywhere in his condition. But, it's a good idea," she said. "If he isn't the killer, then he knows who is."

"With all of the evidence we've collected, do you still think someone else might have killed Schnelling?"

"I'll have to get back to you on that. I have a few people I'd like to speak with."

"If you uncover anything you think we should know, please call. Until that time, Mr. Nelson Belle is our primary suspect."

"Or key witness," she whispered to Nelson after the door closed and they were alone.

Marie and Pierre, the labra doodles, greeted her at the door. Stewart was at the stove.

"You look tired." He gave her a kiss.

She hung up her coat and sat down at the kitchen table. He poured her a mug of tea and placed a steaming bowl of chicken soup in front of her.

"Eat and then we'll talk."

After she finished her second bowl of soup and he'd refilled her mug, he asked with a slight touch of sarcasm, "So how was your day?"

She laughed. "I started out in a five star hotel in Watch Hill and ended up in a hovel by the railroad tracks. In between, it was interesting."

"You said when you called that the police believed Nelson Belle was Bartleby's killer but I detected doubt in your tone."

"It's all too convenient. And once again, it comes down to a phone. Where is it? How did he call in to the library? Was it even him on the other end of the line? And then there's this." She took out her cell phone and showed him a series of photos she'd shot.

"Looks like a dirty floor." Stewart was unsure of what he should be seeing.

"Yes, the floor. Look at the marks. It appears that something heavy was dragged and placed in front of the bedroom door."

"Something like that couch?" he asked, pleased that he was following her line of thinking.

"Exactly like that couch. I believe he may have been kept in that room and unable to escape. He was weak and sick. And I think the person who did that to him is our killer. All I have to do now is narrow down the suspects and figure out the motives."

"Maybe this could keep until later. Right now, I suggest you get some sleep. You and Ruth are not meeting with Durst and the lawyer until later in the afternoon. I'll make sure Celia is fed, bathed and dressed when she wakes up and I'll put her in the stroller to take her and the pups out for a long walk, so there's no need for you to get up early." He gave her another kiss and began to clear away the dishes.

She brought the phone with her into the bedroom and as she looked at the photos again, she became more convinced that someone went to a lot of bother to frame Nelson Belle. But where was his phone? When she found that out, she'd have the answer to her questions: Who killed Bartleby Schnelling and Why?

∽

*Writing is something you do alone.
It's a profession for introverts who want to tell you a story
but don't want to make eye contact while doing it.*
John Green

Thursday, December 19

WHEN TERRY DROVE HOME on Wednesday evening, she had every intention of telling her aunt the truth, but there was a note on the refrigerator.

Be back late. Casserole in the fridge.
Love, Auntie

She poured herself a glass of juice and brought it to her room. The memory of Nelson's pale face as he was carried on the stretcher into the ambulance haunted her. She'd told Virginia about Bartleby and now there was another serious incident tied in to someone connected with the library. Terry wasn't sure how her aunt would feel about her continuing with the workshop. She wasn't even sure how she felt about it. But if Nelson was the one who killed Bartleby and tried to run down Milton, they were all safe. He was in no condition to hurt anyone else.

She'd decided to tell her aunt that Bartleby's killer had been caught but not that she'd been on the scene when he was found. Kara had managed the whole situation well. And she was smart to figure out where Nelson lived and to arrive in time to save his life. *Aunt Virginia would really get along well with Kara. Two women who could deal with any situation.*

It brought back her fear the day she was confronted by the man in her aunt's office. *I wish I was brave, but I'm not. I wish I'd been honest, but I haven't been. Dr. Eddleman will be so disappointed in me. I'm such a coward.*

If only Bartleby were alive, but he was gone from her life and she could never confide in her friend again. She'd told him about the source of her play and he'd entrusted her with a copy of the final chapter in his book. She was the only one who knew the ending he'd finally written. She'd given him a copy of her draft and he knew the truth about where her story had originated. He knew it wasn't even her story. She crawled under the covers and fell into a fitful sleep, waking each time Nelson's pale face appeared in her nightmares.

Later that night, she woke to a knock on her bedroom door. It opened and a crack of light from the hallway seeped in.

"Terry, are you awake?" her aunt whispered.

She wanted to ask her aunt to sit with her and stroke her head. But she stayed under the covers until she heard the door close.

The comforting aroma of coffee and cinnamon rolls filled the house. Virginia called up the stairs, "Rise and shine, Sleepyhead."

Terry had decided to tell her everything, but when she went to the kitchen, she noticed her aunt was wearing a suit.

"You're dressed pretty fancy for work."

"Did you forget? I'm going to be in Connecticut. I have to take care of some business at the institute and then I'm meeting my old friends at Foxwoods. I haven't seen them in a long time so we decided on a girls' night out. We've got reservations at a fancy restaurant and tickets for a show. I might try my hand at the slot machines. We're going to spend all day Saturday at the spa."

"I did forget. When will you be back?" Terry poured herself a mug of coffee and sat down.

"Saturday night. What are your plans for the weekend?"

"I'll be at the bookstore and I have the workshop on Saturday. I'll probably usher at night."

"Okay, well, you'll finally have some time to yourself without your old auntie around. You should invite some friends over on Friday." There was hope now that she'd learned about the people in the workshop. Her phone rang and she left the room to talk. When she came back, she was wearing her coat and carrying her suitcase. "Sorry I have to run. I won't be too far away. I'll try to check my texts every day, but I can't promise. Love ya!"

Terry sat in the kitchen sipping the rest of the coffee and licking the frosting off the tops of the rolls. She wasn't scheduled to go into work until the afternoon. She threw away the coffee grounds, rinsed out the carafe, and put the mugs into the dishwasher. It was only eight thirty. She decided to go back to bed.

While Stewart was out taking a walk with Celia and the Curies, Kara called Detective Sergeant Perez, her old partner.

"How's that case coming along? Is there anything I can check for you?"

"Yes, Schnelling's body was found and his stepson came in to identify it. But his story isn't matching up with the information I have. His name is Deighton Durst. I'll text you his business address and cell phone number. "

"No business phone?"

"None given. I found that strange, myself. He admits meeting with his stepfather for dinner at the Plaza Hotel."

"Swanky Place," Perez commented.

"Yes, I thought the same. Durst says he was attending a conference. Could you check to see what conferences were being held at the hotel last week and if he was registered for one? Get dates for me. Durst says he came to RI on Monday night, December 16th, directly after he was called by the police. But he signed into the Ocean House here in Westerly on Thursday, December 5th according to their register. He lied to me and never blinked."

"Two weeks at The Ocean House? Wow! This guy must be loaded."

"See if you can obtain any information on his finances for me. I have information on the rental car he's driving, if that might help."

"Text it to me. I'll see what I can do. What's the name of his business?"

"Funny thing about that. I handed him my card and you'd think he would have given me his. Have you ever met a New York City businessman who doesn't carry cards around with him?"

"Sounds like this guy flies under the radar. I'll do my best."

"Also, could you check at the desk to see if Bartleby left his suitcase at the hotel? He had it with him when he left on Tuesday, but no sign of it, so far."

Her next call was to the hospital. Nelson's condition had not changed. She called Fannie to relay the information.

"I want to visit him as soon as he's awake. I don't believe for one minute he killed Bartleby. He doesn't have a mean bone in his body," she declared. "You tell me when he can have visitors."

Kara didn't have the heart to tell her that might never happen. She heard noise in the hallway. Stewart peeked into the room and on seeing her sitting up in bed, returned with Celia who was holding a leaf in her tiny hand.

"And where did you find that, Sweetie?"

Celia waved it around. "Buh, buh, buh. Buh, buh, buh, buh."

"It floated from a tree into her stroller. She's been quite enthralled with it. I think she may become a botanist," Stewart said.

"Please, don't mention this to Sophia. She'll be signing her up for the Master Gardener Program at the college."

"I thought you were going to sleep in?" He looked at the phone in her hand.

"I slept soundly and am ready to rise and face the day. I've made a few inquiries and later I'll call to inform Ruth of what's been happening. Rick's been keeping a close watch on her and Gino has insisted on driving her to school and attending her classes. He's become her shadow."

"She must love that. Do you think she's still in danger now that Bartleby has been found and Nelson implicated?"

"Until we find out who the real killer is, I think everyone associated with Bartleby or with Ruth's workshop is in danger."

"It appears you have another busy day ahead."

Celia interrupted with a series of gurgles and chirps. After squashing the leaf in her hand, she tossed the pieces into the air. The puppies heard her and came bounding in, jumping up on the bed to join the family gathering. Much to the baby's delight, Pierre's long, pink tongue scooped up what was left of the crumbled leaf and unceremoniously ate it. Marie licked his face trying to get a taste of the treat.

"Oooooh! Mum, mum, mum mum, mum."

"She says she wants them to share," Stewart translated.

"I do have a lot going on, but right now I'm going to spend some time with the four of you. It looks like you've been having too much fun without me."

༄

Professor Hill was in his office when Kara arrived. "I wasn't sure if you were coming in today. You still have some vacation you need to use up for this year."

"Now that we have more evidence to work with, I want to spend time on this case. I don't want to see the wrong person charged with Bartleby's murder."

"You have to admit, much of that evidence incriminates Nelson Belle. His fingerprints are on the portfolio and the wallet. We even found a partial on the motorbike. And the marks on the floor from the couch could have been made at another time. He'll have a lot of explaining to do if he ever regains consciousness."

"Were you able to get anything from Bartleby's cell phone?" she asked.

"It's being examined now."

They went down the hall to another room where one of the technicians was taking notes. He commented on the condition of the smart phone. "Smashing them results in a broken screen. Someone might assume, because it isn't lit up, that it's not working, but it's usually still running. I'll see what I can extract from it."

"Anything you find will be helpful," Kara told him.

"I'll need to get a warrant for the company to release the data. They're sticklers about privacy issues, not that it's important to him now. But it may take time."

"No other phones have been turned in?" she asked Hill.

"None, but you're right, I checked and Nelson does have a cell. I dialed the number, but received a message that it wasn't in service. It's probably turned off. The team searched the area around his house and found nothing."

"There's something else I've been wondering about. Bartleby's suitcase. Sergeant Perez is checking at the hotel in New York. If he didn't leave it there, I have a hunch it may be somewhere around the train station. I did a cursory search, but I intend to return."

While she was going over the fingerprint evidence, Sergeant Perez called to tell her he'd checked the hotel and yes, Bartleby did arrive with a small suitcase, but it had not been left behind in his rush to get home on Friday.

"I went over to the Plaza and they confirmed they'd made dinner reservations for two under Durst's name on Tuesday. The manager informed me there were three conferences at the hotel on the dates I gave them. Deighton Durst was not registered for any of them, although, he was a guest at the hotel on Tuesday and Wednesday and spent time at their spa both days. He left on Thursday using his own name, not a company, on a rental car. I've got someone checking on his business and his finances. So far, nothing. He really does keep a low profile. I'll call you when I have more to report."

Kara spent the rest of the morning reviewing what they'd found out so far. Mr. Whitcomb called to tell her Deighton Durst had canceled their afternoon appointment.

"Did he have a reason?" she asked the lawyer.

"He was quite perturbed when he called to confirm our meeting and voiced his objections to anyone else being present. Thus, I was compelled to inform him a new will had recently been filed and Professor Eddleman was now named as the executrix. Mr. Durst seemed completely taken aback that he was no longer the executor and said he would be consulting a lawyer and then he informed me there was not going to be a memorial service. His instructions were that Bartleby Schnelling be cremated and laid to rest without further ado next to his wife at River Bend Cemetery. I'll inform you and Professor Eddleman when we schedule the reading of the will. This is most inconvenient." He hung up. Kara called Ruth to tell her about the change in plans.

Kara shared her conversation with Professor Hill who agreed it was strange behavior on the part of the stepson. "I think I'll take a ride to Westerly and see what else I can find out. And while I'm there, I need to see a man about some life insurance."

Conrad looked at his messages. Carolynn had sent him a text that she was going to stay at her mother's for the rest of the week. He texted her back, "Why?" He felt he deserved some kind of explanation.

She'd sent back a caring emoji with the words "Mom's sick and needs me."

He was annoyed and relieved at the same time. Annoyed his wife hadn't checked with him first and relieved he wouldn't have to make excuses about coming home late. And he would have the house to himself. Maybe his new little waitress friend would like to come over for a nightcap after she finished work? She liked riding in his Corvette and he'd be picking it up from the shop later today.

He looked up when he heard the door open. It was the woman he'd met at the library on Monday night. He couldn't remember her name. The cop. Dangerous profession. He thought she'd be someone who might need an insurance policy. Especially if she had any kids. He jumped up.

"Hello .... What brings you here today?"

"Kara Langley."

"Of course. Have a seat." He moved a chair to the front of his desk and moved around to his chair. "Terrible business the other night. We received a message from Ruth that it was, in fact, Bartleby Schnelling. Have you learned anything else?"

"I'm still working on the case, but there's nothing to report except to confirm he was murdered."

"Who would kill such a nice man? Do the police have any suspects?"

"No one's been brought in, yet. Do you know of anyone who would wish him ill?"

"We weren't friends. He was a client. He bought a policy for his motorbike from me some time ago. I recognized the name when we met for our first workshop meeting. We all enjoyed listening to him speak about his spy novel. Such an interesting old man. Did you know him well?"

"I never met him but knew of him through Professor Eddleman. She was concerned when he stopped attending the classes."

"As I told you, we weren't friends. He seemed close to Terry, the young woman writing the play. And he spoke with Milton, the other old guy in the group. The one writing about horse racing. I'm not big on outdoor stuff. I'd rather place my bets sitting comfortably in a casino at a roulette wheel with a gin in tonic in one hand and a stack of chips in the other."

He laughed and Kara noticed a nervous tic. He rubbed at his left eyelid, but it seemed to get worse as he sat waiting for her to say something. When she remained silent, he asked if she would like a drink. "I have juice and soda in the fridge or something harder, if you like."

"No, thank you Mr. Renzulli."

"Please, call me Conrad. Are you interested in an insurance policy? In your line of work, I hope you're well covered. Do you have family?"

She felt she needed to lower the stress level in the room. "I have a little girl. I agree, it's important to make sure she's taken care of. I definitely would like some information on insurance coverage. My husband and I are looking for a company with good rates for homeowners."

"That's what I'm here for." He gathered some informational pamphlets from a drawer and showed her a comparison chart for different companies. She put them in her bag and said she'd take them home to discuss with her husband.

"And don't forget about what happens to those you leave behind." He had relaxed as he went into his schpiel trying to sell her something. She let him explain the difference between term and life insurance. When he was through, she picked up the folder he'd made for her and thanked him.

"Again, I'll take this information home to discuss with Stewart. You've been very helpful."

He smiled and she noticed his eyelid had stopped twitching.

He opened the door for her.

"I was thinking of going by your house to speak with your wife." She looked at the watch. "I believe she should be home by now."

"Carolynn texted me she was going to visit her mother after work today. But if you'd like me to give her a message, I can."

"I'd rather talk with her myself. I have some questions I'd like to ask her about Bartleby."

"She knows less about him than I do."

"I have her number. I'll contact her later on. Again, thank you for all of this information, Conrad. I'll share it with my husband and we can decide exactly what we need."

"My pleasure. I hope to see you again soon. You know where to find me."

Kara noticed that the tic had returned, this time in his right eyelid. She wondered exactly what he was hiding and she thought his wife could probably give her a clue. She sent a text to the number Ruth had given her and waited for a response.

She responded immediately by calling Kara's number. "Detective Langley, it's Carolynn Renzulli. I just got your text. I'm at the library. I stopped by after school to see how Fannie was doing and she told me about Nelson. That poor man. How is he?"

"He's still in critical condition. I intend to go to the hospital later on. I was wondering if I could speak with you this afternoon?"

"Of course. I'll be here working on my book. Are you nearby?"

"As a matter of fact, I'm at your husband's office."

"You're with Conrad?"

Kara sensed tension in her voice. "I just left him. I'll be there in a few minutes."

Fannie was at the circulation desk. "Ruth contacted me this afternoon and said she was still planning on holding the workshop this Saturday." She hesitated. "I can't help think that none of this occurred until the group began meeting here. First Bartleby, then Milton, now Nelson. What is happening?"

"I'm not sure, Fannie. I'm still gathering information."

"You'll let me know if you believe it has anything to do with the library, won't you?"

"I'll make sure I keep you informed. I'm here to talk to Carolynn."

"She's in the alcove of the reading room."

Carolynn jumped up when she saw Kara. "Oh, you gave me a start." She closed the laptop.

"How is your story coming along?" Kara asked.

"Much better now that I'm writing it alone. It's hard to create a plot line and characters and settings and dialogue when you have to check everything with someone else."

"I listened to you and your husband discuss your books the other night and I think it was a wise decision to go your separate ways. You seemed to have different slants on pretty much everything."

"Yes, you're right about that." She began pulling at a stray lock of hair.

"As I said, I was at Conrad's office this afternoon. I asked him some questions about Bartleby. I never met him, so I'm depending on others to give me an idea about who he was and if he had any enemies." Kara watched her reaction.

Carolynn wound the hair around her index finger and put it in her mouth. She took it out. "Conrad didn't really know Bartleby at all. I don't think he could tell you anything that would be of help."

"And you?"

"Me?"

"How well did you know him?"

"He was more of an acquaintance. I'd spoken with him at the library and in the park during the past few years. And we discussed our books in the workshop. That started in November. I liked him. He wandered off the subject sometimes, but I think most old people tend to do that. My mother will start telling me something and before I know it, she's going on and on about a totally different topic than what we were talking about in the first place." She twisted and untwisted the strand of hair around her finger.

"Did he like to discuss his spy novel with you outside the group?"

"No. He did summarize it for us and read bits of the dialogue. It sounded really good. He already had a publisher. I was impressed. I think he was only in the group to get help on writing his final chapters. I can understand what he was going through. My draft was moving along just fine but now that I have to create a rational conclusion that my readers will believe, it's become a chore. I could go on and on writing chapters about the characters and their lives, their relationships and the complications with the people they meet, but trying to tie everything up in a mystery plot is near impossible."

"Maybe you shouldn't try to make it a mystery. It sounds like you may be more comfortable with the Romance Genre," Kara suggested.

"Oh, I wouldn't want to disappoint Dr. Eddleman. After all, we're supposed to be writing mysteries."

"I think you'll find she's very openminded. She tends to be focused on writing style and I know she believes you have talent."

"You know, I'm feeling a lot better now. I was nervous when you said you needed to talk to me. I honestly don't know anything about Bartleby except what we discussed in relation to his book and our conversations in the park were mostly about trees and flowers. He loved perennials. He said they gave him hope because they'd rest underground during the dead of winter and then pop back up in the spring."

"Did your husband know him better? He mentioned he'd written an insurance policy for Bartleby."

"Conrad told you that?" Carolynn looked surprised.

"An accident insurance on his motorbike."

"Oh, his bike!"

"You seem to think I was referring to something else."

Carolynn put her head in her hands.

"Is something wrong?" Kara moved closer toward her.

"I'm not sure."

"Do you want to tell me about it?"

"It could be nothing. Just my overactive imagination. And I don't want to get Conrad in trouble." She lifted her head up. "I found a folder on his desk and it has me worried. I know he wouldn't hurt anyone, but I can't help but wonder why Bartleby would have made my husband a beneficiary on a life insurance policy."

"When did you come across the policy?"

"I wasn't snooping. They were just there on the desk. Out in the open. You wouldn't leave something out like that if you were hiding something? Would you?" She looked to Kara for affirmation.

"You said *they*. Were there other policies?"

Carolynn took her phone from her bag and opened to the photos she'd taken in the study on Tuesday.

"It appears he was beneficiary on at least one of the other policies he sold," Kara noted.

"Yes, he's persistent. An excellent salesman. You should see all the awards he has from the insurance companies he represents. He's really good at what he does."

I've no doubt about that, Kara thought to herself. To Carolynn she said, "I think we may need to have a talk with your husband. This could be totally innocent if the policy holders are aware, but you must realize it seems somewhat suspicious."

"It does look odd. I've thought about it. Why would they name him as beneficiary? None of them have family, so maybe he made a deal with them and paid them money. That's not illegal, is it? If he had their permission?"

"Does he know you've seen these policies?"

"No, I don't use the office. I usually correct my papers on the dining room table where I can spread out. I came across the folders on his desk by accident. I put everything back, and I don't think he noticed. He hasn't said anything to me."

"I don't want you questioning him until I can look into this. Play dumb. Can you do that?"

"I won't be seeing him for a few days. I was nervous so I made plans to stay at my mom's. I told him she was sick."

"Good. We can have this conversation together with him at a later time."

"I'm relieved that somebody else knows. I'm positive there's a reasonable explanation. A wife should stand by her husband. But if I can be sure he's not a murd … a crook, I'll feel much better about it."

Before leaving, Carolynn emailed the photos to Kara. "Don't show these to anyone else. Contact me if you need me and be careful."

Kara went outside to the terrace and sat on a bench to think before phoning Milton.

"Did you ever purchase insurance from Conrad Renzulli's agency?"

"He gave me his card like everyone else, and he even went so far as to prepare the forms and arrange the requisite physical with his doctor for me, but I never bought anything from him. I have to say, he did put some pressure on me and I did have second thoughts after I was nearly run down. Like I told you, insurance nowadays is pretty darned expensive. Not like the old days. I'm just going to have to be more careful and not have any more accidents."

"I think that's a prudent idea, Milton."

Bartleby, Milton, and Nelson. Kara drove to the hospital and spoke with the guard at the door. Inside the room, she pulled up a chair beside

Nelson's bed. She placed her hand on his arm and whispered, "As soon as you wake up, I have a lot of questions for you to answer."

*I have a feeling that inside you somewhere,
there's somebody nobody knows about.*
Alfred Hitchcock

Friday, December 20

SOPHIA SPENT THE MORNING at Vida's house helping her get ready for the Ugly Sweater Party that night.

"I have to admit, Sophia, you are the most organized person I've ever met. This place has never looked so beautiful. I didn't think anything could be better than the job you did for last year's party."

"Glad to help, Vida. I'm just about done. Gino should be back here soon with the outdoor decorations."

"You're an inspiration! I gotta say, all I had planned was to lop off the top of that old fir tree that blew down last week and stick it in a bucket of sand in the corner of the living room. I figured I'd get some Jiffy Pop and let people string popcorn and cranberries to hang on it."

"You could still do that, Vida. A tree can never have enough decorations." Sophia peeked into the food pantry and opened the refrigerator. "Just out of curiosity, what have you planned for refreshments?"

"I stocked up on Narragansett Beer. It's on the porch packed in those styrofoam ice chests. And I figured I'd order a bunch of pizzas as soon as I got a head count."

"That sounds marvelous, Vida." Sophia went out to check and then called from the porch. "Would you mind if Ruth and I brought some snacks?"

"Mind? I think that's right kind. You can never have enough snacks," Vida came outside to slap her on the back. "This is gonna be some party.

Loralei's comin home from college and it'll be nice to get the old gang together. Before I met Kara, I could count my friends on one hand. Now, I'm not sure the house will hold everyone I invited. It makes me feel all warm inside." Vida wiped her eyes and blew her nose noisily on a dishtowel embroidered with prancing reindeers. "Oh look, here comes Gino up the drive!" She ran to meet him. "Hey! Wotcha got there in the back of your truck?"

He jumped out and began handing her decorations. Sophia stood pointing to where they should go.

"You got a ladda somewhere, Vida? Looks like my wife wants Santa's sleigh up on da roof."

It was early afternoon when they turned on the Christmas lights and stood in the yard looking at the winter wonderland they'd created.

"Wow, this is awesome. Now all we need is some snow," Vida said.

"I'll see what I can do about that. We have to get going." Sophia called to her, waving out the window as they drove off. "See you tonight."

"Where to now, Honey?" Gino asked.

"Let's stop at Belmonts for a few food platters. And we'll need some of those famous suppis to go with the beer."

"Don't worry about that. I picked up plenty. I was gonna give em as Christmas gifts, but what's a party without suppis?"

"Fantastic! Then, you and I are going to spend some quality time in the kitchen baking Christmas cookies," she announced. "Let's put this truck in high gear!"

Terry could hardly stay awake behind the counter of the cafe and went out to her car at lunch to take a short nap. She'd spent a restless night alone in the house checking the locks of all the doors and windows and turning on the outside spotlights. In the hall closet, she'd found her aunt's golf bag and took out a nine iron to keep by her bed. Strange noises kept her up and she almost called Greg around midnight, but thought better than to bother him at work. She hoped he'd stop by the store later on and kept looking at her watch throughout the afternoon.

She was making a fresh carafe of coffee when she heard his voice. "Hey, are you making that whole jug just for me?"

He stood there smiling and she had to stop herself from running around the counter and throwing her arms around him. Knowing how bashful he was, she instead gave him a gentle pat on his arm. "Give it a few minutes and I'll pour you a jumbo cup. Meet you at our table."

When she was sitting across from him, she put her hand out and touched his wrist. "I've missed you. A lot has happened in the past couple of days. I needed to talk with someone."

"What about your aunt?"

"She's out of town for the weekend."

"Sorry. It was crazy. Cops out sick with the flu. I did some extra shifts. But I'm here now. I'm all ears." He attempted to wiggle his ears, his nosed crinkled up in the effort, but couldn't pull it off, so he moved them back and forth with his hands. "Good or bad?"

She managed a weak laugh at his antics. "It's mostly bad."

He became serious and took her hand in his. "Do you want to talk about it?"

"There's so much to tell and in ten minutes, I couldn't fit it all in."

"How about you give it a try and anything you can't squeeze in now, we can continue tonight."

"I won't call you while you're working. I almost did yesterday and realized it wasn't a good idea."

"No problem. I've managed to get tonight free. People owe me. My time is your time. Unless you're scheduled at the theatre?"

"No, I'm ushering at Saturday's matinee. Wow! I can't believe we actually both have a night off together."

"Do you want to go to a show or something? I can make reservations at a nice restaurant and we could dress up like big people."

"I'm really tired. I didn't get any sleep. Maybe you could order take-out and come to my place? We can pick a movie to watch on Netflix."

"Sounds great." He looked pleased. "Our first official date."

"How about coming by at eight? It'll give me a chance to take a nap."

"Eight it is. But I need you to tell me who gets to choose the movie?"

"You're the guest, so you do."

"That's a relief. One thing you should know about me is I hate chick flicks."

"I'll keep that in mind for further reference."

"So, what's been happening?"

"We can talk about it tonight. Right now, let's decide what we're going to have for our first real meal together."

"I'm picking the movie, so you can choose the food. Win-win for me cuz I eat everything."

Terry smiled. She was feeling better already.

Ruth and Rick arrived home to be met with the aroma of baking. The dining room table was filled with platters of warm cookies in the shape of trees, bells, reindeer, and angels waiting to be decorated. In the kitchen, frosted cupcakes took up most of the counter space. Gino was sprinkling them with red and green jimmies.

"What is going on here?" Ruth asked as Sophia slid a cake in the shape of an elf from the oven.

"Good timing. The baking is all done. But you can help finish icing the cookies."

She tossed aprons at them. Rick grabbed the one with Mrs. Claus on the front.

"I guess that makes you Santa. Turn around." She slipped the apron over Ruth's head and tied the strings in a bow. "We were at Vida's decorating and her idea of party refreshments left much to be desired. I ordered food from Belmonts since it's last minute. At least the desserts are homemade. "Oh, and I made you a birthday cake. We can have it tomorrow for dessert."

"That was thoughtful of you. Thanks."

"So, how did you spend your day?"

"Rick took me out for breakfast at the Weekapaug Inn and then we went for a walk on the beach. It was perfect."

"To each his own. Quiet is not how I prefer to celebrate any of my birthdays. Keep that it mind." She pointed a spatula at them. "But I guess as you age, less excitement is better for your heart." Ruth let the jibe pass without comment knowing Sophia had wanted to plan a "big birthday bash" for her. But, unlike her sister-in-law, Ruth was not one for bashes and she let it be known she wanted to celebrate quietly with Rick.

"We stopped by Kara's to find out what she's learned about Bartleby's murder," Ruth said, as she concentrated on coating the angel's wings with creamy white frosting. She finished by sprinkling them with silver sugar and stepped back to admire her creation.

"If you're going to take that much time with one cookie, Christmas will be here and gone. Step up the pace," Sophia instructed. "Look, Rick's finished an entire plate." She examined them closely, picking one up, and wrinkling her nose. "And you call yourself an artist! They'll have to do."

"So what's goin on wid da murda case? Does Kara know who done it?" Gino asked.

"No, she's been interviewing everyone. Getting to know the members of the writing group. She has some leads she needs to follow, but it appears more than one of the authors has a motive."

"Maybe it'll be like dat Orient Express movie where dey all did it?" Gino suggested. "Nevva trust anyone who kills people off, even if it's just in a book."

"Does she suspect one of them more than the others?" Sophia asked.

"She's looking at motives. The stepson is sly and for some reason did not want Bartleby's book published. And he lied to her. Never a good idea. Kara can always tell when someone is not telling her the truth."

"What about the romance writers?" Sophia swirled green icing on the trees.

"The husband owns an insurance agency and it appears he wrote policies for Nelson, Milton, and Bartleby."

"That's not so unusual, is it? You said he handed everyone his card at the first class."

"It wouldn't be odd except he's listed as the beneficiary on each of them. If they agreed, then it would be above board, but Bartleby's dead and Nelson is lying in a hospital bed hooked up to machines. He can't confirm it. And Milton mentioned that Conrad had tried to sell him a policy, but he didn't see the point of spending the money, so he never signed the papers. He's had second thoughts since he was almost run down by the motorbike."

"Two, possible suspects with different motives. And then there's Nelson. The police are convinced it was him. All evidence would seem to corroborate that," Rick said.

"And the motive?" Sophia asked.

"Theft of the motorcycle. And maybe jealousy. He had a crush on the librarian who had a crush on Bartleby," Ruth explained.

"Ah, I geddit. It's dee ole lover's triangle." Gino stopped and gazed out the window shaking his head knowingly.

Sophia patted him on the shoulder. "Keep working. These cookies are not going to decorate themselves. Wait a minute. Are these crumbs? Have you been eating them?"

He brushed at his shirt, "You know I can't resist your cookin."

Ruth stepped in. "Kara's been busy at the forensics lab today. They'll probably be a little late for the party. She wants Celia to nap as long as possible so she won't be cranky tonight."

"When has that child ever been cranky? She's the sweetest little angel."

Everyone kept their eyes down, concentrating on the pastry in front of them. No one was about to contradict Auntie Sophia, especially when it had anything to do with her godchild.

"That reminds me, I have to wrap some gifts for the kids. The Sullivan boys are invited, too, and I don't want Celia to be the only one opening a present. Don't stop working. They look pretty good. I'll be back to touch them up a bit when you're done." Sophia breezed out of the room.

"Dares nuttin dat woman can't do. When dee angels were handin out wives, I got da best. No offense, Ruth," Gino declared.

"None taken," Ruth laughed as Rick threw his arms around her and gave her a kiss.

Dr. Walden called him from the institute. "Where are you?"

She'd made all the arrangements for him to return and expected he'd meet her there. But, he was having second thoughts and had written her a note. He drove around the block trying to decide if he should put it in the mailbox outside her office door. He didn't look forward to facing her when she came back on Saturday. He parked on the corner in front of the wooded lot. Taking out his phone, he found her number under *favorites* and sat staring at the screen. A car pulled into the driveway.

Terry drove into the garage. She was exhausted and went straight upstairs to her room. She was looking forward to her date, but right now all she wanted to do was curl up under the covers and catch a few hours sleep. She set the alarm to give her enough time to take a shower before Greg arrived then turned off the lamp and closed her eyes.

She left the garage door open. Careless of her. A light went on upstairs. He waited. Minutes later, the room went dark. No other lights were on in the house. *She must be sleeping.* He looked around. The neighborhood was quiet. *No cars, no people.*

The light from his cell swept around. The garage. *Garden tools. Rakes, shovel, shears, gloves and clippers, gas can, bicycle.* The beam moved across to stairs leading up to the door on the back wall. He turned the knob. It wasn't locked. He found himself in the kitchen. *No sounds overhead.* He opened the refrigerator. Sitting at the table, he drank the juice straight from the bottle until there was none left. He hadn't realized how thirsty he was.

People began to arrive at Vida's early in the evening. Samuel took their coats and hung them in the closet. Arthur immediately escorted them to the Christmas tree where he took photos of them in their ugly sweaters. Clay was in charge of directing the carolers grouped around the piano in the living room. Out on the back deck, people were dancing to Brenda Lee's Christmas album.

"Good thing my nearest neighbors are five miles down the road or you'd be haulin us all off to jail for disturbin the peace," Vida said to Detective Carl Sullivan. Sophia traveled from room to room with a tray of hors d'oeuvres and Gino had set up a wine bar on the kitchen counter. The dining room table was filled with the platters of food and three-year old Connor Sullivan was already on his third cupcake when he suddenly stopped mid-bite and ran to the front door announcing to everyone, "Celia's here. My friend Celia's here!"

His nine year-old brother Billy breathed a sigh of relief. "He'll be okay now. He's always on his best behavior when his girlfriend's around," he assured Vida. "But I'd still guard anything you might want to protect. Like the Christmas tree." Billy threw himself into a chair to take a well-deserved rest from chasing the toddler, trying to stop the little menace from creating a catastrophe.

Stewart set up the bouncy chair in the living room and Kara placed the baby into it. Connor knelt on the floor facing her and began a game of patty-cake. She babbled at him. "Goo ga oooooh. Buh buh buh buh."

"Are you hungry? I'll get you some food. I ate candy canes, and cupcakes, and popcorn, and cookies. There's lots of good stuff. Do you have teeth yet?" He checked inside her mouth and found one little tooth in the front just beginning to emerge. "Hmm, we'll stick with soft stuff. No Soupies for you! Stay here. I'll be right back." He waved and ran into the kitchen. Billy jumped out of the chair and followed. He tugged on Kara's arm, warning her of the potential disaster. She gave him a jar of baby food from her bag.

"Here," he thrust the jar and a spoon into his brother's hands, "start with this."

"This is orange mush," Connor replied making a face.

"Babies like mush. You loved it when you were a little kid," Billy said.

His brother was overjoyed with the implied comment that he was now a big kid. "I remember those days," he told his brother. He returned to his best friend and began carefully spooning mashed squash into her mouth while telling her about his younger years when he was her age.

Greg arrived early with a bouquet of flowers, a bottle of wine, and a take-out bag of Thai food. He rang the doorbell a few times and when no one answered he called her number from his cell.

"Hello, I was just drying my hair. Are you going to be late?"

"Just the opposite. I'm at your front door."

"Oh, no. I'll be down in a few minutes."

"The garage door is opened. I could let myself in."

"Sounds like a plan," she said.

He had everything out on the coffee table in the den and had placed the flowers in an empty orange juice bottle on the kitchen counter.

"This looks nice."

"You still look tired. Did you get any sleep?"

"Not really. I kept hearing strange noises around the house."

"That's your writer's imagination working overtime." Just then a sound from the cellar startled them.

"It's just the old furnace cycling." She laughed and switched on the television.

"Since I get to choose the movie and seeing we both like mysteries, I thought an Alfred Hitchcock might be fun."

"Anything except *Psycho*. I would never watch one of his if I were alone." She moved closer to him.

"That over-active imagination again?"

"Yup. My favorite is *Rope*. I like it when movies based on a play feels like a play. And of course I love *Stage Fright*," Terry said.

"Mine is *Rear Window*. The whole concept of looking in on the daily lives of other people when they don't know you're watching fascinates me. My second favorite is *Dial M for Murder*."

"Oh. I like that one, too. Great character development. Unfaithful wife having an affair with a writer. Vengeful husband. Scotland Yard detective. Let's watch that!" Her phone rang just then causing Terry to jump. She looked at the caller ID. I have no idea who this is," she said.

"If you don't recognize the name, don't answer, I always advise people. Lots of scammers out there," Greg said.

They settled in and Greg poured the wine as Terry commented on the opening credits. The floor creaked overhead, but she wasn't afraid. She rested her head on his shoulder as the movie began.

Outside, the party was in full swing. Loralei walked around with ballots for voting on various sweater categories, the top honor going to Ugliest Sweater on the Planet. It was a foregone conclusion that Vida would win that prize. It had become a tradition. She always wore the same tattered, shapeless, purple sweater upon which she pinned various Christmas ornaments and stickers to it as it grew into more of a Christmas mish mash every year.

On the lawn, people were catching up on the latest news. Gino's and Rick's cousin, Mimi Carnavale and her fiance Darren Coleman were passing out "Save the Date" cards for their wedding the following June. Leo, the dispatcher at the South Kingstown police station, added logs to a fire pit in the middle of the yard. Sergeant Shwinnard, Carl Sullivan, and Detective Brown were sitting around deep in conversation with Professor Hill and Harry Henderson, the medical examiner, about an old case they had worked together to solve.

Vida moved around the house, inside and out, all night long, joining in the festivities, smiling and laughing. At the end of the evening, she handed out the prizes. As her guests prepared to leave, she and Loralei passed around home-made wassail in paper cups to toast to the best Ugly Sweater Christmas Party ever. Clay lead everyone in a chorus of *Auld Lang Sine.*

∽

The movie had ended and Terry and Greg were finishing the last of the wine. She'd given him a copy of her manuscript and they were discussing the best way to approach the situation with her aunt when the phone rang. Terry checked the caller ID.

"Hey, Auntie. No, I'm fine. Everything's okay… Yes, I have a friend over and we watched a movie. How about your night? Oh, that's too bad. Well, I'll expect you back in a little while, then. See ya."

"What was that about?" Greg asked.

"My aunt is coming home tonight instead of tomorrow. Something about having to make other plans regarding her patient."

"Good, you won't be alone and hopefully you'll get some sleep. You look exhausted."

"Oh, she won't be back for at least an hour. Let me splash some water on my face. I'll be right back."

While she was upstairs, her phone rang again. *Nelson Belle.* She panicked and ran back downstairs calling for Greg. He wasn't in the living room. In the kitchen, she found the door open. Floodlights lit up the back yard.

"Greg? Greg are you out there?" she called. She heard a groan and went outside to find him lying on the grass. "Oh, my God! What happened?"

"I was reading over your play and I heard a noise. I thought someone was in the kitchen. I called out and the back door slammed. I turned on the outside lights and when I went to see who was out there, someone lunged at me with those cutting shears." He nodded to a garden tool nearby.

"Greg, my phone rang again. The caller ID said *Nelson Belle*. I didn't answer it. How could it possibly be him?"

"I don't know." He struggled to get up. "Terry, I'm sorry, but whoever it was attacked me stole your play and your laptop." Greg was now standing clutching his arm. There was a cut in the sleeve and blood on his hand.

"Don't worry about that. You're hurt." She took off her scarf and helped him tie it around his arm. "I'll call an ambulance."

"No, it's not bad. I tripped and fell and he got away. I heard a car start up."

"We should call the police!" She was now in tears.

Greg consoled her. "Terry, I am the police. I'll write an incident report and make sure there's a cop patrolling the neighborhood until we find out who this guy is and what he wanted."

"Greg, he was inside the house! I locked all the doors. How could he have been inside with us?"

"Terry, the garage was open when I got here. You're going to have to be more vigilant. He won't be back tonight. He knows I'm here and I scared him off. And your aunt will be arriving soon. You have to promise me you'll be extra careful until we get to the bottom of this." He put his arms around her and kissed her forehead.

"I promise."

"I'm calling the station to tell them what happened. My friend is on desk duty tonight. He'll be right on it." He spoke with the sergeant to tell him to place a patrol on the house immediately. "I'll be there in fifteen minutes to file a report. Thanks, Sarge." He ended the call. "I'll be in touch when I finish up and if you want me to come back, I'll be here in a millisecond. Lock up the place and wait for your aunt. Don't answer the door or go outside."

"Are you sure you're going to be okay?"

"They'll fix me up at the station and if I need stitches, I'll go to the emergency room. Don't worry about me, I'll be fine."

Her aunt arrived home minutes after Greg left. When she came in the door, she looked at her niece and knew something bad had happened. Terry had brewed a pot of tea and they sat talking for a long time before they finally turned out the lights and went to bed. Greg called to check on her and she assured him she was much better.

"Thanks for being here with me tonight. I had a long talk with my aunt and she knows everything. It's a relief and she wasn't as angry as I thought she'd be. More concerned about my safety."

"What are you going to do about your play?"

"I'm not sure. Luckily I have another copy I was going to give to Dr. Eddleman. Aunt Virginia and I are planning to talk about that some more in the morning."

As Terry pulled down the shade in her bedroom, she noticed a police car slowly pass the house. And she remembered the quote from Sir Walter Scott, "Oh, what a tangled web we weave." She climbed into bed and under the covers vowing never again to deceive anyone.

Life is about working out who the bad guy is.
Sophie Hannah

Saturday, December 21

THE WEEKEND BEFORE CHRISTMAS and the beginning of the mad rush to get everything done before the big day. Gino was up bright and early, as usual, but he made sure he was extra quiet so as not to wake the others. He had a project to do and spent the morning gathering materials and making plans. There was nothing more he loved to do than think up surprises for other people and this one was going to take some real thought if it was to work without a glitch. He knew he may have to enlist Sophia's help, because he could never keep a secret from his wife. Nobody could! He packed everything into the back of his truck and went inside to make a pot of coffee and cinnamon muffins for everyone. That would bring them all downstairs and he could map out his grand plan for them.

Carolynn was settling in nicely at her mother's but she'd needed some things she'd left at her house like her homemade yogurt shampoo. She waited until she was sure Conrad would be at work and let herself in through the back door.

As she left the upstairs' bathroom, she heard noises coming from their bedroom. The door was opened a crack and she tiptoed over to peek inside. Her husband was still in bed watching a very young woman getting dressed. "Are you sure you don't want to stick around? I'll make us breakfast," he offered.

Carolynn burst into the room and asked him through clenched teeth, "When have you ever gotten your butt out of bed to make breakfast? You don't even know where I keep the coffee filters." She ran out.

He tried to follow her but one foot got caught in the sheets and he fell flat on his face.

The girl stooped down to help him get untangled. "Who was that?"

He rubbed his forehead. "Would you believe, the maid?"

~

Milton glanced up at the flag on the roof of the Ocean House. *Wind's coming in from the northeast.* He hadn't been inside the hotel for years and thought he might treat himself to a five-star meal on Sunday night. He would make a reservation when he got back to the house. There was reason to celebrate. His first draft was finished and he was pleased with the manuscript. It would need editing, but he was confident Ruth would give it her sign of approval. He'd followed all of her advice to the letter.

Other joggers were out today and two attractive young ladies bid him a good morning when they ran past. One of them looked vaguely familiar, like that popular singer he'd seen on The Grammy Awards. He tried to remember her name, but all he could recall were the lyrics to the song she'd performed. *Catchy little tune.* He often sang it when he did his exercises and he began to run a little faster as he turned the corner.

"Shake it off, Shake it off … Shake it off, Shake it off." He did jazz hands, waving with abandon while performing a short skipping step. "Baby, I'm just gonna shake, shake, shake, shake, shake …"

Rounding the corner to Plimpton Street he spied Elaine who was reading in her favorite chair in her sun room. *I'll make a reservation for three. Elaine and Gerald are such good neighbors. They deserve a night out.* "Shake it off, Shake it off …."

He ran up the stairs to his house still singing, "I keep cruisin, Can't stop groovin … Shake it off, I Shake it off." He loved that song so much he'd bought the album. It always made him feel younger and run faster. Milton suddenly decided to send the cute little songstress a fan letter. He'd look up her address on the internet and tell her how much he appreciated her tunes. He went in search of the album cover so he could find out the title of the song. "I keep cruisin, Can't stop groovin … Shake it off, I shake it off," he sang as he danced merrily around the house.

∽

Sophia called to ask Stewart if he wanted to take Celia Christmas shopping with her later that afternoon. They could go to the malls and have the baby's picture taken with all the Santa Clauses. Then they'd pick the best one and have it framed. "Kara and Ruth will be at the library and Gino and Rick are busy, so I thought it might be nice for the three of us to spend some quality time together." Stewart thought that was a lovely idea.

Kara hid her surprise. "I thought Sophia was working today."

"She said she had some time coming to her and she needed to use it up before the end of the year," he explained. "She gave me strict directions on which outfit I was to dress Celia in for her Santa photos."

Kara looked at the picture of Celia with Santa on the mantelpiece. Sophia had insisted they get it taken at the beginning of December when all of the Santas looked fresh and happy. "The last thing you want is a holiday photo of your child with a raggedy old Santa who's counting the days for the season to be over," she'd advised Kara. "And of course, she'll have a special one taken opening her gifts with Gino as Santa on Christmas Day."

She waited until Stewart left the room, then phoned Sophia to find out what was going on, but was sent to voice mail. "Stewart said you're all going out on another photo excursion. Much like the one we took with Celia right after Thanksgiving when you had her picture taken with at least five Santa Clauses until you found one you liked. Your memory must have had a slight lapse. Call me when you get this."

Stewart was hollering from upstairs. "Kara, do you know where the green taffeta dress with the gold and white ribbon is? I can't find it in Celia's closet."

"I'll be right there." She'd get answers from Ruth. For now, she'd have to hide her suspicions from Stewart and play along with whatever it was Auntie Sophia was planning.

∽

Virginia went to her office right after Terry left for work. Her niece had given her a good description of the man who'd frightened her in the office on Sunday. From that description, she knew exactly who it was and after a heated phone conversation, he admitted he'd been there and agreed to come in to discuss the matter later in the day.

She purposely scheduled all of her sessions when Terry would be at the Savoy. She was cautious not to have her niece and her clients ever meet up. Virginia was upset he'd appeared without making an appointment. Setting boundaries was something she'd insisted upon with the few clients she'd retained from her time in Connecticut. Even though they were not the most serious personality disorders she'd treated, these patients were still dealing with anger issues and she was well aware something could trigger them to act aggressively under certain conditions. She was trained to handle this. Her niece was not. It hadn't presented a problem until now because Terry never came into the office unless she'd specifically asked her to help with some filing. And these occasions always were on the days no appointments were scheduled. She had only five patients and now one of them was being re-admitted to the clinic. Given the nature of her work, she began to reassess the potential danger of having her practice so close to home. When she'd moved to RI, Terry wasn't living with her. But now changes needed to be considered. She called a colleague and after explaining her situation, he agreed to take her clients if she decided to retire. It was a major decision in her life, but her niece's safety came first.

Greg was waiting outside the bookshop when Terry arrived. He looked tired and she made his coffee extra strong.

"Did you get any sleep at all last night?" she asked.

"Like I said on the phone, I went to the station to give them a description and filled out the report. One of my EMT friends came by to look at my arm." He pulled up his sleeve.

"I'm so sorry you got hurt," she said lightly touching the large bandage covering the bottom half of a tattoo. "And don't worry about the play. My aunt gave me her old desktop and I can scan in the script from my extra copy."

"That's a relief at least. I'm glad I was there. I was worried about you. Did you sleep okay?"

"I wasn't as scared when my aunt came home. She's fearless. Aunt Virginia can handle anything."

"I think I'll take your advice and go catch some zees. What are your plans?"

"I'll be working here and my aunt is coming by the store to drive me to the theatre. I'm ushering for the matinee."

"How will you get home?"

"My aunt is going to pick me up."

"Make sure you stay around other people. If you'd like, you can call me and I'll come by when you're ready to leave for home. I'll be your police escort."

She kissed him on the cheek. "That's a good idea. I'll tell Auntie when she comes to get me. I have to start work. Thanks for everything. It must look like I'm not so great at managing my life."

"You're still young. Lots of time to learn about making better decisions."

She went with him to the back door. He gave her a hug. "What do you think you'll do about the play?"

"Auntie suggested we might work on it together. She'll write her book while I finish the script. She's thinking of retiring, so she'll have more time to spend on her case studies."

"She's retiring? Your aunt must really care about you to give up her practice. I hope you know how lucky you are to have someone like her in your life. I'll see you tonight."

Terry waved as he drove away in his car. She definitely did realize how fortunate she was to have her Aunt Virginia and him in her life.

Nelson Belle regained consciousness. Kara had stopped at the hospital before her meeting with the police chief. She was sitting by his bed when he opened his eyes.

He immediately became agitated. She gently took his hands to stop him from pulling at the tubes and wires connected to the monitors.

"Nelson, it's Kara. Detective Langley. You're safe now. You're in the hospital."

She was able to calm him. He tried to talk, but his voice was raspy. The nurse took a cup of crushed ice and held it to his parched lips. He licked at it stopping to stare at them, his eyes wide and frightened. The nurse left to inform the doctor his patient was awake.

"Don't try to talk. There'll be time later to tell us what happened. There's a guard at the door and he won't let anyone in to hurt you."

He closed his eyes and his breathing steadied. He kept squeezing her hand. His grip was weak but it was as though he was trying to tell her something.

"Nelson, did you see the person who locked you in your bedroom?"

He shook his head no.

"You need to rest and get stronger and we'll talk about what happened to you later."

The doctor entered the room and Kara stepped outside to speak with the guard. If Nelson was a witness and not the prime suspect, as she believed, it would be imperative that the guard be extra vigilant.

The nurse came out of the room. "Mr. Belle has been sedated and the doctor is allowing no visitors." Kara left the hospital and drove to the police station. The Chief Baker was in a meeting, but came out to speak with her.

"It will be important to get his statement when he is able," he said. "Have you found out any additional information that could help him?"

"I have a list of suspects who may have had motive to kill Bartleby Schnelling." She handed a sheet of paper to him with a short explanation. "It would help if you could call them in and ask where they were on the night of December seventh and if anyone can vouch for them. I have two more people I need to interview and I'll give you their names when I'm done. I'm still looking for Bartleby's valise. I believe it holds information which is important to this case. He had it when he left New York and did not take it with him when he began his walk home from the train station. Detective Perez reported the ticket checker spoke with Bartleby on the train and he noticed a small suitcase on the empty seat beside him. Nothing had been turned into lost and found at the end of the trip which means I have to find out where he could have stored it. I spoke with the artisan volunteer and no suitcases had been left in the station that night. She checked for me. It has to be some place where he could retrieve it the next day."

"I'll call these two and arrange for them to come in to be questioned."

"You may have difficulty finding Deighton Durst. It appears he left the Ocean House rather abruptly and has not been answering his phone. Unfortunately, he's a sly character. He works in New York. You might want to call the car rental service he used. They should give you some information. The registration is on file at the hotels. He stayed for two nights at the Plaza and was at the Ocean House from the fifth until the nineteenth."

"In addition to Renzulli and Durst, how many others do you have on your suspect list?"

"I'll be looking into two more. One is a patient of a Dr. Virginia Walden. She's a psychiatrist. Her office is connected to her home at the end of Montauk Avenue in Misquamicut. I'm going to see her later. It's a long shot, but I'll feel better if I follow it up."

"Could be a coincidence, but we had a report of someone roaming around that neighborhood last night," Baker informed her.

"I'll ask her about it when I see her. Thanks and I'll get back to you if I find out anything else which could help the case."

Kara went next to deliver the good news about Nelson to Fannie.

"Oh, that poor man. When can he have visitors?"

"They have a guard on his door. They won't let you in to see him until I can clear him as a suspect."

"Suspect? What a perfectly ludicrous insinuation. Nelson Belle wouldn't harm a fruit fly."

Jake had been checking out books nearby and he turned to say, "I think I saw him eat a fly once." He waited for them to laugh at his joke. When they ignored him, he added. "He didn't kill the fly. He licked it off the swatter. It was already dead."

Fannie shook her head in dismay and glanced at the clock. "Isn't it time for your break?" she asked him.

"You don't have to tell me twice. I'm outta here." Jake took his jacket and went outside.

"You'll have to excuse him. I was hoping he would have shown some improvement on his attitude by now, but apparently I was wrong."

"How long has he been working in the library?"

"Since early fall. His probation officer needed a job for him close to his home since he'd lost his driver's permit. I've been part of the intern program in the past and anyone they've assigned to me has gone on to do well. I still have a sliver of hope for Jake. He loves being around books and has become interested in our local history. He spends most of his lunch time and his breaks in the reference room. But his sarcastic attitude remains the same. He's clever enough never to be insubordinate, so I really have no basis to fire him."

"When I was here last Friday, he went out of his way to be very helpful to my friend Sophia."

"Yes, I'd noticed. Jake has an eye for pretty women. He can really turn on the charm. I've seen him do it with Terry. I think he's rather smitten with her. He stays late whenever Ruth holds the writing workshop."

"Speaking of Terry, I'm meeting with her aunt in an hour. I'll see you this afternoon," Kara said.

"Please keep me informed about Nelson. If there's anything I can do …."

"I will."

Jake sat on a bench over by Christoforo Colombo. His head was down. Every few seconds he brought his hand up to his mouth and smoke would circle around him. He looked up at Kara. "So what are you gonna do? Arrest me?" He tossed the cigarette on to the slate and stubbed it out with his boot.

"I'm not a cop. I would like to ask you some questions about Bartleby Schnelling."

He turned away from her, focusing on the statue. "What about him?"
She sat next to him. "Did you know him well?"

"We weren't best buddies, if that's what you mean. My brother and I did some work for him around his yard. Raking leaves, cleaning gutters, painting. Odd jobs. He paid us well and he let me borrow his motorbike."

"Was there anyone who may have had a problem with him?"
"Enough to snuff him out, you mean?"
She waited for an answer.

"I never saw anyone come around his place except for an old lady who cleaned and, of course, Terry. They were friends. I don't think either of them would have big enough cahoonas to push him into the skating pond, do you?" He turned to look at her.

"No, I don't imagine they would. If you can remember anyone else coming to his house while you were there working, I'd appreciate your help."

"Sure thing." He stood up. "That lady who you was with. Last Friday. Is she single?" he asked.

"No, she's married."

"Tell her if she ever gets tired of her husband, I'm available." He swaggered back into the library leaving Kara alone on the bench.

"I wonder how Gino would feel about that?" she mused out loud then laughed. "Luckily, I'll never know because I don't think there'll ever be a situation where that topic would come up."

Dr. Walden was in her office when Kara rang the bell. She unlocked the door and introduced herself then led her into the office where a pot of tea and an assortment of pastries were set out on the coffee table. The two women spent some time socializing, chatting about their jobs and family.

"I really appreciate your taking time to tell me what's been happening. I'm afraid my niece hasn't been very forthcoming. I know you advised her to explain about her play and the incident with one of my clients. She realizes now, she should have been more honest with me."

"Lies of omission. In my experience, sometimes the most lethal of all," Kara said.

"Yes, I run into a lot of that in my profession, too."

"Terry mentioned you specialize in treating patients with personality disorders, particularly males with anger issues."

"Something else we have in common. My husband and I ran a clinic in Connecticut. I worked mostly with children of wealthy parents who exhibited behaviors which can be dangerous to themselves and others. When we divorced, I returned to Westerly where I grew up, and set up a small practice."

"Terry spoke to you about the man who came into your office while she was there. He frightened her."

"Yes, the person she described is the father of one of my patients. He later apologized for his behavior and for coming to the office without an appointment. He had a concern about his son which he wanted to discuss and explained to me he was having a bad day. It's common to find that the patients I treat come from homes where anger issues are also exhibited by a parent or another family member."

"I'd like to know about the patient Terry has used for the main character in her play? Anything you can tell me without infringing on his privacy would be helpful. Can you describe him for me?"

"Yes, he's young, has pale skin, sandy blond hair, and is of medium build. A complete opposite to the older, dark-haired man who confronted Terry."

"And are you still treating this patient?"

"I was seeing him on a regular basis and he'd made great strides coping outside the institution. But he came by the office last week exhibiting the paranoia that has plagued him all his life. He imagines he's being watched and his movements monitored, although he can't tell me why this would be happening. I suspect he may be off his meds and something triggered this behavior. Fortunately, he's astute enough to realize he should return to the institute. I went to Connecticut to make arrangements for him on Friday. He never showed up for the appointment we'd scheduled to re-admit him and I haven't heard from him. I left him messages, but it appears he's turned off his phone."

"Do you have any idea what the trigger was?"

"I believe it may center around his application for a job recently. He expressed concern about the questions on the application and felt they were too intrusive. And he wasn't able to obtain the references he needed. He's angry and feels he's being singled out because someone he considered less qualified was eventually hired and he'd not even been given an interview. When I attempted to delve into why he felt he was more qualified, his explanation was simply, 'She's a woman. You can never trust a woman.' And there are other problems. He's not adjusting as well as I'd hoped outside the confines of the institution."

"And he's had no contact with your niece?"

"Not that I'm aware of, but you need to know about an incident last night. Someone came here while I was in Connecticut. When Terry arrived home from work yesterday, she apparently left the garage door open. She believes someone may have used the opportunity to gain entrance to the house. Fortunately, she'd invited a friend over and he ended up chasing the intruder into the yard."

"Can her friend identify him?" Kara asked.

"Maybe. There was a scuffle and the intruder slashed him with cutting shears from our garage. Her laptop was taken along with a copy of the script. One other thing – Terry received a call that night from someone she said is in the hospital, unconscious. The caller ID was Nelson Belle."

"Have the police been notified?" Kara was alarmed.

"Yes, fortunately, Greg's on the Westerly police force. He filed a report and had them place a watch on the house last night. I'm being extremely cautious. I drove her to the bookshop this morning and will pick her up this afternoon. She's ushering at the Granite Theatre. She should be safe with all the people there and I'll be bringing her home directly after the performance."

"It would be better if she came home from the bookstore and stayed with you. I told her not to come to the library. I've canceled the workshop and scheduled individual sessions for the authors."

"She's insistent on continuing her routine and not letting her fears stop her from carrying on as usual."

"But there's nothing *usual* in what has happened in the past two weeks and she could be directly connected in some way to a murderer. Until we find out who killed her friend, Bartleby Schnelling, and the reason why, your niece needs to be extremely careful."

"I'll make sure she's never alone and I'll do anything I can do to help you with this case."

"I have some other things to deal with today. Thank you for the information on your client and clarifying the incident with the man who visited your office. You've ruled out one suspect for me. I'm still looking for any possible connections to the murder." She helped Virginia clear away the dishes and then left Misquamicut to head into downtown Westerly.

The 1912 Spanish Revival Style station with its curved red brick tiles and stucco covered surfaces reminded Kara of a Mexican hacienda. It was quiet inside. The next train wasn't scheduled to arrive for an hour. She'd calculated that the train Bartleby had taken at 3:30 PM from Penn Station on Friday had arrived in Westerly at 6:40 PM. It took about two minutes, at the most, to walk from the depot and cross the street to the bookshop. He'd placed the call to Ruth at 6:50 PM. *What had he been doing in those eight minutes?*

Kara spoke with the volunteer who assured her no lost articles had been handed in during the past two weeks. The building now was used mainly as a gallery for local artists. Passengers leaving from the Westerly station purchased tickets online. Artisans volunteered hours to staff the gallery from Thursday to Sunday.

"I wasn't scheduled to work on Friday, but I filled in for another artist because I live in an apartment nearby and they were predicting a storm. I kept the gallery open until the regular closing time of seven and checked everything before I left. I can assure you, if anything was left behind, I would have found it unless it was purposely hidden."

They walked in and out of the exhibits in the area where passengers were allowed to wait on the old wooden benches, once a part of the station house. *No suitcase.*

"What about other places people would have access to?" Kara asked.

"There's a small room down at the other end next to the office. It's not locked. I was busy closing up and I wouldn't have noticed if someone walked in and out."

It took her a few minutes, but Kara found the valise wedged behind a screen in the corner. She went outside to her car to examine the contents. Sandwiched between items of clothing and toiletries were Terry's script and two documents: a birth certificate and a death certificate stapled together with a photo. She sat in the parking lot for some time reading and then returned to the police station.

The desk sergeant was surprised to see her again. "Did you forget something?" he asked.

"Could you show me a copy of Friday night's report regarding an incident on Montauk Avenue in Misquamicut?"

He searched through the records. "It was a pretty quiet night but, wait, here's one. Filed at 11:36 PM. I'll make a copy for you." He left the room and returned with an envelope. "Chief Baker instructed us to give you anything you need. Hope this helps."

"Is the chief in his office? I'd like to talk to him."

"He's gone to lunch."

"That's okay. I have his cell."

Kara returned to her car and placed a call. "Sophia, it's Kara. You need to cancel your dubious plans with Stewart and Celia. I want you to go to the library with Ruth and Rick this afternoon. It's important. I'll meet you there. I've put most of the puzzle together and now I'm going to require your help to catch a killer."

In lieu of their Saturday workshop, Ruth had scheduled individual sessions with each author. Rick had stationed himself in the corridor outside the reading room keeping watch as she was finishing her meeting with Milton.

"This has come a long way from the chapters you brought to our first class. I feel it's ready to send on to a professional editor, although I do have one more suggestion." She returned the shirt box filled with letters and notes.

"Kara didn't find anything in here to connect someone with your accident or with Bartleby's murder, but I looked through them and think you should include some in your epilogue. It could be about what happened to you in the years after the trial. And add your photos from *Time Magazine*. This would make an interesting ending to a murder mystery that is also a memoir. I'd be glad to continue working with you after the holidays."

"I'd like that. These classes have become the highlight in my week. I'm going to miss them." He got up to leave, stopping to greet Carolynn as she arrived and gave him a hug. He helped her off with her coat then turned to wave as he went out the front door.

Carolynn sat down next to Ruth and took the manuscript out of her briefcase. "I like the way it's developed since I spoke with you about changing genres. I'm using my original story line as a basis. I'm now viewing it as a romance novel in progress."

"Kudos for a positive attitude. I'm glad you didn't give up and I agree it is coming along fine." Ruth had her copy open on the table and she went through her notes with Carolynn for the next hour.

Fannie interrupted to give Ruth a message. "Conrad called and he will not be able to meet with you this afternoon. He has some unfinished business to take care of."

Carolynn commented, "The story of his life."

"The good news is it gives us more time to work together," Ruth informed her.

While Rick was busy standing guard, Sophia had been given her own assignment. She went in search of Jake and found him upstairs in the reference room. His face lit up when he recognized her.

"Miss MacAlister sent me up here. She said you may be able to give me some direction."

"I remember you. You were here choosing books with the little girl last Friday. I heard you reading to her."

"Yes, you were very helpful. We weren't properly introduced. Sophia Carnavale." she shook his hand.

He blushed. "Jacob Wolff. Jake. What can I do to help you?"

"I'm researching medical conditions. I'm a nurse but I'm applying to med school to be a doctor and I'm not sure what I'd like to specialize in."

"You should do something with kids. You were really great with that baby the other day. I'd be happy to show you where to find those books. I'm interested in medicine, myself."

She followed him over to the stacks holding the volumes in which she might find what she needed. She removed some titles. "Is there some place I can spread out to look through these?"

"Sure, I can set you up in one of the reference rooms." He went into the office and opened a desk drawer to retrieve the key which opened the room. "Make yourself at home." He took the books from her arms and stacked them on the table. "Can I get you anything else?"

"No, you've been extremely helpful. I'll be fine, now."

He left the room but came back a few minutes later and placed a bottle of water and more books in front of Sophia. "It gets pretty warm in here. I know cuz it's where I like to spend my free time. I picked out some books for you."

"Thank you, Jake. That's very thoughtful of you. You mentioned you were interested in medicine. Is there something you could advise me to look at for ideas?"

"Well, I don't know about you, but I'm not interested in cutting people up or anything like that. I'd prefer a practice with no blood. Like psychiatry." He chose one of the volumes he'd placed on the table and handed it to her. "There's lots of good stuff in here on personality disorders." He opened to the table of contents and read some of the titles to her. "There's your antisocial personality disorder, your histrionic personality disorder, your paranoid and schizoid personality disorders. Those last two are doozies, but all of them are really interesting. And, look, there's a whole section on treatments."

"How long have you been studying this, Jake?"

"Years. I bet I could pass all the tests and get my degree in this stuff without ever stepping foot in a college."

"But a degree from a college entails studying other subject areas, too."

"I know. I'd have to get a bachelors, then graduate school, and more courses. Then, maybe they'd let me become a psychiatrist. Too bad, cuz I'm not really interested in most of the other classes I'd have to take. I looked into it. And you have to have money. I don't make much, but maybe when I get off probation, I can get a good job."

"Do you mind telling me what you're on probation for?" Sophia closed the book and sat back in her chair.

"I've got a lead foot. I like to race around when I can get wheels. I borrowed my brother's car and rammed it into a telephone pole. Nobody was hurt, but there was some damage. In my defense, the road was icy."

"You're young. You have time to make amends."

"Unfortunately, it wasn't the first time I've been caught speeding."

"Maybe you should plan on being a race car driver?"

"Or join a demolition derby?" he added.

"We all have hidden talents lying in wait for the opportunity to show themselves." She patted his hand. "Whatever you decide to do in the future, I wouldn't give up on your dreams."

"Yeah, but I got other problems, too. Some of what I learned about psychiatry was cuz I've been in counseling."

"Counseling can be something positive you could use when you become a psychiatrist. Your experience will certainly make you more empathetic toward your own patients."

"Empathy! Now that's a word I've heard a lot. Do you know there's a portion of your brain called the amygdala. It means 'almond'. That's the shape of it. There are nerves running all through it and it's hooked up to other senses. It controls the emotions and if it's damaged, lots of bad things can happen."

"Like what, for instance?"

"They've done studies with prisoners on death row who killed people and didn't feel one bit sorry afterwards. Psychopaths. These guys couldn't empathize with other people's suffering. Neuro-scientists actually saw their brains on MRIs reacting with pleasure when imagining other people in pain. Sometimes not even cognitive-behavior therapy works on them. The damage to their amygdala is too great."

"Jake, this is fascinating. I think you should continue to pursue your ambitions."

"You talk like you believe I could actually do this."

"I do. Is your family supportive?"

"I told my brother about wanting to be a psychiatrist once and he punched me in the stomach and told me to get real."

"What about your parents?"

"It's only me and my brother. I did spend some time in foster homes, but I didn't stay in touch with any of them people. Now that my brother's back, at least I have a set place to live. And he's a pretty good guy when he's on his meds."

"Your brother was away?"

"Yeah. I'm not supposed to talk about it. He was in an institution but he got cured."

"I'm glad you have someone in your life, now, although he shouldn't be hitting you."

"He's not a bad guy – just having one of his off days. Sometimes he doesn't take his medication. I was telling him about the mystery authors' group and how I thought I could write a great story about what happened in my life in foster care. I even told him about Terry's play. Have you had a chance to read it? The patient, Drew, is so much like him."

"No, but Dr. Eddleman has spoken about how well Terry writes."

"Yeah. From her character description in her play, you'd think she knew my brother and the awful things he did. I told him that once and he got really mad. He busted up some furniture and I hightailed it out of the apartment for the night. It's the best way to handle him when he gets triggered. That's another term I learned in counseling."

"Jake, I'd like to talk more about your future plans again. Maybe I could bring you some information from URI?"

"I'd like that. And if I can do anything for you, just email or call me. I live right around the corner." He wrote down his information and placed it in her hand. "I should get back to work. Without Nelson, I have a lot more stuff to take care of. I don't want to lose my job, even though it pays squat. I like it here. Plenty of interesting books to read and you meet nice people." He flashed her a smile before he turned to go. "Thanks for listening to me. The day started out bad, but I feel better already."

After he'd left, Kara came into the room and sat next to her. Sophia gave her the paper with his name on the top. Jacob Wolff.

"Did you hear all that?"

"I did. It's as I suspected. I spoke with the desk sergeant and according to him, Terry's friend, aka Patrolman Greg Wolff, has never been on the police force, although he did apply for a position. He gave me a copy of the application. I looked at the paperwork from Friday night and although Greg told Terry he'd officially reported the intruder and the theft, all he did was call to ask if someone would drive by and check her house because someone was seen in the backyard."

"We need to warn her about him."

"I think I'll leave that discussion to her aunt. It will be easier coming from someone she trusts. I'll phone Chief Baker and give him this information. He can send someone out to go by the house and bring him in. Terry will be a lot safer once he's in custody."

Saturday matinee right before Christmas and the seats were filled with blue-haired ladies who had season's tickets to the annual presentation of *A Christmas Carol*. Many of them had grandchildren in tow and the excitement level was high with the volume louder than usual.

It took a few minutes to calm the kids down after Santa made a surprise visit and handed out candy canes to everyone. When the curtain went up, he came over to Terry and gave her a handful of candy along with a wink and a whispered "Ho, ho, ho". He skipped up the aisle to stand in the rear of the auditorium and watch the performance.

She had to leave her seat twice to usher latecomers, but saw most of the show sitting in the back row without interruption. Thankfully, there was no intermission, making her job a lot easier. She went to the lobby just before the Ghost of Christmas Future made his entrance, to call her aunt, reminding her of the change in plans that Greg would be bringing her home. She left a message on his cell. "Don't hurry. I'll be staying longer than planned to help straighten up after everyone leaves. I'll make sure the back door is unlocked for you."

The audience gave Scrooge a standing ovation. He had seen the light and had made his transition from bad guy to good guy. The house lights came up after curtain call. Terry stationed herself at the door saying goodbye to those heading out to their cars parked along the street. Santa joined her on the front steps to pass out candy. When his toy bag was empty, he proceeded to jog up and down the lawn waving goodbye to the last of the people honking their horns at him.

Terry went inside and began to collect some of the trash from under the seats. She'd told the house manager she'd take care of locking up, since the cast and crew all had to rush home for dinner and return for the night performance.

"Are you sure you're going to be okay by yourself? I can at least stay and help you sweep up," one of the stage crew offered as he handed her a broom.

"No, you get going. You'll hardly have time enough as it is before you come back to open up again. I can handle this and I have a friend coming by to take me home. I don't think he's ever been here and I want to show him around."

Terry loved the quiet that fell over the empty theatre when the players and the audience were gone. It was a magical place. After she finished sweeping, she took a break and sat in the front row imagining her own play being performed on stage. Her phone rang giving her a start. She thought it might be Greg explaining why he was late and answered it quickly.

"Hey, where are you? I left the back door open, so just come in." She was met with silence. "Greg? I can't hear you. Bad reception." This was followed by a low, snarling sound on the other end of the line. "Greg?" Terry checked the caller ID. *Nelson Belle.* Sensing danger, she quickly hung up, looking desperately to the foyer now shrouded in darkness. Someone was out there. She could hear footsteps.

The house lights went out suddenly. She looked up to see who was in the booth. A door opened and slammed shut. She hoped it was Greg. She turned and ran up the stairs onto the stage. Glancing back, she glimpsed a shadowy figure in the hall. She needed to find a place to hide and something she could use to protect herself.

In the wings, stage right, the props were kept on a long table. She used the light from her cell to illuminate the objects she'd helped to organize before the performance. Grabbing a tarnished, brass candlestick, she moved the heavy, velvet curtain slightly to look out into the auditorium. Someone was standing in the shadows.

She felt a gust of cool air coming from close by and realized the side door must be ajar. Terry determined she had enough time to make it to that exit before the figure in the hall could get up to the front of the theatre, but as she ran toward the stage stairs, she tripped on Marley's chains lying on the floor and not in their set place on the props table. Pain surged from her right ankle. She stifled a cry and dialed her cell phone. She heard Greg's ring, the intro from the TV series CSI. It was coming from somewhere in the theatre. She was afraid he might be lying hurt or tied up and called softly to him. "Greg. Where are you?" she pleaded. A slight rustling came from off stage left. Costumes sliding along the racks.

She had to decide whether to stay in the theatre or to run outside. She chose to limp to the side door now open into the darkness. Outside, all alone, she clutched the candlestick. Her phone rang again and she answered it. A brittle laugh and then, "I'm out here and I'm watching you". She wondered if she could make it to the road but her ankle throbbed and she knew he might intercept her before she reached the sidewalk.

She ran back inside to the safety of the theatre, but before she could redial his number, *Greg Wolff* came up on the screen. "Greg, I'm inside the theatre ... I'm not alone ... Someone's stalking me. Please answer me! Where are you?"

"I'm right here." She looked up and he was standing above her at center stage.

"Greg, someone's here. He was watching me outside."

"I know. I chased him away. You're safe now." She collapsed into a seat in the front row, relieved and breathing heavily.

"My heart is still pounding. I need a minute to catch my breath and we can leave."

"I thought you were going to give me a tour of the theatre," Greg said.

"Some other time. Right now I just want to go home. I've twisted my ankle. Could you get my coat? It's on the rack behind the curtains with the costumes."

He disappeared and then returned to the apron of the stage wearing the flowing black robes of Christmas Future.

"I've always wanted to be in a play." He spun in circles, the black cloth swirling around his body.

Terry managed a weak laugh. "Wouldn't you prefer a more cheerful role?"

"I was thinking more along the lines of Andrew, the main character in your play. I can identify with him. Maybe you could cast me as Drew? Although the real Drew might not like it if he found himself sitting in the audience one night and suddenly realized his life was being played out up on stage in front of strangers. People judging him. I don't think he'd like that at all, Terry." He stood glaring down at her.

"Maybe you're right." Her voice shook.

"Betrayal. Such an ugly word. The worst of the worst sins. Have you ever been betrayed, Terry?" His voice was a raspy whisper. She wanted to run away from the sound of it, but she felt paralyzed in her seat.

"Answer me! Have you ever been betrayed?" His scream echoed through the theatre.

Her throat was dry. She couldn't talk and nodded her head *No*.

"Then you have no idea how it feels, do you, Terry ... **Do You!**"

"No," she said.

"First your mother leaves. Tries to abandon you. Then your father has you locked up, because of a stupid accident. And when you finally get free and you think you're fixed, it's all a sham. There's no return to normal. No magical cure. It's just a bunch of pills making you act like someone you're not, because you're really not good enough to live in the world as the someone you are. First your mother, then your father, then your lousy psychiatrist decides to quit on you. No one left to trust. No one will hire you, No one will even give you a reference. I'd have made a great cop. But they ask all kinds of questions. They want to know what you've been doing during all those lost years. It's none of their business. And then good old Bartleby reads your play, Terry. He makes the connection. But still, he decides he's going to help get it published. He was going to help you put me up on a stage, like I am at this minute, for all to judge. What right did he have to make that choice?"

His voice had slowly gone from a crescendo to barely a whisper. "Do you know what the worst betrayal was? Do You?" He flung out his arms on each side and the black robe made a wall from which she knew she couldn't escape. "Answer me!"

"Yes." She looked up and there on stage, directly behind him, along the flats, she saw someone opening the door to Scrooge's house. She gripped the arms of her chair as Greg continued his rant.

"It's when someone you hardly know, who hasn't the foggiest idea what you've been through, uses you as a character in her play. It's when some stranger decides to tell your story for all the world to see. Your story! As if it weren't enough that everyone close to him knows and makes his life hell. It's like being stabbed in the back over and over." He brought out a knife from under the robes and bent his arm at the elbow as if to heave it at her. Terry screamed, leaping out of her seat. A costumed figure lunged forward and grabbed him, wrenching the knife from his hands.

"Oh, no ya don't. I been watchin you." The person in the Santa suit grabbed Greg by the back of the neck and pushed him face down on the floor of the stage. Kara appeared from the wings and kicked away the knife.

She handed Santa a set of handcuffs. "Cuff him, Gino." She walked down the steps and embraced Terry. The blare of sirens could be heard outside and suddenly, the theatre was filled with police.

*We write to taste life twice,
in the moment and in retrospect.*
Anais Nin

Sunday, December 22

A THICK MORNING FOG CREPT over the waves and enveloped the mansion on the cliffs in a misty white haze. Gino, usually the first one awake, slept soundly after the previous night's excitement. Sophia was seated at the dining room table wrapping presents, when Ruth and Rick came downstairs still in their robes.

"Coffee's brewing."

"Where's your hubby?" Rick asked.

"Gino's out cold," Sophia informed them.

They spoke softly, so as not to wake him, keenly aware that these would be their only moments of respite from the heroic tale he'd be recounting for them all day long. Sophia had taken his Santa suit from their bedroom and hung it in the hall closet to spare them from having to relive the night's events with him appearing in full costume.

"I don't remember a time when I ever got up before my brother. He must really be exhausted," Rick whispered.

Ruth returned with the carafe of coffee which she placed on the table. "The excitement must have knocked him out."

"That and the cocoa I poured for him before he went to bed last night." Sophia said raising her mug in a toast. "Here's to the makers of Ambien!" She took a long sip and began placing bows on the packages.

"Sophia, how many sleeping pills did you slip him?" Ruth gawked at her sister-in-law.

"Don't give me that look. I'm a nurse. I know how to figure out the right dosage and he's had exactly enough to get us through a peaceful morning." She poured them each a cup of coffee. They looked into their cups, waiting to drink until she'd taken the first sip. "And you're entirely welcome," she informed them.

Ruth knew when it was time to change the subject. "So, what do you both have planned for today?"

"I'm going to spend a few hours in my studio. I need to frame some photos for the exhibit at the artisans' gallery and it will be pleasant to have some free time to work on it." Rick said. "What about you, Sophia?"

"I've planned a little party for the pediatric unit. Old Sleeping Beauty loves to play Santa for the kids every year. I just finished wrapping their gifts, but I don't think they'll all fit into this toy bag. If you'll excuse me, I'm going to stitch up a larger one." She topped off her coffee and brought it with her.

"And what about you?" Rick moved the pile of presents in order to see his wife's face across the table.

"Last night, at the police station, Terry gave Kara a message for me. She asked if she could see me this afternoon. I think she wants to talk about Bartleby. Kara senses that she's feeling guilty about his death. I'm going to call and ask her to come by for lunch."

"What are you going to advise her to do about the play?"

"I wouldn't be surprised if she's already made up her mind on that. She has talent and I'd like to see her continue to write, but after what she's been through, I'm not sure how she feels about it. I think I'll just listen."

Rick went to the window. "I can see my studio out back. I think the fog is beginning to lift."

Ruth joined him and he placed his arm around her. "I hope so. We could all use a little sunshine today," she said.

Kara was up early writing a summary of everything that had happened when Stewart came downstairs with Celia. "Look who I found wide awake in her crib eating a book."

She reached out her arms for the baby and held her close, the curly head tucked under her mother's chin. "What a smart girl. And can you tell me what it was about?"

Celia looked up into her mother's eyes. "Oooo,oooo, duh,duh, duh, buh, buh, muh, muh."

"Well that was a wonderful story, wasn't it, Daddy?"

Stewart was in complete agreement. "Her vocabulary is expanding exponentially."

The three of them sat together on the couch, taking turns telling a short tale and clapping enthusiastically in appreciation when each ended with the words, "And they lived happily ever after." Stewart put on his old Bing Crosby Christmas album. They were singing and dancing along with The Crooner and the Andrew Sisters when the phone rang. It was Sophia.

"I called to invite Celia to a party in the pediatric ward this afternoon. You and Stewart can come too."

"I won't be able to make it. I'm meeting with the investigating team at the police station. But I'm sure Stewart and Celia would love to join you." She relayed the message to her husband over the music and singing.

"What is that caterwauling in the background?" Sophia asked

Kara held up the phone so she could hear Stewart and Celia harmonizing.

"Mele Kalikimaka is the thing to say on a bright Hawaiian Christmas Day …"

"And here I was hoping her second language would be Italian," Sophia said.

Stewart brought Celia to the phone. "Say Merry Christmas to Aunt Sophia."

"Muh ka muh ka," the baby said attempting to kiss the screen.

"Mucka mucka to you. Now, can you say 'Buon Natale' for your Auntie?'

"Muh ka muh ka," Celia answered.

"We'll work on that later, Sweetie."

"When do the festivities begin?" Stewart asked

"Any time after two."

"We'll be there with bells on," he said giving the phone back to Kara. He resumed the celebration with his daughter. She went into the kitchen where it was quieter.

"How's Gino this morning? I want to thank him for his help last night," Kara said.

"I'll give him your message when he wakes up."

"He's still in bed? It's past nine o'clock. Is he okay?"

"He's fine. Kara, I'm concerned about Jake. I called him this morning but he didn't pick up. If you see him, could you give him my number and ask him to get in touch?"

"They'll be bringing him in for questioning today. Now that they have his brother in custody, the police are going to want to fit more of the pieces of the puzzle together and Jake can certainly help them."

"If there's anything I can do for him, please let me know," Sophia said. "Plan on coming by tonight. We'll all be here after the party. And Celia will be practicing her Italian with me. Ciao."

♾

Terry did not want to get out of bed. Her aunt knocked on the door and brought her a glass of orange juice. "Fresh squeezed. Can you smell the cinnamon buns?"

"Why haven't you left for church?"

"I'm taking the morning off to be with you. You had quite a scare last night. Do you want to talk about it?"

"Maybe later. I told my story over and over at the police station and I'd like to forget all about it if that's even possible."

"I'm afraid forgetting easily is not something that happens after all the things you've been through."

"They told me I'd have to testify. Get up in front of people and let them know how stupid and gullible I was."

"You are far from stupid. And trusting people who don't deserve your trust does not make you gullible. You made some choices that resulted in a set of events that just toppled out of control."

"And Bartleby is dead and it's my fault. I killed my friend."

"Bartleby made his choices and he chose to help you. He saw a talented young writer and he wanted to see you succeed. He had faith in you. You didn't kill him. You were his friend and you made his life better."

"I thought Greg was my friend and what a fool I was not to see who he really was."

"People like Greg Wolff spend their lives hiding who they are. He could have been honest with you, but he chose deceit. He could have explained how he felt about your play and asked you not to continue writing it. Instead, he led you on. He had his own plan he was following. You can't fault yourself for that."

"And now I have no friends."

"That's not true. You have me and Dr. Eddleman and Milton. And you reached out with your writing and joined the workshop. Your writing will bring you close to people who are like you with stories to share. Dr. Eddleman called me and said you were having lunch with her today. She has faith in you and sees your talent. What more could you ask from a friend?"

"I think I'm about ready to face the day," Terry said.

Her aunt kissed her. "I'll save a cinnamon bun for you. See you downstairs."

∽

Milton was up early choosing the suit he would wear when he went for dinner with Elaine and Gerald at the Ocean House. He couldn't wait to tell them about his book and he had an inscribed copy of the manuscript to present to them. His phone rang and he picked it up. He recognized the voice on the other end of the line.

"Mr. Stafford, it's Jake Wolff."

"Well, hello young man. And what can I do for you?"

"I wanted to call to apologize to you for something I did."

"And what might that be?"

"I was the one on the motorcycle who almost ran you down. I didn't mean it. I started going faster when I recognized you. I was showing off. I wanted you to look at me and I hit a slippery patch and lost control. Bartleby said I could use his bike while he was gone but I shouldn't have been out on an icy road. I should have known better. And I'm really sorry. I'll take whatever punishment I deserve."

"Well, that took courage to admit your mistake. You could have gotten away scot-free, but you owned up to it. That's a brave lad."

"Thank you, Sir."

"Will I see you tomorrow?"

"Yes, I'll be at work. Miss MacAlister is here with me in the library. She's the one who said I should call you. She'll be taking care of me for awhile. I'll explain it all when I see you."

"Then I'll come by early and we can talk. Give Miss MacAlister my regards."

"I will, And thanks for giving me a second chance, Mr. Stafford."

"Everyone deserves a second chance, Son." Milton hung up his phone and looked through his closet. He put out his best suit, shirt, and tie and decided it was going to be a good day. He took the envelope from his bureau and placed it in his suit coat pocket. He'd have to remember to mail it to that cute, leggy blond. He'd remembered her name. Taylor Swift. Coincidentally, she lived right around the corner. Maybe he'd just drop it off?

∽

Conrad was in the study packing up his desk. He and Carolynn had decided to separate and for now, she was going to remain in the house and he'd rented a bachelor pad. He had to admit, he was looking forward to being free again. Carolynn had agreed to edit his book when he'd finished the draft. She was being a good sport under the circumstances.

He looked for the files, but they were not in the top drawer where he had placed them. "Carolynn, could you come in here for a minute. I need to ask you something," he called to her.

She appeared at the door but did not enter the room. "Yes, what is it?"

"I left some files in my desk. You don't happen to know where they are?"

"You mean these?" She brought the folders from behind her back."

Her soon-to-be ex was momentarily speechless. "What are you doing with them?" He managed to find his voice.

"I was just on the phone with Detective Langley. After I got a good look at these, I wanted to make sure I wouldn't be considered complicit in a crime."

"Crime? What nonsense are you spreading? Those are legal documents. Bartleby and Nelson allowed me to take out insurance for them. They had the requisite physical exams. I paid them a large amount of cash for the right to be named as their beneficiaries. And I paid the installments. It's all legal. Ask Nelson. He'll tell you."

"Nelson's may be legal because the date is correct. But Bartleby's is questionable. You see, I believe when Bartleby died, not enough time had elapsed for dispersal of the funds. You changed the date."

"You weren't there. You can't prove that."

"It may not become an issue. We could make a deal."

"What kind of deal?"

"You, as beneficiary, could give the money coming from Bartleby's claim to Nelson."

"Why should I do that?"

"Because you don't need it and he does. And if that doesn't strike you as a good enough reason, then how about if I testify against you in court for fraud. You changed the date and if you try to collect, you could be arrested. Give Nelson the proceeds from the claim. You're still named as his beneficiary and will get money when he dies. Win-win, I figure."

"That old guy could outlive me."

"I'd put some serious thought into your final decision."

"A wife can't testify against her husband in court."

"But an ex-wife can. Now I'm going to visit Nelson at the hospital." She left the room.

Fannie and Jake were sitting with Nelson when Carolynn arrived. He was in good spirits and drinking through a straw. His intravenous tube had been removed. The nurse came in to check on his vital signs. "You are one tough cookie," she announced. It looks like we might be releasing you tomorrow. Amazing!"

"It's this Newport Creamery *Awful Awful* Jake brought me. I feel better with every sip. He remembered I'd said it was my favorite drink."

Jake was sitting quietly next to Fannie and she reached out to pat his hand.

The nurse left and they continued their conversation from where it had left off.

"You can't go back to your place. You'll need someone to take care of you until you're well again." Fanny said. "Jake's condo is in the same complex as mine and I can keep an eye on the two of you."

"But I told you, Miss MacAlister, I can't afford the rent."

"I think your problem might be solved," Carolynn informed him. "I was speaking to Conrad this morning and he told me that Bartleby had named you as beneficiary on his insurance policy."

"But why on earth would he do that?" Nelson looked at them in amazement.

"He was a good and generous man. It's as simple as that," Fannie said.

The nurse returned and told them that the patient needed his rest so they reluctantly said their goodbyes. Fannie told him to sleep tight, they'd be back soon. She leaned over and tucked the sheet up around his chin. "And I think it's about time you started to call me by my first name."

When they'd left, the nurse gave him his medication and looked over at the monitor. "Mr. Belle, you heart seems to be getting stronger."

He looked forward to his friend returning. He would never tell her about how all those Sundays they'd spent together in the library were the best hours of his life. Even though she had no idea he was there. That would have to be his secret. As he closed his eyes to sleep, he saw her tap dancing her heart out in the Hoxie Gallery. "Fannie. Dear Fannie. Ah, wuv, twu wuv ...."

Late on Sunday morning, Marilynn called from the Ocean House to inform Kara that Deighton Durst was back and his sister was with him. Kara knocked on the door of his suite and a woman answered.

"Can I help you?"

"I'd like to talk with Mr. Durst."

"He's at the spa. You'll need to come back later."

"I'll wait." She walked into the room and took off her coat, placed it over a chair, and made herself comfortable on the couch."

The woman used the phone to connect with the spa. "This is Miranda Durst. Would you please tell Mr. Durst I need to speak with him." Some time lapsed before he was on the other end of the line. "Deighton, there's a woman in the room insisting on seeing you." She turned to Kara. "Excuse me, but who are you?"

"Detective Kara Langley." She said it loud enough for him to hear.

"Deighton will be up in a few minutes," Miranda informed her. She sat on the edge of a chair and crossed one long, shapely leg over the other. "So, you're a cop. Why do you want to talk to my brother?" She nonchalantly flipped the long platinum blond sweep of hair with the back of her right hand.

"Actually, it was you I'd come to discuss, but since you're here, maybe I won't need to speak with him."

Miranda uncrossed and crossed her legs. "I suppose it has to do with my stepfather's will?"

"In a way. You've been out of the country for a long time. How did your brother find you? The last time we spoke, he seemed to have no idea where you were."

"Oh, he knew where I was. I'd asked him to respect my privacy. I didn't really want to be found. But under the circumstances, when he called, I realized I had to be here to get my mother's books."

"First editions. Worth quite a lot, I'd say."

"I didn't realize they were so valuable until Deighton explained it all to me. If I don't claim them, they'll go back to the estate. And who knows where they'll end up?"

Kara looked at the woman's long red fingernails and matching lipstick and wondered where Deighton had found her. "So what have you been doing for the last decade or so?"

At that moment, Deighton burst into the room. "Miranda, I'll take care of this." The woman left the room. "Why are you here? I thought I'd told you what you wanted to know."

"Actually, I had a few more questions to ask, but you left rather abruptly and I wasn't able to get my answers."

"What else could you possibly need to know?"

"Why have you brought this woman here to pose as your sister?"

"How dare you accuse me of subterfuge. Please leave."

Kara reached into her bag and brought out two documents which she held up for him to see.

"Where did you get these?"

"Does the imposter you've recruited know how much trouble she'll be in if she tells Mr. Whitcomb she's your long lost sister and attempts to claim her inheritance? I've given him the original of that death certificate and I'm sure you both will be arrested in less time then it took you to concoct the story you intended to use."

The woman had been listening in the next room and rushed in with her coat on. "I'm out of here, Deighton. Thanks for breakfast and maybe we'll get together next time you're in town."

They were alone and he began pacing around the room.

"Are you ready to tell me why it's so important to obtain the novel Bartleby was working on? I know you don't really care about the other books. It's the manuscript you want."

He sat in the chair facing her and took a deep breath, then exhaled. "My father was an important man in the government. He was well respected. No one knew he was leading a double life. He was a spy. He was responsible for people's deaths. When he died, my mother found papers. Documents, letters, a diary. She was devastated. Bartleby was his best friend. She trusted him and showed him what she'd found. They agreed to keep my father's secret. But at some point, she must have decided to write down his story. She showed it to me explaining she owed it to Miranda and me to know the truth. That book belongs to me."

"How did you find out Bartleby was going to publish it?"

"He told me himself. He said he intended changing the ending where the spy is revealed. No one would know it was about my father. But he was never a writer and the editor was not having any of it. The style was different and she insisted he continue working on it. He was actually considering keeping the original ending. Bartleby asked to speak with me in person and he wanted me to contact Miranda."

"And you met with him in New York."

"Yes. I warned him he had no right to the manuscript. It was part of Miranda's inheritance. It was clear in the will. She was to get my mother's books and that certainly qualified if any of them did."

"I suppose he contacted you again when he had found out about Miranda. He had a meeting with a private detective on Wednesday."

"Yes, he called and said he had Miranda's death certificate in hand and was planning on going forward with the book. He had a meeting with his publisher. I asked him not to do it. I'd get money together to buy the rights and we could negotiate at a later time."

"So, you came to Rhode Island with the money and when you found that Bartleby was missing, you waited to hear from him."

"And then I was called to identify the body. I thought everything would work out until the news about the will."

"And you decided to use someone to impersonate your sister. You really should have been more careful in your choice."

"What are you going to do?"

"I doubt whether you intend to carry on with the charade, so no laws have yet been broken."

"What about the manuscript?"

"I believe Bartleby's will gives the books to Fannie MacAlister, the head librarian at the Westerly Library. She's a woman of honor and I know if you explain the situation to her, she'll listen and make the right decision." Kara stood up to leave and he helped her on with her coat.

"The will is going to be read in January and will have to be probated. I'll speak with Miss MacAlister before then. Thank you, Detective Langley."

Kara's next stop was the hospital where she found Nelson sound asleep. The nurse informed her he'd had visitors earlier and arrangements were being made for him to be released on Tuesday into the care of a Miss MacAlister, so he could be home for Christmas. Kara placed a note by his bed and left for her meeting with the police chief and the detectives who'd worked on the case.

Kara opened her notebook. It was time to fill in the dots. She'd been in on many of these sessions when she was a detective lieutenant on the South Kingstown force and this was second nature to her.

She began with a review of the events leading up to Bartleby's murder on Friday night. "Some of this information I received through phone calls and meetings with the people involved. Detective Sergeant Perez of the NY City Police, provided me with additional information he collected on my behalf. All of it is fully documented by first person accounts.

"On Tuesday, December 3rd, Bartleby Schnelling walked across Wilcox Park from his home on Grove Avenue to the Savoy Bookshop and Cafe. He told his friend Terry Ricitelli, the barista at the cafe in the store, he would be meeting with his publisher, Mr. Pinkham of GreenTree Press in New York City and would return on Saturday night. He took a copy of her script to give to Pinkham for consideration.

At 10:46 AM he boarded the train to Penn Station and at approximately 2:30 PM he checked into his hotel. We've since retrieved the data from his cell phone showing he made a series of calls that afternoon to his publisher, his editor, and his stepson, confirming times to meet with them. Another call was made to a private detective agency he'd hired to do some investigative work for him. On Tuesday evening, Schnelling had dinner with Deighton Durst, his stepson. Durst threatened to legally stop him from publishing the book, asserting the rights did not belong to Schnelling but had been left to the stepdaughter, Miranda Durst, in her mother's will.

On Wednesday, December 4th, he met with the private detective who gave him a packet of information on his step-daughter. Included in the packet was her death certificate.

Thursday morning, December 5th, Schnelling met with Ms. Albright, his editor. She was insisting he rewrite portions of the novel and he left the office threatening to have her fired. He kept his 11:30 AM appointment with Mr. Pinkham where he demanded to be assigned another editor. Pinkham refused and Schnelling stormed out of the office at 11:45 AM taking his manuscript with him and declaring he was terminating his contract. We're unclear how he spent the rest of the day. He placed numerous calls to his stepson's number apparently trying to arrange another meeting on Friday but Durst was already in Rhode Island and did not return the calls.

Schnelling received a call from Gregory Wolff prior to leaving New York on Friday afternoon, December 6th. He arrived in Westerly at 6:40 PM, hid his valise behind a screen in a back room of the station before he left, and walked across the street to the Savoy where, at 6:50 PM, he placed a call to Dr. Ruth Eddleman, leaving her a message which was unclear probably due to the storm. He slipped the envelope containing his manuscript into the store's mail slot and proceeded up Canal Street turning left onto High and entering Wilcox Park through the Serpa Gate. Schnelling was taking the shortcut across the park to his home on Grove Avenue when he was attacked and killed."

Kara gave them hard copies of the information gathered by the detective agency that Perez had sent her. "I became involved in the investigation when my friend, Dr. Eddleman, expressed concern that Bartleby Schnelling had not been attending the writer's workshop she was conducting at the Westerly Library. We questioned his housekeeper and determined he hadn't returned home on Friday night . A missing person's report was filed and it became a homicide investigation when his body was found by the park superintendent on Monday, December 16th."

At this point, the lead detective gave his report on the findings of the autopsy and a summary of the subsequent events around the attempted murder of Nelson Belle.

"Evidence collected at Mr. Belle's house first led us to believe he was the prime suspect in Bartleby Schnelling's murder. On further investigation, it was found this evidence had been placed at the scene to incriminate Mr. Belle. The official statement taken from Mr. Gregory Wolff confirms this. Wolff admits he was angry with Schnelling and had asked him not to pursue publication of Terry Ricitelli's play. He called him on Friday. Schnelling said they would discuss it later that night and he would be home around seven. Wolff was in the park waiting. He shoved him, causing Schnelling to hit his head, then drowned him in the pond. He stole the victim's portfolio and cell phone in order to get the copy of the play Ricitelli had given Schnelling which was based on Wolff's psychiatric treatment that he did not want to be made public. The script was not in the portfolio and he later used the victim's phone in an attempt to intimidate Dr. Eddleman into ending the workshops. In order to cast suspicion on Nelson Belle, Wolff entrapped Belle in his house and left him to die. Incriminating evidence, including Schnelling's motorbike, portfolio, and phone were placed at the scene. Belle has dictated a statement and has positively identified Wolff from a photo brought to his hospital room this morning. Last evening Gregory Wolff made an attempt on Terry Ricitelli's life. He was arrested and is awaiting arraignment on charges of murdering

Bartleby Schnelling and of attempting to murder Nelson Belle and Terry Ricitelli. A full statement will be released to the press later this afternoon."

Later, in the Chief Baker's office, Kara asked about Jacob Wolff.

"It has been confirmed that he was allowed use of Schnelling's motorbike so there are no charges of theft and none for driving without a license as we have no witnesses who have come forward to his having done so. Although he provided information to his brother about the playwriting group, he was unaware his brother had initiated a friendship with Terry Ricitelli nor that he had killed Schnelling. The worst he did was agree to leave a window in the library basement unlocked. Greg used it to get in and try to steal copies of the manuscripts Jake had informed him Fannie MacAlister kept in her office. We have no reason to believe he knowingly abetted in the murders or the attempted murders. He was as much a victim as the others. Miss MacAlister and Mr. Stafford brought Jacob to the station and spoke on his behalf. They've agreed to take responsibility for his well being. He'll be eighteen in another year, but they have made a commitment to provide guardianship until he's completed college."

"I'll pass this information to my friend Sophia. She'll be relieved to know he's being well cared for."

The Chief thanked Kara, assuring her they had enough solid evidence to convict Gregory Wolff on all counts. She left the station knowing the case would never get to court. She was confident Dr. Walden would be advising Greg Wolff's lawyer to plead insanity and they would eventually strike a deal which would probably put him away in an institution for the rest of his life.

∽

*There's no real ending.
It's just the place where you stop the story.*
Frank Hebert

Tuesday, December 24

"SOPHIA IS ON THE phone and she wants to know if you can give her a ride to Westerly this afternoon. Her car is being washed and detailed and the rest of us are tied up." Kara handed Stewart the phone.

"Sure, no problem. What time should I come by? I'll be there with bells on." He gave the phone back to his wife.

Kara left the room to whisper into the phone. "You do realize he meant that literally? He found a strand of bells we usually drape around the tree and is wearing it as a belt ... Okay, just warning you. And he's stuck the red reindeer nose and the antlers on his car. I thought I'd hidden them better this year, but he'd attached one of those tile devices that track things on the inside of the Styrofoam nose ... All right then. Have fun. I'll see you tomorrow."

The Curies came running into the kitchen. They each were sporting bows around their necks. Marie's was green with red polka dots and Pierre's was red with green stripes "I think they're finally getting used to these reindeer antlers," Stewart said. "We're going for a stroll around the block before I leave to get Sophia."

"I'll just finish up here and dress Celia. She's coming with Ruth and me to welcome Nelson home from the hospital. Fannie is bringing him to stay at Jake's where she can keep an eye on both of them."

"Sounds like a good arrangement for everyone. Whoa!" He'd managed to hook the leashes on the dogs before they dragged him from the kitchen. "On Dancer, on Prancer, on Donna and Vixen ..." Stewart called out as he was pulled out of sight..

⁓

"Happy Christmas Eve Day," Terry said, as Virginia came into the dining room.

"What's all this?"

The table had been set with the Christmas Spode plates and red plaid napkins were tucked into silver rings. A boxwood tree sat in the center with a golden angel on the top.

"I've made us breakfast for a change. You're always waiting on me and now it's my turn." Terry pulled out a chair for her aunt. "Alexa, play Christmas music."

"I guess we have cause to celebrate, although I have to say I'm not sure how I should feel about Ruth's news," Virginia said as Terry filled her plate with a veggie and cheese omelet.

"I feel the same. I know I should be happy that Bartleby left me his house, but I'm not sure how I'll make out on my own. You could always come to live with me," she suggested.

"No, you'll be fine and I'm not that far away. I'll stay right here where I grew up. I don't think I'll ever leave Misquamicut again. I've reconnected with old friends and I'm settled in. Lots of comforting memories. Did I tell you how our families would spend the summer days at the beach and then we'd go to the pond to go clamming? Your grandmother made the best chowder. And when I was in college, my girlfriends and I would barhop along the main drag and get home at all hours of the night. I have to say, it's a relief you're not wild like I was."

"I've given you enough cause to worry lately, and I'm sorry about that. I am glad you've decided to stay here and aren't retiring. You should keep working as long as you continue to love what you do."

"Wise advice. What time will you be heading out to Fannie's?"

"Milton, Jake, and I are going to decorate Jake's place to have it ready for when Fannie brings Nelson home later this afternoon. We have to pick up a Christmas tree somewhere, so I'll leave after we have breakfast. Do you want to join us?"

"No, I have a date. Enjoy yourself." Virginia was pleased her niece was going to be spending time with her new friends. It was the first sign Terry was finally coming out of her shell. When she'd returned from Ruth's on Sunday with the news about her inheritance, she also mentioned they'd discussed her returning to college. It looked like there'd be much to celebrate in the New Year.

"I made us some mimosas. Here's to a new year full of surprises!" They raised their glasses in a toast.

"Mmmmm, that's delicious."

"Maybe I should trade in my barista job and get a bartender's certificate? Bigger tips I've heard." Terry laughed as her aunt shook her head vehemently.

"That's one change I'm not going to encourage unless they start combining bookstores with barrooms. But you can invite me over to your new place anytime to try out any homemade concoctions on me. I think I'll go by the Savoy today and pick you up another Christmas present. In what section will I find books on making designer cocktails?"

Rick and Gino sat drinking coffee in the truck which was parked around the corner of the Langley house. They were waiting for everyone to leave for the day. The moment Stewart's SUV was out of sight, they pulled into the long drive and began unloading the supplies.

"This shouldn't take us too long, cuz we just gotta dig a trench, put in da frame, lock it togetha, and fill it wid da hose. Sophia's gonna keep Stewart busy for most of da afternoon, and Ruth won't bring Kara and Celia back home 'til I call her and tell her we're done. She'll make sure it's afta dark," Gino informed his brother.

Inside the house, Marie and Pierre jumped up on the couch to get a better look at the goings on out in their back yard. They barked for awhile but finally settled down.

"Hey, Gino, that would make a great holiday store window display." Rick pointed to the picture window where the black labradoodles sat watching the show dressed in their fancy holiday bows and antlers and surrounded by red and white poinsettias.

◦◦◦

Fannie pushed the wheelchair through the entrance of the hospital. A nurse helped her get Nelson into the car. He was still weak but he didn't want to give them any reason to readmit him, so he tried to act as perky as he could. He was going home. He'd asked Kara to pick up a few possessions from his shack and bring them to Jake's. He explained to her that he never wanted Fannie to see how he'd been living.

When they came into the dining room, they were greeted with a chorus of "Welcome home!" The table had been prepared and for the first time in years, Nelson sat down to have a meal with friends. And he was given a place of honor at the head of the table with Fannie at the other end. The Christmas tree was lit and he could see brightly wrapped presents underneath. Nelson could hardly keep himself from bursting into tears. He made sure he kept smiling because the thought of crying in front of Fannie was out of the question, even though they would be tears of joy. And he thought about all the books he'd read and the movies he'd seen and realized that finally he was going to have his own happy ending.

◦◦◦

It was dark outside when everyone returned to the Langley house. Stewart and Sophia had bought pizzas and a tired group of friends sat around the table eating and discussing the day's events.

After the table was cleared, they agreed they were all exhausted, except for Celia who was wide awake. She'd managed to catch a nap in the car. They would return the next day to open presents together. Before they left, Sophia took something from her bag for Stewart.

"It's to thank you for chauffeuring me. Open this now," she told him.

He unwrapped a special edition of Clement Moore's "Twas the Night Before Christmas".

"Sophia, this is such a thoughtful gift. Thank you. I'll read it to Celia when we tuck her into bed tonight."

"And I'll make sure I capture it on video," Kara said.

*He was conscious of a thousand odors floating in the air,
each one connected with a thousand thoughts, and hopes, and joys
and cares long. long, forgotten.*
Charles Dickens

Christmas Day

THE FRIENDS SLEPT LATE the next morning. "I didn't even have to drug Gino," Sophia announced to Ruth as they got ready to return to the Langley's to watch Celia open her presents on her very first Christmas Morning.

Santa did the honors, passing out the presents and having his picture taken with Celia surrounded by her gifts. After they were done and a mountain of wrapping paper was under the tree, Kara presented Stewart with his ice skates. Ruth gave him two pillows with a belt to wrap around his body and a first aid kit. Sophia tied colorful pompoms on the shoelaces. And then Gino and Rick told everyone to put on their coats. The brothers escorted them all out to the back yard where the ice had formed overnight in the skating rink they'd constructed the previous day.

Stewart walked around with the skates slung over his shoulder staring at the gift they'd made for him. "I'm gobsmacked!" he said wiping his eyes. In the center of the rink was a handmade baby's sled filled with more wrapped boxes.

"You can hold on ta da handle in da back of da sled and push Celia around on dee ice. It'll keep you standin up til you get use ta skatin widout it," Gino informed him.

Inside the boxes were ice skates for each of them with different colored pompoms tied on the front. They put on their skates and glided around.

Sophia instructed Rick to photograph them taking turns singing Christmas songs and dancing with each other for Celia's album.

"It's gettin cold. I'll be by to build da fire pit dis week. Den we kin stay out as long as we want and toast marshmallows."

"Gino had figured out how to get everything done on Saturday, but we all ended up embroiled in helping solve the mystery, so we had to change our plans. Gino put the pieces together at our house and we assembled it in your backyard yesterday," Rick explained.

"I've sent out invitations for New Years Day. You're hosting a skating party. Don't worry. You won't have to do a thing. I've got it all covered," Sophia announced.

Stewart stepped safely off the ice. "Have I got a surprise for you. I made a special holiday brunch from all the favorite recipes you told me you loved so much."

A groan slipped from all of their lips.

"I knew you'd be excited. It's my gift to you. Who needs a turkey dinner with all the fixins when you can have a Stewart Langley Smorgasbord? You keep skating and I'll call you in when everything's ready."

"Don't worry," Sophia assured them, after he'd gone inside, "there's a whole turkey dinner waiting for us at the mansion for later this evening."

Gino breathed a sigh of relief. "What's Christmas wid no turkey leftovers for da week?"

They skated around taking turns pushing Celia on her sled until Stewart's voice beckoned them. "All set in here. I think you're really going to enjoy this. You'll recognize highlights from some of my best recipes. And I made sure I have every color of the rainbow represented."

"For his birthday present, we're all chipping in for Stewart to get formal cooking lessons," Sophia announced and they all agreed this would be the best gift ever. To themselves.

They all ate sparingly, knowing a turkey dinner awaited them. Much of the food was surreptitiously slipped to the puppies lying blissfully under the table.

"Looks like I'm going to send everyone home with leftovers. Good Sophia gave me a set of Tupperware containers for Christmas," Stewart declared.

Celia was totally enthralled with all of the colorful food set out in front of her. She clapped her hands and gurgled, calling out, "Guh buh uh ebba uh," as she waved her hands in the air. "Guh buh uh ebba uh."

"Stewart, do you know what she's saying?" Ruth asked.

"Of course. We've been reading *A Christmas Carol*. She loves all the ghosts, but her favorite character is Tiny Tim."

Celia repeated it again looking around expectantly at the smiling faces of everyone who loved her. "Guh buh uh ebba uh."

"It's clear as a bell." And as Sophia took a video, Stewart translated for them. "God bless us everyone."

Thoughts on Westerly

I decided to set this next book in Westerly because of all the amazing history contained inside the borders of this southern Rhode Island town separated from Connecticut by the Pawcatuck River. The library was built in 1892-1894 in conjunction with the town of Pawcatuck to give regular folk the ability to access the books acquired by the richer townsfolk. It was a memorial to the veterans and town heroes from the Civil War and provided a place where people could gather to commemorate and celebrate special occasions. At the heart of it all, throughout the years, were the loyal librarians who lovingly helped it to grow into a thriving and nurturing center for the townspeople.

In the beginning, the philanthropists Harriet Hoxie Wilcox and Stephen Wilcox and their well-to-do friends developed a shared vision of the library and donated time and money for its construction. Under their watchful eyes, the townspeople picked up the mantle and gradually, the building grew with its many additions into what it is today.

And of course, it was Harriet who resoundingly announced, "The people shall have their park" and though she never was able to walk through the paths and meadows created because of her steadfast determination, she well understood the legacy she was leaving for the families who would call Westerly home in the decades to follow.

Little did I know, when I chose this next setting, that the people of Westerly would generously share so many stories and help me to understand the rich background of all of the places I chose to feature. Misquamicut, "place of the red fish", was once a summer fishing grounds for Native Americans. It became known as Pleasant View when between 1894 and 1903 cottages were constructed along the beach. Hurricanes, fire, and floods have taken their toll on the growing settlement over the years since 1913, but the village has proven to be resilient through it all. It even went through a honky tonk phase in the 1990's but business owners and residents turned it back into a family-friendly beach area in the 2000s. Misquamicut is not only a state beach but a village which stretches 3 miles westward from Weekapaug to Watch Hill and separates Winnapaug Pond from the Atlantic Ocean.

Now, Watch Hill is a horse of a different color. In the 17th Century, it was inhabited by the Niantic Indian tribe. Situated high above the ocean, it was used by colonists as a lookout point and this is where it got its name. In the 19th and 20th Centuries, it evolved as an exclusive summer resort of Victorian style "cottages." But even money couldn't protect against the force of nature living along a coastline brings. During the 20th Century, fire and hurricanes destroyed the huge Victorian hotels which had lined the waterfront. The Ocean House was completely rebuilt in 2005. This grand seaside hotel, along with the lighthouse and yacht club, the famous Flying Carousel, and the mansions with their affluent owners perched high above the cliffs are the survivors of days gone past.

And no discussion of Westerly can take place without bringing in the North End Historic District, 150 acres which now, along with the Downtown Historic District, is part of the National Register of Historic Places. Between 1832 and 1955 the North End was home to immigrants coming from Europe to work in its water-based textile mills and in the famous granite quarries . The community is now dedicated to revitalizing the cultural, social and historic character through arts and educational initiatives for all its citizens, young and old.

There is so much pride of place and I could feel it emanating in each conversation I was privileged to have with residents from all of these neighborhoods making up this historic part of Rhode Island.

I hope you enjoy some of the information, postcards, and photos I've gathered and used as sources while researching the town of Westerly for this 6th installment of my South County Mystery Series.

THE HISTORY BEHIND SOME SETTINGS IN THIS BOOK

The Westerly Train Station

Circa - 1941 postcard mailed with a 1 Cent Stamp, no less!

In the early 20th Century, inspired by the admission of Arizona and New Mexico as states, the New Haven Railroad built Spanish Revival style stations across southern New England. In 1912, the Westerly Station was constructed in this style.

Eighty years later, the station manager in his five-sided ticket booth was replaced by the more convenient on-line ticket purchase. The building was repurposed when a dedicated group of artists moved into 14 Railroad Avenue and it became the Artists' Cooperative Gallery of Westerly. It is the perfect venue for displaying creative works because the building, itself, is a work of art evident in its description in *The Great American Stations:* "Although constructed of rich red, textured brick laid in Flemish bond,- most of the building is covered in stucco to keep with the Spanish Revival aesthetic. Spanish design is especially noticeable in the choice of roofing material: tejas, or curved red clay tiles. The hipped roofs all display deep eaves that cast strong shadows onto the station walls when the sun shines bright in the summer sun."

In the 1990s, a full restoration of the building returned it to its 1920s appearance. Rail passengers have access to the indoor waiting room and can enjoy the artists' works when the gallery is open from Wednesday-Sunday.

westerlyarts.com
www.greatamericanstations.com Westerly, RI (WLY)

The United Theatre

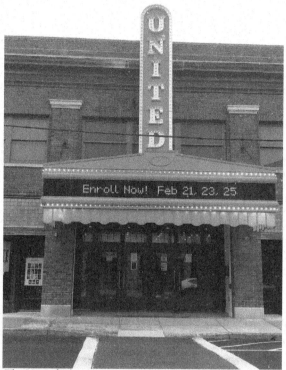

The United Theatre marquee

Along with his renovation of the Ocean House and his latest project, The United Theatre, Charles Royce has been instrumental in utilizing historic venues and restoring them into amazing modern spaces for the betterment of the town. In 2006, community members and the Westerly Land Trust had a vision of uniting the community through the arts by creating a hub of activity and entertainment. In July of 2021, The Ocean Community United Theatre, once a vaudeville theatre and cinema, once again opened its doors to the public as a center for the arts and arts education.

https://www.unitedtheatre.org

The Westerly Library and Wilcox Park

Westerly Library in its Wilcox Park setting

In 1717, Reverend William Gibson bequeathed a small collection of his books to the Seventh Day Baptist Church in Westerly. In 1797, these books, under a Charter granted to the Pawcatuck Library Company, moved to various locations until, in 1870, the Library Directors made a decision that the library ownership be vested in the public and free for all citizens.

In 1891, Stephen Wilcox proposed that a committee be established to raise funds for a Civil War Memorial and Library to be built, providing a meeting place for a

Stained Glass Window of Chief Ninigret

Grand Army Post and related memorabilia. Through the dedicated work of Ethan Wilcox and his daughter, Miss Fannie, the collection of five thousand ninety seven books were catalogued using the Dewey Decimal System and found their place in the Memorial Building in August of 1894. Ethan Wilcox served as librarian from 1894 to 1908.

Stephen Wilcox never lived to see his dream fulfilled. He died in 1893. His wife, Harriet Hoxie Wilcox, devoted the rest of her life to carrying out her husband's plans and wishes.

One of her major accomplishments was negotiating the purchase of the adjoining Babcock estate and this was the start of what we know as Wilcox Park today. Over the succeeding years, other properties were acquired and her promise that "The people shall have their park" was fulfilled She also proposed the addition of an art gallery to the library and in 1902, it was completed to house the gallery, a gymnasium, and a stack room. She never lived to see this come to fruition, as she died in 1901. Her bequests have enabled numerous projects which enriched the lives of the people in this community.

Cristoforo Colombo

Throughout the intervening years, librarians and staff have played a major role in the growth of the library. They oversaw the acquisition of new volumes, the further development of programs, and needed expansions to the building itself.

westerlylibrary.org

The Babcock-Smith House

Benjamin Franklin and George Washington were some of the distinguished guests of in this early Georgian style mansion (circa 1734). Their host was Dr. Joshua Babcock, the local physician, then businessman, and eventually politician. He was appointed as the first colonial postmaster and his house was his place of business. After Babcock's death in 1783, the property was sold and later became a tenant farm until 1845 when Orlando Smith, a stonemason, bought it to use the granite discovered on the site for his work. Customers of The Smith Granite Company were welcomed to stay in the home which, in 1884, was renovated in the Victorian style more fitting for wealthy guests who came to Westerly to approve monuments they'd ordered.

Babcock-Smith House

These Victorian details were removed in 1928 when owner Orlando R. Smith hired Norman Isham, a restoration architect, to return the home to its original Georgian appearance. Upon Smith's death, a Trust was established to preserve the house and furnishings. And in 1972, the trust was reorganized so the house could become a museum for which it serves to this day.

wwww.babcocksmithhouse.org

The Granite Theatre

This iconic Greek Revival Style building was first used as a church from 1849 into the 1960s. In 2000, it was lovingly restored with funding from the Kimball Foundation to become a live performance theatre under the Artistic Direction of David and Beth Jepson. Throughout the years, it has presented over 160 shows. A non-profit organization, Renaissance City Theatre, Inc. was established in 2012 to continue with the goals of providing live-theatre, education programs for all ages, and to act as stewards to preserve this historic building. It has proven to be resilient, presenting on-line productions for its loyal fans throughout the pandemic. Happily, live productions resumed in the 2021 season. *A Christmas Carol*, a traditional favorite, is held in December.

Over 160 shows have been presented

granitetheatre.com

A Favorite Local Staple - Soppressata

When I informed people that my next book was set in Westerly, I was given fair warning to make sure suppis (pronounced soupies) was mentioned somewhere in the book. I had no idea what they were talking about but after asking around, I was told to get myself over to Westerly Packing for an education about this beloved Westerly food staple.

I expected to walk into the offices of a meat packing plan, which was what this business has been for five generations. But what greeted me was a large, bright market space chock full of mouth-watering foods beautifully displayed. I explained my purpose for the visit and was escorted to an office on the second floor where Ruth, the woman behind the desk, introduced me to a couple in the room - Medoro and Palma Trombino. I gave them my card and explained the purpose of my visit. They immediately welcomed me with typical Italian hospitality. Medoro proudly gave me a behind-the-scenes tour of this fifth generation business. I watched Josè Salazar as he worked at the machine which stuffed the special meat and spice mixture into casings and met other members of the Trombino family working in the store. It was one of the best mornings I'd spent in ages. Ruth provided me with a copy of the history of soppressata and how it is made which I will share with you. Although the packing label states "No Preservatives, No Nitrates/Nitrites Added and lists Pork, Paprika, Salt, Spices, Beef, Casings," it does not specify which spices and how much. That is a family secret which makes each family's soppressata unique.

Medoro Trombino

After my tour, I was given a suppi to bring home. It will be the first I've ever tasted. I chose the Mild, rather than the Sweet, Hot, or XXXHot. I'm adventuresome, but cautious. Perhaps, I'll work my way up to XXXHot some day because I intend to make this market one of my weekly stops. I did not expect such a lovely respite from the dreary, frigid January day when I headed to Westerly and I am indebted to everyone at Westerly Packing for making my morning so much warmer and brighter.

Notes on the Westerly Packing Company family tradition for making Calabria Soppressata

In the late 1800's the family immigrated from Corigliano Calabria and continued the tradition of raising a pig to make the pork dishes they were accustomed to. They opened a small store on Pleasant Street. Especially popular were sausage and Soppressata. The Paprika used in the sausage and Soppressata provided the nice color.

Calabria Soppressata was made in January when the pig, raised and fattened to provide food for the family, was slaughtered. Just about every part of the pig was used. After being salted and cured, the belly would become pancetta, the hind legs would be made prosciutto, the back fat became lardo and the jowl becaue guanciale.

The word Soppressata comes from the italian verb 'soppressare" meaning to press down. An Italian dry cured sausage was made from a mixture of chopped lean and fatty port mean, seasoned with salt and hoot and black pepper. It was then hand stuffed into the intestines (castings) and pressed down wtih weights and cured.

The blood was scented with citrus fruit and flavored with spices to make Sanguinacccio (blood sausage). The shoulder and loin would be ground to make sausage and soppressata.

Soppressata - from Italian for 'pressing down'

The Prehistoric Days Before Cell Phones

There was a time in Westerly when the mailman delivered mail to homes without numbers on the front of the houses. He knew all of the residents by name. The 1947 Westerly telephone directory includes Pawcatuck, Connecticut and is the size of a small booklet. In this modern age of cell phones, it is interesting to read the pages referring to party lines and the advice regarding dialing and long distance calls. I've included a few excerpts which might be of interest to those not old enough to remember what telecommunication was like 74 years ago before cell towers and text messages. (A shout-out here to Jake Fonseca, Director of URI's Digital Forensic Cyber Center for explaining the intricacies of tracking and acquiring data from cell phone calls.)

Important Calling Information from the Westerly-Pawcatuck Telephone Directory (Actual excerpts, circa July, 1947)

FIRE
When the fire alarm sounds, hundreds of curious but thoughtless people at once go to the telephone to ask the operators or fire station where the fire is. It is impossible to answer these additional calls ever time the fire alarm sounds.

Calls for physicians, the ambulance, the police or for additional fire apparatus may be delayed as a result of your thoughtlessness. FOR YOUR OWN PROTECTION, we ask you not to call the operator or fire station every time you hear the fire alarm sound.

POLICE

To summon Westerly police call operator and ask for ring 2.

HOW TO USE DIAL TELEPHONES

Be sure to dial the right number. Then lift the receiver and with the receiver in your ear, put your finger in the hole over the first figure on the local number dialed, turn the dial clockwise until your finger strikes the stop, lift your finger and allow the dial to return to normal itself. Do not hasten or retard it. In the same way, dial in order the other figures of the number desired.

MAKING CALLS FROM PARTY LINES

Calls from party lines, rural lines or extension telephones are made in the same manner as other calls. They are, however, subject to occasional interference by others on the line. Always listen before starting to dial, to be sure the line is not in use.

If you hear a series of clicks when dialing, someone on your line is dialing. Wait until the clicking stops, then tell the other party you have interfered with his call. Satisfactory party line services depends largely upon the willingness of the several users to cooperate in their use of the service.

TO CALL FROM A COIN BOX TELEPHONE

Do not deposit a coin until told by the operator.

The Savoy Bookshop and Cafe

Savoy Bookshop and Cafe opened in 2016

In 1889, The Martin House was officially opened by Captain Michael F. Martin who passed out cigars for those who came to tour the 42 bedrooms, parlors, and billiard room that comprised his hotel. The price of a room was two dollars. Dinner was fifty cents. He offered special rates for "dramatic companies". Six years later, Martin leased out sections of the building and the name changed to the Foster House Hotel. On the first floor was the Foster House Pharmacy.

In the years to follow, the building went through many names changes. It was a less reputable establishment in 1897 when the Granite Hotel was raided by the police because of illegal liquor sales. Frank B. Cook, the landlord at the time, resigned from the town council the next morning and sold the property later that same year. The Granite Hotel was eventually sold but continued as a lodging house for men only.

The building survived through new owners, police raids, and fires. In 1955, the hotel was given its final name change – The Hotel Savoy, as a tribute to the royal family of Italy. In 2013, philanthropist Charles M. Royce purchased a portion of the building to oversee its renovation into the Savoy Bookshop and Cafe, which opened in 2016.

banksquarebooks.com (Westerly Store)

Postcards from the Past

Watch Hill Lighthouse and Radio Station

From the back of the postcard above: The hurricane of 1938 left a death toll of over 600 with another 100 persons unaccounted for. 6,000 homes were completely destroyed and damage amounted to hundreds of millions of dollars - an amount that today would approach the billions. The wind crippled power, lights and telephone systems and hundreds of thousands of trees were uprooted. Boats and small craft were set flying.

House in Watch Hill after the Great Hurricane of September 1938

Westerly Town Hall, Broad Street, circa 1945

Chief Ninigret Statue watching the entrance to Watch Hill

Ocean House, circa 1950

Acknowledgments

My continued gratitude goes out to the team who help bring these books to life in print:

Dr. Joyce L. Stevos, Ph. D., editor; I. Michael Grossman, publisher; Zachary Perry, cover and map designer; Rick Dyer, beta reader extraordinaire. I'm also indebted to Bill Stoddard for sharing memories of his childhood in Westerly and for use of his collection of books and postcards; all of the folks at Westerly Packing; Westerly Library staff, especially Teresa Peck and Nina Wright; Wilcox Park Superintendent, Alan Peck; my good friends Mary Sullivan and Leslie Chouinard for their support and camaraderie during my research and travels around town.

To all my loyal, fantastic fans, I offer my sincere thanks for your continuing enthusiasm and encouragement to keep bringing out new installments of the South County Mystery Series. You'll be glad to know I've begun writing the 7th book in the series, *Last Step Beyond the Pale*.

About the Author

Claremary Sweeney is a writer/photographer from South Kingstown, Rhode Island. She spent her earlier years in the field of education and now, retired, she uses her imagination to create stories that can be enjoyed by children of all ages and the young at heart. Within her first book, *A Berkshire Tale*, are the original ten ZuZu Stories about the adventures of a kitten born on a farm in the Berkshire Hills. It's filled with the settings that make this area an historic as well as a cultural center in western Massachusetts.

Sweeney's children's book, *Carnivore Conundrum*, is set at the Roger Williams Botanical Center in Cranston, Rhode Island. During one of her school readings, a little boy asked her to create a book about bugs, and plants that eat bugs. Written in verse, the story concerns Adonis, a pitcher plant, who decides one morning he's swearing off meat. His mother, her friends and all the plants in the garden must find a way to coax this stubborn baby to eat again.

Last Train to Kingston was the first in this series introducing Detective Lieutenant Kara Langley of the South Kingstown Police Force. *Last Rose on the Vine* is the second in the South County adult mysteries featuring Rhode Island historical sites. *Last Carol of the Season* is the third mystery and is set in Wakefield at Christmas time. *Last Sermon for a Sinner* takes place in Peace Dale and *Last Castle in the Sand* includes towns along the South County coastline.

The author lives in South County. She sometimes finds time to post in her blog, *Around ZuZu's Barn, Conversations With Kindred Spirits* which you can find at **www.aroundzuzusbarn.com**

Author's web page: https://claremarypsweeney.carrd.com
Facebook: https://www.facebook.com/cpsweeneyauthor
Author blog: AroundZuZusBarn.com

Books by Claremary P. Sweeney

SOUTH COUNTY MYSTERY SERIES FEATURING DETECTIVE KARA LANGLEY
Last Train to Kingston – 2017
Last Rose on the Vine – 2018
Last Carol of the Season – 2018
Last Sermon for a Sinner – 2019
Last Castle in the Sand – 2020
Last Walk in the Park – 2022

THE ZUZU SERIES – set in historic places around the Berkshires of Massachusetts and featuring ZuZu, a charming little tabby born in a barn at Tanglewood
A Berkshire Tale (10 stories for the young and young at heart) – 2015
The Pacas Are Coming! ZuZu and the Crias – 2016

Carnivore Conundrum – 2017
A whimsical, illustrated verse tale set at the Roger Williams Park Botanical Center in Cranston, Rhode Island. After a stressful incident with a fly caught in his digestive juices, Adonis, a tiny pitcher plant, decides he is swearing off meat. His mother, Dee, and the other plants and creatures in the garden explain the conundrum – he is, after all is said and done, a carnivorous plant. But Adonis firmly believes he must follow his heart. Thus, a solution must be found to keep Dee's baby alive.